Totally Bound Publishing books by Landra Graf

Bad Boys of Space
A Talent for Trouble
A Gamble Among Sheep

I0524365

Bad Boys of Space

A GAMBLE AMONG SHEEP

LANDRA GRAF

A Gamble Among Sheep
ISBN # 978-1-83943-832-5
©Copyright Landra Graf 2019
Cover Art by Erin Dameron-Hill ©Copyright August 2019
Interior text design by Claire Siemaszkiewicz
Totally Bound Publishing

A GAMBLE AMONG SHEEP

Dedication

To Lori, you're my best friend, my confidante,
and the only person who will stay on the phone
with me for two hours as I plot out a book
verbally. To Louisa, for helping me pick the
heroine's name. To my husband, never give up,
never surrender.

Chapter One

Caterina Genovese still loved gambling, even after it had brought death to her life over and over. She enjoyed the sounds of cards shuffling, dealers calling out winners or losers, the clink of glasses and the smell of tobacco smoke that left random clouds over tables. A good spin of a roulette wheel only added to the atmosphere. Her appreciation for all that was why she'd closed her tattoo shop, crossed the street and entered the establishment of her father's competitor.

Daddy dearest had competitors in every city on Callisto, but for some reason unknown to her, The Sweet Spot, with its red and gold color scheme, was the one Daddy worried about. Evidence of that was her brother's threats mere hours ago, after she'd wrapped up her work for the day.

She took a seat at a pontoon table, pushing her long ponytail behind her shoulder, the tattoos on her arms visible and gaining a few side glances from a couple of guys already seated. No sense in covering up her personal advertisement for her current profession.

"Ante in," the dealer announced.

She pushed forward a chip before cracking her knuckles.

"I don't think I've ever seen a Genovese in this place before."

Fatch. She'd been recognized. "Surprising what a loaded gun will do."

The dealer laughed and dealt the cards. She chuckled along with him, for appearances' sake, even as her brother's words replayed in her head.

Luca had laughed too. *'You're a regular peace-loving spacecase here and your mourning is over. This is about business, and doing what's right for the family. Our family. If you don't want violence, you'll march your anti-killing ass over to that fatching club as I've requested. I'll meet you there and we'll have a nice evening.'*

'Or?'

Luca had pulled out his gun, the shining surface glaring against the halogen beams overhead. *'Yash's wife and kid are going to find making ends meet a bit difficult if Daddy is no longer around to pay the bills.'*

Her stomach curdled as the other players received their cards. This visit wasn't for her pleasure. Familial obligation laced with the threat that her tattoo shop boss would die. More people killed because she wanted to be rebellious. Their deaths would lie at her feet. So, she shoved down the disgust, heaped bricks of anger on it and focused on the cards.

Rina tipped up the corner of the face-down card. A nine. Then came another nine, face up. She glanced at the three other folks sitting at the table. Each took their turn betting or folding against the dealer's face-up ten. When the dealer, an older man with a bit of paunch, pointed to her, she flipped over the other nine. "Double down." She threw a couple of extra chips into the growing pot in the center of the table.

Play continued and the dealer busted. She won on nineteen with both hands. The pile of chips tripled her original amount. And so it continued, the shuffle, the deal-out, the betting and finally the outcome. She kept playing, winning some, folding on others. Rarely did she go the full way unless she was sure she'd win.

Like riding a hover cycle.

She lit a clove cigarette, taking small drags. In between rounds, she glanced out over the crowd at the other tables, taking a gander at the faces of the gamblers. She could tell which ones were from ships, hardened by a life of never living in one place for too long. There were the women hanging on the backs of the high rollers, most of them house women, sent out by the club's owner to entice patrons to invest their winnings via sexual escapade in the rooms somewhere at the top of a spiral staircase.

Rooms only the women working the floor could take clients to These housewives worked the gambling area and the bar, as well as cutting a rug on the dance floor.

Rina kept watch over everything, something she'd honed over the years she'd spent in her father's club, as first an observer then as a manager.

"Bet's to you." The dealer's voice got her attention back on her cards. She had an ace of spades showing and a queen of hearts underneath—the same as a pair of her tattoos. Instinctively, she reached up and touched the right side of her neck. Then she flipped the cards.

"Twenty-one. The winner is the painted lady."

The patron beside her moved out and someone new sat down. A man, full suit, nice hat, rich brown skin, hazel eyes a gal could get lost in and full lips with a thin goatee. "Quite a run you're on."

"My day is definitely looking up." She'd pack away a nice little sum for her first trip to this place. *And I'm keeping every last leaf.*

"Mind if I join you?" he asked, all half-tilted lips and already moving the seat up to the table. He extracted a stack of chips from the inner breast pocket of his suit jacket and placed them on the table.

"A little too late for me to object and it's not my club, not my choice. Though I question why you're sitting so close."

He winked at her. "Hoping some of that good luck might rub off on me."

I got something you could rub.

The round started anew, the cards falling. Rina was well versed in the addition of players to the table. It meant the cards she would have gotten were going to someone else. As she stared at her three and the upturned five, she grew envious of the showing ten her handsome stranger enjoyed.

Shit, have to fold.

Her new chair companion stayed in and, at the last second, she decided to stay with him. No extra betting had been thrown. She would see what the next card was. The dealer rounded the table and she noticed how the man played, not calling for a card. *Staying. Yes.* They faced off against the dealer, not other people like in Hold 'Em poker, but still she wanted other players to bust, to lose. That way the club manager didn't feel the need to switch out the dealer. How many times had she watched a table switch dealers to kill the players high on lady luck and keep the money flowing to the business.

This was the only time in her life Rina had wanted the majority of the money in her stack. At the very least, she wanted to beat this man who'd woken up her libido by sitting next to her. She tapped the table, signaling for a card.

The dealer flipped it. "Eight of clubs."

A sign. The eight was the date she'd been born on, the club matching one of the cards on the left side of her neck. She threw some chips into the pot, raising the amount of play. The two remaining players and the gorgeous suit next to her followed her lead. Then came the dealer, who ended with twenty, to the groans of the two other players, but she flipped her twenty-one in delight. The man next to her tied with two tens.

"Impressive playing."

Rina was aware of this suit as a man, a good-looking one, but at the same time, she wasn't here for flirting. She'd already caused enough death...her dead fiancé was proof of that. So she played it cool.

She lit another cigarette, inhaling deep. "Yeah, you too."

"Anyone ever tell you that you have some amazing-looking skin?" He smiled, looking her over like a prize animal.

Another one.

She sighed, sticking her cigarette in her mouth and rubbing her hands down her arms. "Yeah, I'm told it would look better without all the ink."

He frowned. "Well, whoever said that is an idiot. The ink tells your story. Like ancient civilizations did on Earth-before-the-nuke. They'd mark up their skin with tales of adventures, courageous deeds and the battles they'd won."

"I've haven't been in any battles."

"You sure about that?" He looked over at the dealer and gave a nod. "You didn't get those without a reason. Each one tells a part of your story."

She'd done what she came for…except getting noticed sat at the bottom of her list. "It's not an interesting one. I can promise you that."

"Table's closing. Please cash in your winnings at the counter or continue play elsewhere." The dealer made the announcement and started tucking away the cards and dealer chips in a drawer beneath him.

"Looks like it's time to go." She scooped up her chips, stuffing them into the pair of pockets on her vest before moving to the ones on her pants.

"You don't have to go."

Oh, but she really did. Especially since she'd figured out exactly who she was talking to. It was one thing to enter the enemy's lair, but another to flirt with him. "I do, especially since you're Akono Sweet."

He grinned again. "I like it when you say my name."

"I'm sure you do. I can imagine you like of lot of things if it lands you a beautiful woman in your bed."

"How about we take this conversation to the bar and you can tell me more about what you like… Is that the offer you're used to receiving?"

She shrugged. "Not sure. I've haven't been in a position to receive offers as of late."

A low profile was what she'd aimed to keep for the last six months. Something to separate her from the person she'd once been, to strengthen her new role as untrustworthy, wayward daughter to the biggest cutthroat business owner on Callisto.

"Well, let me be the first to extend an offer."

She took a long drag. "I think I'll decline and finish my cigarette."

"I heard smoking kills."

Rina smiled this time. "I'll quit smoking the day I find something worth living this life longer for and that will be a cold day in space —"

"Just the two people I was trying to find."

What the hell is he doing here?

Sweet didn't take his eyes off her, but they narrowed and looked more suspicious than she'd seen them. "Do you know this woman, Luca?"

Her brother sidestepped Sweet and put a hand on her shoulder. "I do. Since the day I was born. She's my sister."

Akono Sweet had sat at the table planning to play a few hands with the sexy tattoo parlor owner from across the way. He'd seen the woman plenty over the last several months. She'd caught his eye with her pale skin covered with tattoos. From cards on her neck to the intertwining infinity snakes on her upper arm, he found each tat alluring, in its own colorful way.

So of course, when she appeared in his club, he needed to take advantage of the opportunity and investigate. *Strange how she suddenly appears here for the first time when she's lived across the street for months.* And she wasn't new to the game. Her stack of chips showed as much. Add in her sexy black pants, black vest, white T-shirt, her long brown hair…a bundle of woman that drew his attention.

Except…she turned out to be the sister of his biggest competitor. An enemy.

They'd infiltrated easily enough, and while he'd expected this day to come, he wasn't ready for it.

Akono stood up from the chair, straightening to his full height, which was an inch or so taller than Luca. A good gander between the siblings and the similarities between them started to stand out. Hair color, eye color...though she wore the pale skin better than Luca, who looked a bit sick. "What are you doing here?"

"Came to chat. See you're already talking to my sister." Luca clenched his palm against the woman's shoulder, but if he intended to hurt her, the sister didn't give any hint.

"Say whatever you need to then get the hell out of here." Akono gave a signal to Willie back by the wall. The guard headed toward them, gathering one of the others, Zeke. Akono would have Luca thrown out, the sister too.

Send a strong message.

"I don't like the idea of conducting business out in the open. Better we take this to the back. To talk privately?" Luca had sent spies in before, but never his sister. She'd disappeared six months ago.

If Akono had known it was her across the street from him... "Say what you need to here and now or get out of my club."

Luca grinned, "But it's not really your club, is it?"

"The hell you say." No way would he confess to anything.

Luca shoved a piece of paper in front of his face. Akono skimmed it, taking in the most important parts, the name of the man who'd sold him this place and Vincent Genovese's, both clear as day.

Akono folded up the papers then motioned for his guards. "Fine. Come this way."

Luca looked down at his sister. "You'll be joining us, too. Should have known you'd wait for me at the tables. You could never resist a good round of Arcas Hold 'Em."

So the sister had been a plant. Sweet typically didn't come out on the floor much anymore, with so many of his future plans being focused on ventures far away from the club. But when he'd seen the gorgeous woman on his holo-screens, he'd been unable to resist the temptation. He should have known she'd be a trap. Even worse, a Genovese.

The Genoveses had the moon at their feet, heirs to their father's fortune of clubs and businesses spread across Callisto like an infectious disease. Akono didn't bleed his clients dry, not like that family did. No, those clubs took everything a patron had one way or another. He'd heard the horror stories from other folks who'd worked there and barely got out. Employees paid less than a decent wage, indentured servants bought from the space stations and house women force-fed drugs. *Disgusting stuff.*

Every instinct in his body screamed in opposition to taking these two snakes deeper into the world he'd created. A world he'd once deemed to be safe from these people. *Lies.* "How long is this going to take?"

Akono left the gaming area first, heading towards a set of velvet curtains. He nodded to his guards so they would move in behind Luca and the sister.

"Only a few minutes," Luca replied from behind him.

Through the curtains, up the wrought iron circular stairs to the second level, and only twenty steps away from where his office sat. Select clientele could head down a separate hallway to venture into the house women's entertainment area.

"And you need closed doors to deliver bad news?" Akono kept a steady pace, pulling on the key ring on his belt. A pulley system let the chain extend under pressure. The heft of the keys in his hand seemed more poignant, as if this might be the last time he'd have full control over them. The beginning of the end.

"Closed doors to discuss the nature of what comes next."

He unlocked the door to his office and walked in, flipping the switch to trigger four different lamps to illuminate the room. The paintings, the desk, the chairs...everything in here he'd won or traded for. He couldn't lose all this to them. Refused to.

His guards took up position on either side of the office entrance. Of course they frisked Luca, then the sister. Luca's sister was an enigma. Akono still didn't even know her name. *I shouldn't want to know.*

Except an urge to dive head first into whatever she'd give him still hovered there beneath his skin. He'd heard of her through the years. The ball-busting woman who managed Geno's largest club. At least she *had*, until some mess with an assassin who'd almost killed her father. If she'd been anyone else, he might have summoned an ounce of sorry for her situation, but it was hard to muster up caring for people who gave no hells about him or the people in his enterprise.

Genoveses were greedy, nasty beings. By extension, so were those they associated with. He'd learned over the years to expect the worst from them.

Willy held out a hand for her cigarette.

"What the fatch do you want, a tip?" She spoke right around that damn piece of smoke, like it had melded to her lip and wouldn't let go.

Akono waved Willy to stand down. "There's no smoking in my office. I prefer to leave the smell of shit out here, but it seems like tonight I'm making a lot of exceptions."

She opened her lips, touched the tip of her tongue to the filter and the offensive thing dropped to the floor. Defiance burned bright in her eyes as she squashed the lit end with the tip of her boot, smashing the embers into his carpet. He knew his guards would have someone take care of it, but the disrespectful action wore at his already thinning patience.

Once they were all inside, door shut, Akono stalked to his desk and leaned against it. "You got your privacy, Luca. Say what you need, but this document is going in front of the authorities for verification."

Luca grinned. "The Callisto government seal is imprinted on the bottom. Plain as the stars in the sky. We got the thing in triplicate if you want to keep that copy."

"But I bought this place outright. How in the hell —"

"He never owned it. Not truly. Guess the old fool always figured he'd be too small potatoes to attract our focus. Except you're not running a small business here. And per our contract, we deserve a piece of the action, if the number of patrons coming in and out of here matches my guy's numbers."

Akono frowned, scrutinizing the contract once again. "How much action?"

"Half."

The sister, who'd taken up residence in one of his high-backed office chairs, laughed, throwing her head back in such a way as to expose the column of her neck. Three initials were inked in big script under her chin, and he wondered what they meant.

"Dad wastes no time."

Luca stepped back, lining up with the chair, and looked down at his sister. "Rina, shut up."

Rina...her name sounded a bit blissful. He liked it as much as he enjoyed her saying his. She was so off limits and yet she called to him. A siren in tattoo ink.

Akono set the contract on the desk. "Here's the situation. We can agree to half, if it means I keep my business afloat, but who is going to act on your father's behalf and ensure you get the full amount? I mean, last time I checked, Luca, you were in charge of running the rest of the operation here in Arcas."

Luca touched Rina's shoulder and she tensed. "My sister will."

Chapter Two

"The hell I won't," Rina replied, launching out of the chair and pulling away from Luca's hold on her. She'd sworn off the whole club-managing gig the day Dominic had decided to pull a gun on her father. Her brother had set her up again, moving her like a pawn on some sort of chess board for his own perverse pleasure. Luca's efforts to deceive and manipulate sat heavy in her chest.

"Caterina, remember what happens if you say no." Luca stepped forward and tried to grab her.

She evaded, sidestepping toward Sweet's desk. "I'm not some street trash bought and paid for, damn it."

He smacked her, his hand too fast for her to dodge. "But you're a member of this family, and your duty to the family requires you step up and take care of this."

She growled in defiance. "I may be in a mess, but try to touch me again, you small-sized prick."

The strike never came. No, Sweet stepped in and swung Luca around by his extended arm. "No one hits a woman in my establishment, even behind closed doors."

She used the distraction for her gain, dropping to a crouch position and delivering a couple of blows to Luca's kidneys. "So cute. Mr. Sweet is trying to defend me. But remember Luca…" She circled around, putting her body between Luca's and Sweet's. "I don't need anyone to protect me from you."

She gave Luca a good punch to the jaw and he stumbled back. The sadistic fatch grinned the whole time. Like always, they played the game of pain, blackmail and power. Though she'd never bow to him, his threats were backed by her father. His requests required obedience. Her father used to consult her about all business matters, so to see that her little brother had stepped into her place rankled a bit more than she wanted.

"My big sister, what big paws you have."

Rina wanted to bare her teeth. She glanced around, looking to throw something, guilt and regret like a dozen needles piercing her belly. Her instinct to flee her family had caused this mess. Luca was a fox, sneaky and sly. She never knew when he might try to pull some bullshit or jack a business deal.

"There's more of that where it came from, but no sense kicking your ass. You'd like it too much."

He rubbed his jaw. "You're right about that. Lucky Sweet's here to back you up or we might explore what could really happen."

Those words gave her chills, except heat spread through her as she realized how close Sweet stood. He acted like a solid force behind her, close enough that when he spoke, the deep timbre of his words vibrated within her body.

"There's none of that crap in my place. I'll leave the semi-legal fighting bouts to Geno's. Now get out of here, Luca."

Luca laughed. "Oh, those are nothing compared to a sparring round between the Genovese siblings. Especially no holds barred."

Those words triggered more unsettling reminders, ones that reminded her of the person she used to be, the one who didn't care.

"I've heard the rumors, but I don't run my establishment that way. It's time for you to leave."

As if summoned by Sweet's thoughts, both guards entered the room, swinging the office door wide open.

"Fine. Rina, come. We can chat business tomorrow—"

"No, she can stay. You need to leave." Sweet stepped forward, past her, guiding her brother to the exit. Luca looked unhappy about the arrangement and Rina found Sweet's commanding demonstration attractive. She'd yet to meet a man willing to stand up to her brother.

Luca glanced over his shoulder one last time. "You and I still need to discuss details."

"Which she can do tomorrow, like you suggested. Get the hell out. Papers or not, this is still my place."

For now. She could see the words in Luca's eyes. The idiot just grinned and walked away, escorted by a guard. The fool she was stood and took in the impressive display of power Sweet had deployed. "Interesting."

Sweet pivoted on his heel, his steps back to her smooth and suave. He demanded her attention—everyone's attention—and she'd failed to notice that in her first assessment. "What? The fact that someone defended you, or seeing your brother escorted out of somewhere for once in his life?"

"The escort, because Luca doesn't listen well, and I would think if you've learned anything since we entered this room, it's that I don't need anyone to defend me." Tingles swept up her arms and neck as Sweet smiled and shook his head. This maddening attraction got worse by the second.

"Yes, you're definitely more feral than refined. Surprising, since you're the heir to the richest man on the moon. I guess you wouldn't easily trust people and I'm not the type to do so either."

She cocked her to the side. "Your point?"

"Do I need to worry about you trying to stab me in the back?"

Akono watched Rina closely, the slight widening of her eyes, the hint of blush to her cheeks. The attraction he had for her wasn't one-sided, that much he could tell. Acting on it would be madness.

"Everyone will stab you at some point. But I prefer doing things face to face, unless you attempt to attack me. I've got nothing against you or this club, but surviving in this world requires sacrifices." She moved past him and sat back down in a chair. "I need a cigarette."

"How about a drink instead?" Akono pointed to the bottle of vodka on his desk.

"Fine."

She tapped her fingers against the cigarette case propped on her knee. He liked her fire. Her spark. And he wanted to know if she was a pawn or a larger threat.

"Pretty impressive how you handled Luca." He grabbed two glasses from the bookshelf on the wall and set them on the desk.

She nodded. "I could say the same to you. Though, you've made a permanent enemy of him. Luca hates anyone who tells him what to do. Even our father. So maybe it's a good thing I'll be your contact for this."

The vodka splashed into the glasses, a couple of drops coming back out and landing on the desk. No matter how hard he tried to pour in a nice, controlled manner, shit fell outward. *Kind of the way my life appears to be going.*

"You could tell them no."

She chuckled as she twirled a cigarette between her fingers. "In my family, when father wills it, we do it. But I don't talk about family shit with strangers...so quit trying to pry. Tell me what's in that contract."

Hell of a performance.

"What you already heard. Your father owns half of my establishment and if my attendance hits over a certain level, he's supposed to receive half of the profits for the day." He extended a half-full glass, which she accepted. Their fingers touched briefly, enough of a connection to send a tiny hum through his being. The attraction he experienced toward her was a frustrating complication. She wasn't worth pursuing, and he didn't usually gamble on something unless he knew he could win.

She took a drink, then sighed. What he wouldn't give to inspire that look of satisfaction on her face.

"Bet my brother showing up stings like shine on an open wound, especially since my father will take back every penny."

"Will he really, though?"

Those slender fingers with non-existent nails still gripped a cigarette like it alone kept her from doing something drastic. Rina stared into the clear liquid in her glass. "My father doesn't entertain empty threats, if that's what you mean. You can count on them. The contract is sealed by the moon government and he'll enforce it if needed."

The words echoed the ones his surrogate father, Tobi, had spoken on his deathbed. "Bastard can't leave me be, can he?"

"Vincent Genovese has never allowed competition. He'll find a way to squash it. By legal means and not-so-legal ones. I'm surprised you lasted as long as you did." She took a long swallow and polished off her drink. A small scoot, and she perched on the edge of her chair, pushing the glass onto the desk.

Joseph's balls. "Not my fault people like my atmosphere. Refill?"

She shook her head. "Atmosphere, that's bullshit. I think we can dispense with the lies. You hosted a notorious runner, who's wanted by the APU, and a cartel leader the runner is rumored to have killed. It's enough to put any club on the map. Everyone hopes Emilio Morales will stroll in here. I bet there's a running on the exact time and date. I may be peddling ink stains across the way, but even I hear about the celebrity sightings. Though people can't really describe what Morales looks like, outside of the scar."

She stood up, tucking the cigarette case into her vest pocket, still holding on to the one loose one. "That event alone would have grabbed my father's interest."

"What would grab yours?" Akono asked with a grin. He should have left things be, not fallen into the bad habits he'd cultivated over years of one-night stands and physical release. Flirtation would serve him no purpose with a woman like Rina Genovese.

"Why would you want to do a foolish thing like that?" She closed the distance between them, putting their bodies a breath away from touching. Her heat mingled with his.

Saints above. Foolish didn't come close to describing him. He wanted to do things that might make him a target for his enemies. A part of him wished she'd been an ordinary girl. She walked two fingers up his arm, making him regret always wearing a full suit.

"I noticed you like to cover up all your skin. Ever think about marking it up?" The question came out all innocent-sounding, but her rust-colored eyes met his and chased away any chaste possibilities. No, desirous fire burned there. Hovered between them, like a gambler waiting for the next card turn.

He was lost on whether he'd pull away or ask her to... "Stay with me."

She grinned wide before licking her lips. The fingers turned into a full-on grip of his lapel. Time slowed to a near stop as she moved in closer. Mere centimeters separated their mouths. The clove cigarette became visible, poised between her index finger and thumb. "Very tempting, but a woman like me might" — Rina snapped the cigarette in half — "break you."

Akono swallowed hard and silently willed his cock to stand down, because her words should have turned him off, not on. Right as he opened his mouth to tell her just that, his office door burst open.

"Sweet! Sweet!"

"What is it?" His response came out a harsh growl to the child-screech voice from Dash, his brothel manager's charge.

"Maple says you got to come now. She's up to her eyeballs in trouble. Those were her exact words."

Rina's grip on his suit jacket loosened and she took a step back. "That's my cue. Saved by the messenger...or is it the old saying, don't shoot the messenger?"

She slipped away, past Dash and out of the door. The boy took that as a sign to come forward, wringing his hands. "I should have waited after knocking, huh? But Miss Maple, she's super upset. That silent fury way she gets."

Akono knew that fear and anger part of Maple well. The older woman had been around longer than he had. "It's fine, Dash. Though you should know my anger can be just as fierce."

Dash, all wide-eyed skepticism, stared up at him. "I don't know, Sweet. There's you mean and Maple mean—they ain't the same."

Silly boy. The kid had the type of innocence Sweet would have begged to have at his age. All because of Sweet and Maple protecting him after his mother had died. This club and how Sweet managed it made such a thing possible. "Head on back now and tell Maple I'll be there in a minute."

Before the boy had barely made it out of the door, Akono had already poured himself another drink. He needed to clear his head, get rid of the roiling fire in his blood. The alcohol burned a trail to his stomach. *Replace one problem with another.* Rina was stuck in his mind and he should have been thankful for Dash. *Thankful something stopped me from making a huge mistake.*

Chapter Three

It took Akono fifteen minutes to get from his office over to the brothel's main parlor. Maple stood there, hands on her hips, her curves accentuated by the skin-tight deep purple ankle-length dress she wore. Her hair fell in ringlets around her face, a matching ribbon with a perfect bow off to one side. At one point, she'd led Arcas in fashion, though any admiration for her had died once her profession had been revealed. She'd been the madam here long before Akono owned the place. His mother had apprenticed under Maple, and when she'd passed, Maple had taken care of him. *A second mother.*

"I sent Dash for you over thirty minutes ago, and you take this long?" Irritation dripped from the sentence.

An impatient mother. "I had other business to attend to."

She sniffed. "Yes, I heard. Some pale-skinned, tattooed female. Dash said she looked hateful, fiery."

Rina was all those things and more. Things he would find himself more acquainted with if she followed her father's wishes and became the go-between. "You didn't call for me because of that."

"No, there's a body. One of the girls. She wasn't working tonight and Lily found her sprawled out on the floor. I didn't want to call anyone, knowing how we don't need bad words spread about the club."

"How do you know it's a dead body? Maybe she's just passed out."

Maple stared him down, eyes narrowed. "I might be away from the gambling floors, but I know what a dead body is. Since she's one of my newer girls, stands to reason she wasn't on the straight and narrow like the others."

No drugs, no husbands and no debts. Those were Maple's rules for the house and ones he stood by.

"Where is the body now?"

Maple lifted an index finger and pointed to the ceiling. "Right over our heads, one floor up. I want your opinion before we move her, make sure this isn't a business transaction gone bad, and the question is, where do we move her?"

Akono headed for the staircase. No sense in wasting time, though he'd seen enough dead bodies already to last a lifetime. "When was her last sale?"

"Yesterday evening. Didn't see him leave though, and at bed check everything appeared normal. And you know I don't cut corners."

No, Maple searched under beds and even piles of clothes. Nostalgia mingled with anger at the words. Someone had harmed this woman. A person under his protection.

"She had no visitors in her off time, didn't go out anywhere in the last couple of days?"

"No," Maple replied as they turned on the first landing before they trudged up the stairs, Akono in the lead. "She wanted to spend today indoors, claimed she wanted time to relax. What if she caught some sort of sickness, Sweet? What if we're all in danger?"

They reached the top of the stairs and Lily, one who'd come onboard after her mother had died, stood there with tears in her eyes. "Is that what it is, Miss Maple? An infection? Will we die?"

Maple waved a hand at the woman. "Hush, girl. You'll spread rumors faster than any illness."

"What about our money?"

"We can't earn anything if the doors are barred."

Those statements filtered down the hallway from a small group of house women. All of them huddled around each other, still scantily clad, varying faces holding everything from concern to contempt. *The irony of how they sell their bodies for flash, but can't stand the idea of not making any.*

"That's enough out of all of you. I won't listen to whining. We'll open when we're cleared to do so," Maple hollered.

Akono moved on while the older woman stopped to continue preaching to her charges. She'd get them under control and Akono would examine the body. The women had a point. There was money to be made any given night or day. For as hard as they worked, they deserved every last gold flake. He was going to be taking out of those wages to cover this half mess. *And I'm going to piss everyone off.*

The door to the room Maple had spoken of was closed. Akono took a deep breath before opening it up, but only a faint stench of death greeted him, mixed with a hint of sweat heavy with jasmine. Very different from the dead-body situations he'd been part of in the past.

Akono held up his hand. "Stay at the door, Maple."

"I've already seen the body up close," she countered. She shut the door then stood behind him. "You forget sometimes, we've all lived in the same environment. We're not precious things you need to protect, though the thought is nice. A dead body or two doesn't scare me."

He ignored her and rounded the bed. The young woman lay face up, collapsed in front of the mirror, her face purpled from lack of oxygen, her eyes bloodshot as if she'd been exposed to the cold of space. Such a thing was not possible on the moon.

Akono held no connection to this woman other than that she worked in the brothel he owned. He'd met her once, the day she was hired. One thing he prided himself on was never engaging the services of his house women. No, he sought sexual companions from the patrons within his club. Ones he'd never have to see again, because giving of oneself to another wasn't something he could afford as a business owner.

He examined her neck for signs of strangulation, her hands and arms for defensive wounds, and found none. "She killed herself?"

Maple tsked. "Not possible. Girl had big dreams and everything."

The only thing noticeable on the girl was a tiny butterfly tattooed on her shoulder, its bright yellow a vast contrast to the girl's brown skin. The ink was yellow, but the outline was in a distinctive glitter purple. Ink prominently used by one parlor in the entire city. *Genoveses knocking down my door, tattooing my employees…only fools believe coincidences are random.*

He swallowed hard, then stood up straight and pulled a handkerchief from his pocket. "Maple, I want you to keep the girls under close watch. No leaving the club, not even on their off days or if they beg you."

"That's strange business, Sweet."

He walked over to the ewer of water on the table next to the mirror and wet the piece of fabric down before using it to clean his hands. "Well, times are changing, along with the way we do business. I believe this is a message, one I can't talk about in detail. Until I figure out if my thinking is correct, I want to keep everyone as safe as I can. Understand?"

Maple nodded. "Whatever you say. You ain't steered me wrong yet. What about the body?"

"I'll send in some of the boys to take her to a reclamation facility." Though he wanted a holo-image of the body, keeping it for further observation, even her blood, was against the law. No part of a body was wasted, not in the age of space travel.

"If you want, we can hold a ceremony tomorrow morning, before we open back up." He spread the used cloth over the young woman's face.

"Fine," Maple replied, as she walked over and started rummaging in the girl's dresser. "There has to be something, some clue."

The older woman's motions were a bit frantic, as if the faster she dug around in the silks and negligees, the more likely she'd be to discover the murderer.

Akono put a hand to her shoulder, wishing with everything he could rewind this day, rewind to the fateful day their mutual friend had signed them up for a path of heartache. "Mai-mai, we won't find the answer there."

She sighed before she turned back to face him, tears glistening in her eyes. "I know, Sweet. But I wish we could."

He silently vowed to fix this, not only for those who worked for them, but for Maple. This was why he'd started working on a plan to get them off-planet, every last one of them, when Tibo had died and confessed his greatest sin. Why the Genoveses' interference came at the worst time, before Akono had launched into the third stage of his endgame. But he'd be damned if he let anything stop him now.

* * * *

Rina touched in the tip of the dragon's tail tattoo. "All done. In signature Luna Ink purple. No one in Arcas...hell, Callisto, has a tattoo like this one."

"What do I do now?" asked the recipient.

Rina pulled out the roll of plastic wrap and started to wrap the patron's arm. The guy was a brick shithouse, but damn if he didn't look fearful that he'd move the wrong way and fuck everything up. "You can move the arm. Just keep it wrapped for at least a solar day. Keeps it from getting wet, and lets the ink set in."

"Appreciate you, Rina. You got some raw talent." All wrapped up, the guy hopped out of the chair and fished crinkle out of his back pocket. "I believe it's ten leaves."

She nodded, pocketing the flash. Normally she made less than that, but not often did someone come in requesting a tattoo that covered half their arm. "Welcome. Do me a favor and show that off as much as possible."

He winked at her as he pushed open the front door. "You bet."

Normally, she would have asked her boss, Yash, to get a holo-image of the final product. But he was hunched over some female with a red mohawk, inking a skull above her left breast, and she knew better than to interrupt an artist in his work.

Besides, the moment was lost, and she didn't keep customers waiting around. No, she wanted them out of here and on to the next. No time to make connections or give them a chance to ask lots of questions. Most were too selfish to be worried about her, pre-occupied with the markings they were going to put on their skin. Sometimes she liked the stories accompanying their selection, but usually she enjoyed the customers who gave her creative rein. The chance to treat their skin like a blank canvas.

Plus, when she got lost in the work, she couldn't focus on her anger, her frustration that had become her life. Her confusion on how everything in it had once been so cut and dried, but then had been no longer and was now a muddled mess.

Rina started dismantling the needle injector for her machine, switching out parts, sanitizing tools, wiping down the chair. All muscle-memory things, similar to being in a club. *Fatch.* She'd dreamed about Sweet and his club the night prior. A dream that had left her more aroused than she should've been.

"Hey." The angry greeting paired with the ding of the doorbell and Rina swiveled on her feet, hand instinctively brushing against the handle of the knife strapped to her thigh.

The man who crossed the threshold wore a long shit-brown trench, matching pants, grav boots...the whole thing saying off-worlder. No one from Callisto dressed like that.

"Can I help you?"

"Probably. I'm looking for my brother. We're practically twins, looks a lot like me, but with longer, blonder hair."

She shrugged. "Can't help you. We get so many customers in here a day. We don't keep pictures of them, just the art. Do you know what tattoo he had inked?"

The space traveler stepped forward, frustration etched into each wrinkle appearing on his forehead. "If I knew that, I would have said so. People say he came in here. His friend said he specifically made an appointment."

"We don't make appointments." She didn't care for this spacehole's hostility. She crossed her arms and stared him down, trying her best for a nice passive look, though her bitch-left-her-fatches-in-a-grave look probably showed up.

"Then he was a walk-in." Traveler took two more steps forward, encroaching on her personal sphere and shoving a picture in her face. "What about now? Do you recognize him? I just want to know where he went, what happened?"

The interrogating questions, the crap. She ripped the photo from his hands, took a quick glance then tore it in half. "I don't know where you're from, asshole, but we don't act that way here. Not on Callisto and especially not in Arcas. I barely remember him, but even if I did, I'd have no clue where he went. I don't get chummy with the paying folks. I do my job, I take my money."

The guy growled. "You ripped up the only photo I had. I want retribution. I'll get the pups."

A gun cocked in the background, the sound of the hammer being pulled back unmistakable. Then Yash's voice. "Oy, loud voices disturb the creative process and I don't appreciate my employees being threatened."

Rina glanced over her shoulder. Her boss had stood from his perch, the barrel of his small six-shooter trained on the spacehole. Guns were technically illegal, but Yash had gotten one from some off-worlder in a trade for ink.

"Word of caution." Rina faced their troublemaker. "He's not afraid to shoot. Friends in high places. The pups wouldn't even take the report."

And the gun had no bullets. But most wouldn't take that risk.

The guy shuffled backward, slamming into the door. "I'm sorry, man. I'm just looking for my brother."

Yash motioned with the barrel of the gun at the door. "Then look for him somewhere else."

The guy left, dragging his feet and nearly tripping as he did so. The bell dinged after him and right as the door closed, Rina sighed in relief.

Yash laughed, loud and unashamed, putting the gun back into the small drawer of his ink station. "Never fails to scare the crap out of some off-worlder."

"Only off-worlders? I almost crapped my pants, man. We done?" asked Mohawk woman.

"Yeah, that will be ten leaves."

Rina got back to her cleaning, ignoring whatever conversation played out between the woman and Yash. She was more concerned with the image of the man in the photo. The one torn in half at her feet. She leaned down to pick up the scraps.

"Did you recognize him?" Yash's baritone washed over her.

She stood up straight and brushed her ponytail back behind her shoulders. Concern etched by an abundance of forehead wrinkles and weather lines stared back at her. Yash wasn't quite as old as her father, but she'd known him since she'd been born. His wife Nila had served as a nursemaid to her and Luca, until Nila and Yash had started a family.

"Eh, they all start looking familiar after a while. Especially since I don't look too close at their faces. Only the art."

Yash reached up and took the scraps of photo from her hands. "One-track mind, dedicated to the trade. I'm thankful for that, Rina."

"Yeah, but I'm not." The sound of Luca's voice had Rina freezing in place.

Yash, not so much. He growled, turning to face the back door. "When are you going to learn I prefer you come in the front door?"

Luca's laughter always sounded sinister, a low building chuckle she'd heard in her nightmares over the years. Rina shut it out with sheer determination and a constant need to be faster, stronger.

"But surprising people is what I do best, Yash. You should know that. I need to talk to Rina a minute."

Yash shrugged with some incoherent sound and staggered back to his booth.

Wonder if he'd be so accommodating if he knew Luca threatened Nila and the kids.

"Speak quick. I've got things to do." Rina faced her brother then. He looked the usual, dressed in his business suit finest, a black rose pinned to his lapel.

"You should've stabbed that man when you had a chance. One troublemaker usually leads to more." Luca's swagger matched his ego. If she didn't know him better, she'd think the words were a threat toward her. This visit was expected after Luca's little pissing contest with Sweet last night. One her father was forcing her into the middle of.

"When I want your input on how to handle things, I'll ask for it."

"Whatever. Can we talk upstairs?" he asked, pointing to the ceiling above.

She nodded, though the temptation to tell him to say whatever he had to say right here ran high. Being alone with him was less than ideal.

They walked past the tattoo chairs and tables and down a narrow hall with a shitty blinking tube light. They needed to replace it. *Hell, the light could burn down the building with its peeling paint and crappy cracked flooring.* The damn place was a mess, but it wasn't hers to mess with. No, Yash had run this place since Nila had had their first child. Years of saving crinkle working in her family's employ had yielded a business of his own.

When it had come time to run, Yash had offered her the small apartment on the top floor. The one his family had lived in until the business had afforded them enough to move into a house. She walked all the way to the back of the hall and made a sharp left, then up the stairs, to her private apartment. The stairs creaked, first with her light steps then heavier with Luca's weight. At the top was a little landing and another door. She opened it, leaning forward to flick the light switch, illuminating her little one-bedroom haven.

"Jeez, Rina. This place is a hovel. Why the hell haven't you moved back home?" Luca said that every time.

"I didn't bring you up here to discuss my living choices. I want to know why you and Dad are suddenly going after The Sweet Spot." She walked over to the fridge and pulled out a bottle of Fizzy. Carbonated beverages were supposedly bad for people, but she loved the sweet fake orange taste.

"What happened to you knowing your place?"

"I'm in my place and you're going to get kicked out of it you keep acting like I'm some peon. Treat me with respect or fuck off." She set her bottle of Fizzy on the counter and let her hands form into fists.

Luca puffed up and marched over until he was in her face. "Respect works both ways, and I'd say, since you wimped out and ran when shit got tough, I deserve a bit more."

Rina grinned something wicked. She threw the first punch, straight to the gut. The second, a follow-up across his face. *Talk about muscle memory.* She been in a scuffle nearly every night at Geno's. Working as the manager, she didn't care if the bouncers were taking care of it—she'd throw herself into the fight. But scrapping with her brother? Until the other night, she hadn't done such a thing in years.

And Luca recovered a lot faster than he'd done as a kid, keeping at a half crouch and barreling into her. The air whooshed from her lungs and she lost her balance for long enough to take a few steps backward, until she came into contact with the refrigerator.

That was when he stood, took a step back and feinted for the punch. She moved her left arm up to block. Luca surprised her, coming in for a sucker to the face from the right.

She shook it off and growled, "If all you have is trick shots, you're in trouble, little brother."

Luca sighed, wiping the trickle of blood on his lip with his thumb. "Okay, shit. I'm sorry. Just hold up. While I needed this, I don't need to show up looking like a bloodied, bruised mess."

She dropped her fists to her sides, but stayed semi-ready. Trusting her brother never seemed to work out. "Apology accepted. But you need to get someone else for this Sweet Spot business. Dad wants me back, this is not the way."

Dad…he still wants to play master of the puppets. Wasn't it enough he had the pair of them feeding off fights with each other? A sick, twisted display of familial connection, one that nourished Luca's hidden fetishes.

"That's not an option. There's no choice in this. You're lucky he let you run to begin with. He's demanding you return. To *everything*."

Business, family dinners and the family estate. "I'm not moving home."

"We can burn the bed." Luca grabbed her bottle of Fizzy and downed the rest.

The jab was meant to rile her, but she'd realized over the last six months that her depth of caring for Dominic, the man she'd planned to spend forever with, a man who'd tried to kill her father, had never run too deep. They'd been together out of necessity, a common goal and uniting force against her brother. To ensure she came out on top of the family business. "Forget it."

"Then say goodbye to Yash, Nila, the girls. This place."

He who refuse, runneth over. She pushed off the fridge, opened the door and grabbed another bottle. Popping the cap, she swallowed half of it in record time.

While Dominic had never left a note or anything to explain why he'd ruined the future they had planned or why he'd suddenly despised her father, in her months away from the environment and her limited interactions with her brother, she'd found it easy to embrace distaste for everything she'd once been.

Luca chucked his empty bottle into her waste bin. "Come on, Rina. You don't want to force Dad's hand. People will die, lives get destroyed. I know you don't want to see that. Neither do I. We need you this time, one more job. You might even remember how much you loved the life, huh? Just manage Sweet's crap, give up this inking shit and come home."

"I'll be staying here. If I do any of this, my central location doesn't change. I'll tell Dad as much at the next dinner." She refused to be the cause of more death, but would stand her ground as needed. Going back home wasn't healthy for her.

"Fine. I'll tell him what you said."

She finished off her bottle and dropped it into the bin, enjoying the sound of the two bottles shattering as they hit. "Then I guess *no* isn't the word I'm looking for. It's *when*."

Luca grinned and the Fizzy curdled in Rina's stomach. "You start tomorrow."

Chapter Four

"Antonia Smith." Sweet plastered on his biggest smile and prayed the woman he needed now more than ever was having better luck than he was.

"Sweet. Long time no betrayal."

Yep, the reminder stung. One she continually threw at him whenever she wanted. He stared at the view screen. One of the craziest and most beautiful women he'd ever met gazed back at him. Many a time he'd tried to win her over to his side, subtly…Akono never begged. But Toni was a wild, free spirit who refused to be tamed or brought to heel by any man. At least, until Emilio Morales.

"Yes, why are you calling again, Akono? We said we had things well in hand." The devil himself, swarthy, black-haired, black-eyed, cheek-scarred Morales came into view. The man wrapped his arms around Toni and squeezed her to him. A twinge of jealousy hit Sweet in his chest. Not of the couple specifically, but more of what they shared. The way Toni's eyes lit up at her husband's display of affection.

"I know and I trust you've got Genisys well in hand. This is about the next phase, the final steps we need to take. I know —"

"And you've screwed up." Emilio smiled with those words. The runner loved to poke at him like a junkie with a needle.

"No. My timelines have changed, thanks to other parties. I don't see why it would matter to you. You make plenty of flash. Besides, don't deny I've passed good business your way in the last eight months."

"Business you hoped would get you back in our good graces," Toni countered.

Not a lie. "Yes, and I needed to confirm what I hoped...that I could depend on you."

Emilio leaned around his wife. "It helps that you pay well, too. I guess it's worth hearing what this third phase is. As long as Toni agrees."

Toni nodded once and Sweet let out a small sigh. "I appreciate this. You have no idea what it means to —"

"Keep it short, Sweet. I have other plans for my day." Emilio readjusted his hold on Toni, cinching his arms around her waist, supporting her.

"All right. I'm in need of a ship. A big ship. Something that can carry two hundred people from the Callisto space station and get us to the Genisys destination."

Toni's eyebrows hunched down. "When you said we were helping you create a haven, you never mentioned this."

On purpose. "Telling you the entirety of my plans might put them at risk. There's too much at stake for me to risk everything because someone needs all the details."

Toni scoffed. "Excuse me for preferring to operate on an entire story. I've got people to take care of too."

"*Tsk tsk*. Honey, you mean *we* have people to take care of." Emilio added the admonishment with a sickeningly kind kiss to the tip of his woman's nose.

In turn, she reached up to caress his cheek, her hand covering the gruesome scar on the side of his face. Akono cleared his throat.

Toni narrow-eyed him. "So, you want us to go cruiser shopping for you?"

"Yes...I mean, no. I have a cruiser. It's docked at Callisto station, but it doesn't work right now. I need an engineer and a crew to get it running." Akono had won the thing off an idiot who'd gotten addicted to drugs. At one point, he'd considered selling it to Toni, except he needed it. The dead woman's body in his brothel and the Genoveses on his doorstep expedited the need.

Emilio grinned. "What you're asking for would cost you."

"Whatever you need, I'll pay." He should have put a stipulation on that. While business had been good in the last eight months and his profits near doubled every day, the Genoveses wanted their cut. While he hadn't heard a peep from them in over a day, he had no doubt they'd bang on his door again soon enough. His flash tank, while endowed, wasn't endless.

"Oh, we know you will," Toni replied.

Akono would take that for an agreement, for now. "What is the status on Genisys?"

Emilio and Toni both got serious, all smiles and smirks wiped away. Toni spoke first. "We've brought her to the final destination and our mutual friend with the debt to pay says that he'll be ready to launch in the next six hours."

Sweet nodded his understanding. "Good. I'll expect an update then."

"Sure thing," Emilio offered. "Also, that cruiser is going to take us the better part of a month. You know that, right? That's if we catch a good current back to the station. I hope you're not in a hurry."

A month was like a lifetime on Callisto. Gambling empires rose and fell in less time. Add in hostile takeovers and the occasional hover-by... Anything became possible. "There's no way to speed things up?"

Toni shook her head. "Not if you want us to keep Gen safe and protected. We need to have time to secure everything. I don't think you want us towing your cruiser to a place that's not proven to be safe and sound. Per your directions."

Sweet rubbed a hand over his face, dragging his fingers down his cheeks. "Fine, fine. I'll have payment waiting for you on Callisto station in the usual drop. Just get the damn cruiser done as soon as you can."

The door to his office burst open then, and Rina strolled in. She dragged along his door guard, Zeke, who was moaning in pain, most likely due to the awkward angle Rina held his wrist. He hobbled with her to avoid breaking the damn thing. "One thing you need to learn about me, Sweet. I don't like to be kept waiting by business partners."

The woman was a force, a force he'd like to be directed his way. Akono licked his lips, trying not to be completely aroused at Rina's dominant display.

"Who is that, Akono?" Emilio asked.

Toni's eyes went wide. "Since when do you have a partner?"

He didn't have time for questions. "Afraid I have to cut this short, Morales. I'll be in touch."

Akono clicked the view screen off and focused on his unexpected visitor. "Can you let my guard go?"

Rina did as asked, surprisingly, and Zeke dropped to the floor. An odd scene to be present for, and the imagery momentarily reduced him to an attracted fool with no thought for anything but the beauty before him.

The man's cheeks held a slight pink, though his pursed lips told a different story. "Do I leave her here, boss?"

"You get the hell off the floor and pretend I didn't put you there," Rina replied, whipping her ponytail behind her shoulders. *White T-shirt, black vest, black boots and slacks. With the tattoos up and down her arms, she looks like a member of my security team herself.* "Plan on me showing you a few things if you plan to continue acting as a door guard."

Akono nodded at Zeke, who got up and left the room, shutting the door behind him and leaving Akono to deal with the mess this fiery woman brought in her wake. "To what do I owe the pleasure of your appearance, besides having you embarrass the people working for me?"

"Then let's great straight to business." She smiled then, something sinful and designed to make his pants tighten. Sure, he knew the attraction was strong, but getting hard from a smile? *That's never happened before.* He certainly didn't want it to happen again. Two nights prior had been a different story, but he couldn't afford to play with the temptation she brought.

She crossed the room, bringing with her the scent of orange blossom and a lingering smell of bleach. "I need your books, your desk and the understanding that I'll cut off any appendages that touch me."

The words were rough, to the point, and he almost winced at how a shiver trailed down his spine at her commanding tone.

I'm screwed.

Rina had showed up to ensure the safety of her boss and his family, not because the man staring her down affected her more than she'd ever experienced with Dominic. A kind of sinking and falling feeling, like a ship falling from the sky...at least she imagined that was what falling would be like.

Akono flirted his way through everything, or she was reading too deeply into things. Which was exactly why she needed boundaries in place, to keep things business and stay far from personal. *Cue my barge and bash.* Though Sweet had looked at her as though she was beauty personified. A woman could get stupid with looks like that.

"I'm not sure why I need to give you access to anything." Maybe he wasn't as affected as she'd initially imagined.

She sighed and crossed over to his desk, closing the distance between them. Erasing that safe, invisible line, similarly to how she'd dissolved it the last time she'd been in this room.

Business. Stick to business. "Because it's the fastest way for me to prove to my brother and father that you haven't had high attendee numbers. Therefore, we don't need to step in and they don't need me here."

She spoke the words, but deep down below, the rock lodged in her chest branded her a liar, her confidence lying low.

Landra Graf

"Can you prove such a thing?"

She shrugged. "It's worth trying, right?" *Worth ending this before more people die because of me.*

"Then by all means. Take a seat, look at the books. Maybe I can get you a drink while you work." Sweet motioned to his chair, a high-backed monstrosity that she sank into. "I assume you know how to use holo-screens?"

"I did your job once. So yeah." Hints of leather and cherry drifted by. Sweet's scent, possibly.

The job...focus. The holo-screen took a minute to play with, but she accessed the records. The dollar amounts, the orders for booze, cards and the payouts to each employee. Nothing shady. As she pried into the finances of the club, Sweet poured liberal amounts of whiskey into his glass and a new one.

"Where are the real numbers?"

"Those are the real numbers."

She scoffed and kept digging. There were reasons her father trusted her with everything. She'd been good at burying the real figures, fudging the numbers, along with keeping the patrons happy. Geno's had hit its height when she'd managed the place, super popular and with the lowest turnover rate. That was when people had wanted to work for her family.

Sweet set the glass in front of her, and she accepted it, glancing up with a shake of her head. "No one keeps real books. Not now or ever."

"I do," he said, right before he downed the whole glass. Each swallow punctuated the long column of his throat. His chin and neck showed no signs of emerging hair, meaning he'd shaved no more than an hour or so before. She wanted to kiss that expanse of neck, see if she'd get scratched for having desire for someone she couldn't be with.

"You're staring."

Rina lifted her glass to her lips. "My eyes can wander as they please."

He leaned down over her, a smile on his lips. "Or they can't get enough of me?"

This man, all smooth-skin and clean, seemed to channel some sort of bravado with ease, which prompted her to desire the opposite.

"Talk like that will get body parts on the floor."

Sweet walked around the desk, removing the final object keeping them apart. "You could have all of me on the floor."

Damn. Where did the business piece go again? His offer was enticing, a little distraction to chase away the demons hounding her dreams—with disastrous consequences.

"If you want to keep playing games, I can leave. But that means you're willing to go to war. My brother says your operation is a threat. Genoveses deal with threats in only one of two ways. I'm the less painful version."

"Do you always sound sexy when you're talking about business?"

She smiled—couldn't help it. Not when he kept increasing the bet, refusing to check. "I was going for serious."

He leaned back against his desk, using his palms to brace himself. "All work and no play?"

"Usually the best way to handle things." She wanted to dispense with this thing between them, fold and try for a new hand. "I say we get back to business. Will it be me or my brother?"

Sweet sighed and stood, moving away from the desk, providing the space she wanted. "You, I guess. Your father and brother aren't leaving me much choice. You've looked at the books, and they confirm the reality. Those numbers your brother had weren't staged or fake. They are the real deal. I owe him what the contract stipulates."

Shit. Whoever heard of an honest club owner? "Yes, if you haven't faked anything, then you owe every last penny. One would think you were smarter than this."

"Smarter than? Sorry, I don't get off on the idea of being dishonest. I run a clean place, a solid business. No one in Callisto could say that, until me. My people thank me for it. Honesty is among thieves, at least under this roof." The conviction of his words touched something inside her cynical heart and a twinge of respect for him appeared alongside the attraction.

"You're quite passionate about your business. So I hope you're willing to do whatever you can to save it." She downed the last little bit of her drink and set the glass on the table. The numbers in front of her equated a lot of money. Money, based on his current numbers, he didn't have.

Sweet clapped his hands together. "Then, what's first on the agenda?"

"I need to become familiar with your operation. What you do here that facilitated the ability to purchase all these fine furnishings." She motioned to the wall-set bookshelf, the matching desk, the Diaz painting worth a tiny fortune. The expense was plain to see, though an average house woman or dealer might be oblivious.

Sweet walked toward the door. "Fine, I'll show you around. Though I doubt seeing it will reveal how we save it."

He ignored her question. It seemed she'd hit on a sore subject, one she'd have to push back against at some point.

"Hey, this is as painful for you as it is me." A little bit of a lie, because part of her craved this environment, being back in the nightclub game.

He opened the door and glanced over his shoulder. "I thought I told you before? I like pain."

Chapter Five

Sweet forced his demeanor to change as soon as he crossed the threshold out of his office. He discarded the flirtatious man who teased and smiled, replacing him with an emotionless, fierce creature. And he embraced the fact that he'd lied to Rina in his office. He'd lied about several things. But one didn't trust a fox in the henhouse, as Mai-Mai would say.

"Terrance, this is Rina. Where's Zeke?"

"Went to get his wrist checked. Should be back any minute, sir." Terrance, like all the other guards, had grown up with Sweet and lived the similar stories of turmoil and struggle, exactly why they'd all flocked to his side when Akono had gotten the club. It was why they stayed loyal and another reason why the Genoveses didn't deserve The Sweet Spot.

"Nice to meet you, Terrance. You're definitely taller than the last guy. How long have you worked at The Sweet Spot?" Rina asked the question without looking at Terrance or Akono, instead examining the hallway, sucking in details like a computer mainframe. The question seemed to be in how she planned to use those details.

"I've been here for years. Can't really say it's worth keeping track of time."

Her words about trying to save his business almost made him laugh. How she, a woman of privilege, might save their poor, distasteful souls. Too bad his dick didn't scamper from such insinuations. Nope, the damn thing was still all in where this woman was concerned.

"I agree. Keeping track of your flash passes the time better."

She stared Akono down, intentionally. A nice jab right at him and his books. Was it possible she knew he was lying? He liked to believe no, because he had a pretty damn good poker face.

"That may be your way, but not mine," Terrance offered.

"How many of these guards do you have?" Rina asked.

Akono debated lying about that too. Her presence here, becoming familiar with his operation, potentially left him wide open for a hostile takeover.

"Your hesitation speaks bricks. But I promise you this...my brother already knows the count, the entrances and the best times to hit. He doesn't need me on the inside to supply that information. Me asking either means I want to see if your numbers match his or I don't know them to begin with."

Fatch. The woman appeared to be a mind reader too. "Which is it?"

"You'll have to wait and see." She winked at him.

Akono shook his head, attempting to keep his face impassive. "I have five or six guards, depending on the day or situation. Zeke, the one you assaulted, is one of my top guards, along with Terrance here. There are a few others and my second in command, Ant. Along with the majordomo at the door, Ned. All are loyal to me."

"Loyalty is a commodity too many people trust in and it's an investment most lose out on." Rina wore cynicism and future betrayal like a coat.

"Seems Terrance and I have plenty to disagree with you on. Let's get this tour and round of introductions started." Akono nodded to Terrance, who departed his post at the door and headed down the hall.

Akono motioned to Rina to move on. "After you."

As she walked forward, he locked the door then followed behind the pair back out into the club area, where the sounds of dice, cards, music and laughter made their way to his ears. Every area was packed with people eager to gamble, drink, dance and screw their way to an enjoyable evening.

"Ned takes care of greeting patrons, ensuring no one who is banned enters the establishment, and he tracks the numbers. You can quiz him on his methods if you still doubt the books."

"You should doubt them," she said. The woman had no filter, or ability to hold back from letting loose. He looked forward to her conversation with Ned.

"I think you and Ned are going to get along famously. Ant monitors the gambling tables. We can introduce you later." Akono pointed to the taller-than-Terrance behemoth of his best friend. Ant dressed similarly to Sweet in a suit and tie, but without a hat. Ant preferred to show off his braided hair, the designs changing each solar week.

"You said you grew up with all of them. Any of them work for my father before working for you?"

"No." He spat out the rebuke, because the idea sounded abhorrent. No one from this entire neighborhood would entertain the idea.

They walked down the spiral staircase that stood as the division from the open to patrons and the closed-off areas.

"What about the brothel?"

"We prefer to call it the entertaining rooms. We passed the entrance before we came down."

They reached the bottom of the staircase and Rina swiveled to face him. "I guessed. My question is why don't you have a more accessible entrance? Seems a bit short-sighted to have a major part of your operation with such limited access."

Akono leaned in, and the gap between them melted away. "Because I protect those in my employ, especially the most vulnerable. The previous owner had an entrance like that and his women were assaulted or worse. This staircase detects weapons that might otherwise be concealed."

"An interesting approach."

"I'm not like the other club owners. I value my people."

She frowned. "Risky, but admirable. What other innovations do you have?"

"Not as many as you'd think, but enough to give me an edge when it comes to offering a level of protection to this establishment and keeping things more honest and fair." Akono side-stepped her and headed for the far edge of the bar.

Rina stopped next to him, leaning against the bar. She took in the three bartenders mixing drinks and dropping the crinkle received as payment into a metal tube. One of the dealers walked up from a table and handed over a container of their own.

"That, right there. Is in an innovation."

"The cylinders?"

Akono nodded, pushing off the bar and heading for the entrance to the club. "Yep, in all their glory. That's my way of getting money deposited."

"It's a pneumatic tube system, right? My father has those. They were on Earth-before-the-nuke, rudimentary but still effective."

"This is no simple system. I upgraded it. Instead of dropping all the flash into one safe, it sends it via an AI computer that divides everything up into individual boxes accessed by fingerprint. My employees are paid every day. And I don't have to let the crinkle be touched by human hands. Keeps everyone honest."

"That's...impressive."

He shouldn't have enjoyed how surprised she sounded, yet he wanted to prove to her how he was different from her family—more humane, not ruled by greed. "Thank you. Now, you need to meet Ned, my host."

She chuckled. "We've already met, but I'm good with an official introduction."

Side-by-side, they made their way towards the front. "You employ around twenty to thirty people, no small children?"

"That's correct."

"And you don't widely advertise?"

They skirted between the dining tables and the gambling area. The dance floor to the far side slowly started to populate as the band began a jazzy, snappy number.

"The most important advice I ever received from Tibo, the previous owner, was to fly under the radar. Nothing gets your father's attention as fast as competitive advertising. I've seen clubs go down after one big campaign." He also enjoyed when she looked at him like he'd invented terraforming, wide-eyed and with a hint of a smile. He'd say whatever he had to if it meant she'd keep looking at him like that.

"Sound advice. I would have offered the same."

Patrons walked by and Akono offered simple smiles and kind hellos. The words and actions were part of the game, part of the number of masks he wore on the floor, whether the man an idiot wouldn't cross or the ever-gracious owner. Sleek and suave were needed, which was exactly why he employed the ever-effusive Ned.

"How are things looking?" Akono asked as they reached the podium and he put a hand on Ned's shoulder.

Ned was clothed from head to toe in dark purple. Hat, suit and even his shiny shoes. "It's a good evening to visit The Sweet Spot. I won't lie, people have been asking if the younger Genovese is going to be making more appearances. I keep telling them they'll never know if they don't stay."

Rina rolled her eyes. Akono needed to pay more attention to that. Her blatant dislike for her family lent to her whole I-want-to-help-you act.

He pointed in her direction. "This is Miss Rina, Luca's sister. She's going to be helping us out for a bit."

Ned nodded in her direction with a wink. "Yes, we've met a couple times. Can you tell me if your brother will be stopping by more frequently?"

She leaned up against the podium and gave a wink of her own. "Let's hope not."

"I won't tell people that," Ned replied. "You need to learn how to charm the masses and tease a little."

She can tease aplenty. The last two times they'd been alone in his office had proven her abilities to flirt were not hindered in the least.

Another couple walked in through the door and she chose to step back from the podium instead of responding. Akono greeted them first, then Ned. When they pair moved on, he asked her one more question. "How long will you be joining us, Miss Rina?"

"She won't be, because I thought we agreed to ditch her." Ant marched up, his braids swinging behind him. He wore a suit similar to Sweet's, but not nearly as wrinkle free. Put together, but slightly disheveled.

"Who are you?" Rina growled as she stepped in front of Akono. Her natural inclination to charge forward against a threat wasn't a good sign. He liked people who were cool, calm and collected in the face of trouble.

"I'm Ant, second-in-command. We don't need you. We can deliver the money."

Akono sighed. His tall, growly, mountain of a friend had never been any of those things. The way Ant stared down at Rina as if she was nothing, worth nothing, bothered him too.

"Funny, that's not what your boss said, and I only take orders from the guy in charge." Rina stepped up toe to toe, her fatch-this-guy expression and the clenched fists at her sides a sign he needed to take action.

"And I don't remember when your voice spoke over my orders." Akono moved in between them, shoving at both their arms and forcing them to step away from the entrance.

Once they were a foot or so away from the people still streaming through the door, Akono pointed at Rina. "Ant meant no disrespect."

Rina directed a wide, shit-eating grin at Akono's second. "Then he can apologize."

If Ant scoffed any louder, people would think they had structural issues. "When Arcas freezes over —"

"Do the rounds, keep the patrons happy and the assholes out," Akono interrupted the bastard. No way would he let a fight break out at his entrance a day after Luca Genovese had disrupted his entire enterprise.

As Ant stomped off, Akono turned to her and let out a sigh. "He's a spacehole, but there's a time and a place for pissing contests. My entrance is not one of them."

The smile she'd so eagerly employed disappeared. "Then you should teach your employees not to be so hot-headed."

"I think my people have a right to be scared of your father encroaching on our business."

"Oh, no doubt. But Ant has more of a power trip. I've seen his type often in my father's clubs. More often than I'd like, and I've had to put several in their place. You reacted well. More than I expected, really."

He shook his head. "It would help if you would do your best to avoid him. I'm not a fan of fights, which lead to disruption...unless that's your goal here, to disrupt."

"So it's my fault your second has an anti-female attitude," she replied, hands on her hips, looking as regal and pissed as she ever did.

"No, I'm asking you to be better than him. Now, enough crap, let me show you the rest of the operation." Akono led the way back up the spiral staircase and in the opposite direction of his office...through the entertainment rooms door.

He glanced back at her. "We have the one entrance, the one exit open to patrons. There is one additional entrance for people to escape in case of a fire or explosion... I won't show you where that is, so don't ask."

"What will you show me?" The inflected tone paired with a wink sent a flood of renewed arousal across Akono's body.

"The operation only. Familiarity with the number of rooms, the layout." He recited the words, stepping farther into the main room.

They walked down a little hallway with cream-colored wallpaper and flowers, very feminine and demure. Yet for all the soft element, an underlying smell of bleach remained. He'd paid a hefty price for cleanup after the incident. Except the efforts had left behind a distinct scent he hoped Rina didn't recognize.

The main room boasted couches and chairs, all in reds, purples and greens. Women posed on different ones, some with a man or even another woman. They hung on arms, trailed fingertips along ears, jaws, whispered sweet nothings, and did whatever they had to, short of stripping themselves naked, to entice patrons upstairs to the bedrooms where the real fun would begin.

"Everyone is over-age?" she asked, coming to a halt beside him.

His knowledge of the Genovese brothels included little children and other taboo practices on display — Rina's father catered to depraved interests, making the rumors that her brother Luca ran the thing even more disturbing.

"Yes. I would think I've already expressed that I run clean and legal." The only thing he hid was his endgame.

"What other aspects are there besides willing bodies and rooms? I don't see the need for me to be here."

He motioned to the women in the room. "Do you find these women less than you for having to resort to this way of life?"

"I don't judge them. They can't be faulted for selling the only thing they have worth anything. I only wish they had other options, other means."

"I'm sure they do too, but your father has made it nearly impossible for those of us in the poorest of positions to get anywhere further than where we are now."

She looked down, her fists balling up again. But Akono wasn't sorry if he'd hit a sore spot.

"Follow me. You should at least see the layout of the second floor and rooms." Akono started up the staircase without her. *Maybe I've scared her off.*

"What's the rush?" she asked, four steps behind him.

He didn't bother responding and kept moving up the stairs. Once on the floor, he motioned to the different rooms. "These are all entertaining rooms. The girls have ones assigned to them. There are specialty areas as well for those with certain needs."

Rina walked past him, glancing at each door and stopping in front of a solid black one. She rapped on it. No answer came. "What do you keep in here? The ones who misbehave?"

Akono reached around her, the temptation of her scent, cloves and vanilla, wrapping around him. He breathed in deeply, and his whole body tensed as he grabbed the doorknob, turned it and gave a slight push. "We use this room to punish those who seek pain."

He flicked on the light right inside the door. "Something you mentioned you were interested in inflicting before."

Rina's head moved as her gaze tracked the various instruments in the room. Walls lined with whips, canes, devices with feathers, beads, spikes and so many more. Stationary tables where people could be restrained upright, face down… The possibilities were endless.

Akono would never admit that he had never stepped foot in here. No, his desires were unfulfilled, deep-seated things he refused to let emerge when they could be used to end his very existence. *Unnecessary risks.*

"I like to drive needles into people's skin. There's something soothing about breaking into flesh. A far cry from what I really would like to do with them, but some things are not legal." Her words came on a breathless whisper, like this was the first time she'd voiced them out loud.

Akono opened his mouth to respond when a shrill scream rent the air.

Sweet reacted before Rina did, taking off in a sprint down the hall. The sound came from the second floor, somewhere behind them. She acted on instinct, switching off the light and shutting the door, still surprised that a room filled with so many weapons had no lock.

She headed in the direction Sweet had gone, relishing some sort of action. Anything to take her mind away from whatever moment she'd just shared with Sweet. He'd smelled her, and showed her a room of things to torture him with. If that wasn't foreplay, she didn't know what to call it.

Sweet's destination appeared to be a room on the opposite side of the stairwell, part of the floor she'd glimpsed but not paid close attention to. He was attempting to work his way around a small group of women who were milling about the open doorway. An older woman stood near the center, her hair piled on top of her head and wrapped up in shining fabric.

Slowing her steps before she plowed into him, Rina barely stopped herself in time. "Sweet, what's going on?"

Akono pivoted, but his attention focused on whoever was behind her. "Ant, Zeke, get the patrons out of here. There's been an accident and we'll reopen tomorrow."

"Should we remove her too?" *Ant with his big man complex again.* At some point she would need to show him exactly who he was messing with.

"She is not a patron. Stick to business and deal with your personal issues later."

Rina smiled. "I'm so glad there's a time for pissing contests."

"Don't give me a reason to have them kick you out," Sweet said before turning away to face whatever was in that room.

"What's wrong?" The expression on his face, all dread and displeasure, prompted her concern.

"Nothing I haven't dealt with before. Follow me in." He stepped back into the throng, gently moving the women out of his way by pushing them on their shoulders.

Rina followed suit and, judging from the mascara-lined tear tracks on some of their faces, someone was injured or worse.

Sweet made it through the door then turned to face the group. "Excuse me, ladies. Probably time to head back to your rooms."

Rina frowned. *Fool's idea to just gloss over everything with dismissal.* "How about all of you head across the hall, instead? We'll get something to drink up here for you. A good shot of whiskey."

The gals nodded in agreement and moved away, not far but enough to provide a little space. Sweet didn't dismiss her statement, but his attention moved to the older woman with the shiny-wrapped hair.

This woman appeared important, judging by the way Sweet held her hand and stood as a stable body for her to lean against. The older woman shook as he held her. "Sweet. I swear…"

Sweet appeared to be taking in the state of the room, so Rina did the same. She glanced into the room and saw the lower half of the body lying on the bed. "Maple, did she have company?"

Maple nodded. "He's the one who came and told me. I compensated him a refund and sent him on his way. I thought maybe she faked it. Didn't like the patron or something. But instead I found her body."

Rina glanced at the lifeless figure on the floor as the old woman uttered the last syllable. Rina couldn't help but walk toward the body.

"Do we have the patron's name?" Sweet asked.

"He's a regular," Mabel offered.

"Good. You'll tell his name to Ant to track down. We need to question him. Was he here the night of the last one?"

Rina reached the bed and grabbed the woman's wrist. No pulse. She looked over her skin, searching for the tell-tale signs of drug use, as overdose was a common cause of death in Arcas. "What do you mean, the last one?"

Sweet looked up, meeting the questioning gaze in Rina's eyes. "It may be better if you stay outside."

She frowned, disturbed by this turn of events. "If your housewives are dying on a regular basis, it may be something I'll have to inform my brother of."

"It's not a regular occurrence, just a strange coincidence. Someone else overdosed here at the house." Sweet guided Maple to a chair in the corner of the room. "There's no reason to tell your brother anything."

"Aren't you required to report it?"

Sweet crossed to where she stood, squaring up. "It's most likely an overdose, in a city of hundreds of them a week. This is the moon of souls destined for fuel reclamation—one more body makes no more difference. Especially one that's poor."

"I don't see any evidence of drug use." Rina stepped closer, to the point where she could see a small scar above his left eye and the stubble on his chin.

He reached around her and pulled the sheet completely off the dead woman. "Then you're not looking in the right place."

Rina swiveled around, sighing in frustration. "This is not a competition, but we should do right by…" The words died on her tongue at the braided blonde hair, the nose ring and a tattoo she was familiar with.

"What? What do you see?"

Funny how she no longer wanted to see. For all her bluster about her recipients blurring together, some she remembered. "This girl, I know her. She came to the shop three days ago. Wanted a simple flower above her breast, her namesake, she said. Talked about life after Arcas, said she planned on surviving."

Another lie we tell ourselves.

"A damn shame," Maple mumbled.

Sweet walked around to the other side of the bed, grabbed the sheet and covered the body again. "Maple, get the girls some drinks. Question them and remind them of the prudence of being quiet."

"And when they want to know who killed her?" Maple stood, tears in the corners of her eyes. Rina didn't miss the accusation in the older woman's gaze.

Sweet looked at the older woman, straight on. "Mai-mai, it's got to be this way. She took her own life."

"There's no proof of that," Rina countered again. The girl she'd met in her shop wouldn't have killed herself. Just like her fiancé had had no reason to attack her father. Senseless deaths where people deserved answers.

Sweet threw his hands in the air. "This is the best option of all. You feel like Luca needs to know? Fine, but I'll be damned if I risk anyone else's life or livelihood because a lady died. None of this can get out. The reputation of everyone is at stake."

"What about truth?" Rina had moved to comfort Maple. No one deserved to die without those who cared knowing why. "What about her family?"

"The truth will be uncovered soon enough and retribution swift. If you think otherwise, then allow me to tell you a little about me." Sweet stomped over to her and Maple, putting his face inches from Rina's. "I don't deal in speculation, I don't deal in guesses. Once I know the truth, though, trust I'll act. Besides, what do you care?"

Maple's eyes went wide, as if seeing something she couldn't believe, and Rina hoped she would lay into Sweet later. Thankfully, before the conversation could continue, Ant appeared in the doorway.

"We've got the patrons cleared out, boss. What's next?"

Sweet took a couple of steps back and pointed at the body on the bed. "Wrap her up and get her out of here. Clean everything. Maple will take care of the ladies. Rina and I will handle things next door in the club with Terrance."

With that he left, expecting Rina to follow. She did, after one last glance at the dead woman hidden by a sheet, erased from the world. "If you expect me to act like some dog at your heels every day, I'd like to correct you of the notion right away. And say what you want, but one more lie and I take everything to my father and brother. Let you deal with the consequences if you keep lying to me."

He wheeled on her, a short, sarcastic laugh emerging. "If this is how you plan to treat every disagreement with me, then you're about to find out how much I dislike people trying to handle me. I manage this business. Your sudden interest in me and mine is a shock and surprise, but don't believe I'll fall for the act."

Attraction surged in her veins at his ability to call bullshit, equal amounts of frustration and anger following. She'd thought Sweet might be a bit of a pushover—it appeared not. Her reaction? Fists at the ready, because damn if someone threw her caring back in her face. "My emotions are not an act. I'm not heartless or cold. It's why I left my father's employ, because I refused to be the detached person anymore."

Sweet shook his head. "No. You don't get to throw some sob thing at me. Not when your family's arrival into my club's business has brought nothing but trouble and death."

The lifeless look in that girl's eyes came rushing back. The same look had been on her fiancé's face. If she'd been smacked, Sweet's theory might have hurt less. "So, you think I did this?"

He turned away and resumed walking. "I'm not accusing you."

Through the hallway, back into the main part of the club and down the stairs, each step on the metal clanged within her body and shoved her back into memories of all the bodies, lives she remained responsible for. "You should accuse me."

They'd reached the bottom of the staircase and Sweet scoffed. "I've been told of the mystery of women, but you take the cake. I misspoke and seeing such a thing isn't good for anyone. It's a tough way to start out our evening."

"You're not hearing me clearly. I'm cursed." She'd thought as much before, but dead Rose proved it. Nothing good could come from her life, from her being here.

He laughed. "You're joking, right?"

"No, I never joke about death. It tends to follow me." Ever since her mother's. "I thought I'd escaped it when I left Geno's and went to Yash's parlor. Now, I'm not sure."

The lost brother, Rose...how many more?

"Rina? Rina, look at me. You're no more responsible for their deaths than I am." Sweet's hand came to her shoulder, kneading gently there. The touch was thrilling and she leaned into it, the club melting away around them, until a glass shattered at her feet.

"I refuse to pay for this shine-swill. I want top-shelf liquor and I demand to talk to the owner!"

Sweet looked at her, eyebrows raised. "I am the owner, sir."

Rina nodded her agreement. Her pity party could wait. She'd stuff it down into the dark hole where all her emotions lived, and summon the anger. *Time to go to work.*

Chapter Six

Rina winced as her fork clinked against the china. "I've looked over the books, toured the operation. I believe we can run a fifty-fifty split to start and slowly increase until full takeover."

Three days after her first night at Sweet's and she'd arrived for her first family dinner in six months. *And I'm already bungling it.*

She barely remembered the protocol for clothing and eating etiquette. Even now she still debated if she'd grabbed the right spoon. The girl raised in sophistication, losing it with barely any effort.

Her father, Vincent Genovese, ignored her comment, focusing on the grilled lamb shank in front of him. He sliced off a good piece and gently brought his fork to his mouth. No sounds were made in this entire process, at least not jarring ones. He followed the bite with a sip of wine.

"He runs a clean operation."

Vincent looked at her, full-on, his dark blue eyes boring into her. "Dig deeper. No one runs clean. It's not possible in the world we live in. Each person has some dark secret, bones and flesh they're trying to hide."

Dead bodies were the only thing she was sure he was hiding, but she refused to tell them about that. She worked on cutting off another piece of lamb.

Luca sneered at her. "Maybe she doesn't want to dig too deep because she's too busy looking at his dark skin and fucking him."

Rina shot daggers at Luca. "I'm merely stating facts, not opinions."

"Oh, but you think so highly of him. As if his fake clear operation was something to admire. You don't build empires unless the house always wins," Luca replied before stabbing into his lamb so hard his fork squeaked against the plate.

She growled. "An empire forged through fear is weak, whereas one built in friendship yields more reward."

"Save Yash's shine-soaked beliefs for someone who cares." Luca pointed his lamb-speared fork at her. "If you want to screw him, let's not be in a rush to bring him home to meet father. Remember that the last exclusive screw almost killed him."

The words sent fresh guilt spilling over her like a wave of water...for Dominic and not the man she should feel it for. She glanced at her father, who remained impassive. Since the attempted assassination, things had not been the same between them, but she had no clue how to go back to the relationship she'd had before her fiancé's death, because she warred with what was right and wrong.

She'd been sure of her future, a future without her family as soon as she and Dominic had enough funds to get away. That had been cut short, ruined. Her father could never let things go. Even her self-imposed exile hadn't been allowed for long.

Luca, though she hated to admit it, was right in that father would never let her leave. Not willingly.

"I'll keep that in mind."

"That'll be enough, Luca." Her father's words were a growl, his face menacing in its frustration. When he glanced at her, his features softened. "Caterina, I think you've punished yourself enough and should move home. Stop living above that tattoo parlor. It's an insult to who you are, who your family is."

Ice, cold and numb, spread through her. She enjoyed her freedom, enjoyed the chance to express all the pent-up rage and anger in her artwork. She'd spoken the truth when she'd confessed to Sweet how she enjoyed putting needles into people's flesh. Though it was controlled, she got a rise from their pain, the pain they fought against to gain the art's acceptance of their skin as a canvas. To no longer have an outlet, to be forced back into a world of glamour and lies… *No*. Her mind raced, searching for an excuse as she ate a large bite of yellow squash. *It's rude to talk with your mouth full.*

"I agree, Father." Luca licked his lips and she swallowed hard to stop herself from gagging on the vegetable in her mouth.

The harsh gulp required a dose of water and she ended with a small cough. "That's not the best for business though, not yet. With me staying at the parlor, I'm closer to Sweet's. If I'm running our operation and working to see how we can close it down, being right across the street plays to our advantage."

That was how her father controlled everything. It started with getting her to work for him, then encouraging her to come home. She would retain what freedom she could.

Her father shrugged. "Eh, you have a point. Though I don't like it. Allow me to give you a bodyguard."

"Father, I've been protecting myself for years. I need nothing, want for nothing. A guard would only slow me down and be a waste of good manpower." The hypocrisy lived on, because he already had her watched, aware of each movement, through her work for Yash.

"Fine, but if you change your mind, speak the word and you have whatever you need to ensure your success with The Sweet Spot. Now, what other news do my children have for me?"

Rina took a sip of wine, silently reveling in her little win, and considered the next question on her mind. One that had been brewing since her encounter with Rose. One that had sent her all over the city. "There was a man in my parlor a few days ago. Severely upset and looking for his lost brother. I found it odd he came to the shop to look for him. I wondered why he'd go missing after visiting the parlor."

"Are you serious?" Luca slapped a hand against the table, rattling the glasses, the plates and the unused coffee cups against their little saucers. "This isn't news. Druggies overdose every day. People get killed stealing. Do you know how many people are missing daily?"

She did. The dead woman, the missing brother...the fact that they both had tattoos from her shop had prompted her to investigate. The numbers of missing, the rising numbers of dead were a marvel. "Over a hundred at the last count. I looked into it."

And found no answers. Her sleep cycle being shit anyway, she'd gone searching for the missing man herself, but had found nothing.

"Then you'd know it's like a needle in a haystack. Most of these fools become victims of their own vices." Her father chimed in with those gems and she glanced between the two of them. How similar they'd started to sound.

"Vices we supply by the armful. Is it right?"

Her father smiled, a look designed to placate and pander. "It seems Yash and his foolish beliefs about ethics and morality are wearing off on you, though you both are quite hypocritical. Tattoos are a vice just as destructive and a waste of money. Besides, we feed more mouths with those vices. Morality and ethics are fine, but when people are starving, I do what others do not have the guts to do. I supply a way to make money."

There was no sense in arguing with a man who believed he was justified in all that he did. "How are the clubs faring?"

"Well, we continue to operate from a position of strength, even in your absence. Those who try and say otherwise are merely jealous of continued success."

She'd heard these words a dozen times over the years, and usually following their appearance dead bodies appeared. She was familiar with her father's theories about the jealousy of other clubs and their owners — theories that were usually unfounded. "Who's saying such things?"

"I do," Luca offered. "You're not around our business anymore, Rina. There's a lot of turmoil amongst club owners. Speculation and rumors have spread like drugs in a vein since father has taken more of a back seat."

She frowned. "Sweet hasn't mentioned anything like that."

"And why would he?" her father asked. "He's a man with a single establishment, in the most downtrodden part of Arcas. No one wants that business because they are too stupid to see the potential."

"He's a business owner. I imagine if there are threats to you, since we're his business partners, he might feel them as well."

Luca rattled the table yet again, stabbing into a beet cube. "If he does have problems, let me know. She brings up a good point, Father."

"Yes, she does, but then Rina could always see things in a different way than others do." Her father picked up his wine glass and nodded to her. "You do your family a service. I'm so happy you came back."

She wanted to yell. To scream. The old anger spread like a rampant fire, licking and biting at her flesh. She clenched the silverware in her hands as she sawed into the lamb. For all her seeing things in a different way, *they* certainly didn't bother attempting to view things in any other way than they always had.

They easily excused their warmongering and hostile takeovers as defense against those who would otherwise threaten Geno's, threaten their livelihoods and those who worked for them. Though, if asked to give up their own wealth, they would spill blood by the barrel and laugh.

Unlike another man, a man she couldn't stop thinking about, or the way he took care of business with a deep fire burning in his eyes. Even when tested by death and seemingly protecting himself, he vowed to fight for justice, to protect his own.

She longed for someone like that, who protected those he cared for with a fierceness worth more than any possession, any piece of flash. Sad to know she'd once believed her father to be that man, until he'd become a monster.

* * * *

"Are you really betting so low, Web Spinner?" Akono threw a few more leaves in, and not the rough stuff either. This was pure and cut. He needed every one of the seven players milling around this table playing deep. It was an old Earth game, but they'd changed the name a gazillion times. For now they called it Arcas Hold 'Em. Seven cards on the table, two in the gambler's hand and the best five won. He had a pair of aces face down.

"You play like a Neptuner, Sweet." Funny, the words came from Sir Bastian, the sole owner of clothing stores on Callisto. Some said he didn't sell fashion—he created it.

"I might be coming up in the world, and wouldn't you like a chance to?" he replied, throwing one more leaf into the growing pot.

Bastian joined in, as well as the Web Spinner, an additional runner from some obscure group, and two of the other patrons. The dealer flipped the cards— another ace, an eight and a seven, all the same suit— and Akono caught a couple of grins. They thought they had him, but a flush would do nothing. A straight... *I can risk it.*

So he bet more. Let his money do the talking instead of his mouth, and in the seconds after placing the bet, he searched for Rina. She walked alongside Terrance, doing a sweep of the dance floor and bar area.

The woman had successfully integrated herself with his staff over the last couple of days. She appeared at sundown and worked the room until closing time, followed by reviewing the books when Sweet finished with them.

Sweet checked on Ant next, hovering at the edges of the gambling area. His second had followed Sweet's direction to avoid Rina, though he voiced his dislike for the woman who could stare him down at eye-level without blinking.

He wasn't the only one voicing concerns either. Bartenders, dealers and house gals alike worried that her presence meant the solar days of fair wages would soon come to a close. Some even wondered why Sweet didn't discreetly get rid of her. But it boiled down to a growing amount of respect, never mind the desire and lust he still experienced every time he saw her.

No, she took care of issues he didn't have time for. Did things to help enhance security, walking in the door. She locked eyes with shady characters and had devised a system to keep the girls safe. No more people had died, no brawls. He'd run a successful four solar days without issue.

He glanced again and this time she caught him. *Fatch it.* He admired her openly, let her see exactly how she affected him. She wore the same thing every day. The black pants and matching vest, with a white short-sleeved shirt, black boots and her hair pulled back from her face. Long hair, tresses he could grip with his hands as she sucked his —

Landra Graf

"Sweet. Are you in or out?" Bastian quizzed.

He looked back to play, shaking off the image of Rina supplicant before him, her lips wrapped around him. The final card was ready to drop—he just needed to add in his bet. "In, of course."

The final card flipped, another eight. Akono waited his turn as each player showed their cards. Some hands were definitely better than others and Bastian's three-of-a-kind made him the frontrunner.

"Looks like I'm winning, Sweet." Bastian said with a big smile.

Akono flipped his own cards, reveling a little in Bastian's dropped jaw. "Not yet, I'm afraid. If you want, we can play again."

Cards flew, as Bastian threw his at the dealer. "I should have known better than to let you goad me, but I did. No, I'm done for tonight. I think I'll get a drink then head next door. I'm sure Maple has someone lovely to keep me company."

Akono shrugged, gathering his winnings to him. "Eh, it's a good idea, but you won't win your flash back that way."

Bastian's chair groaned as he stood up and placed his hat on his head. "I wouldn't win it back if I stayed. These other gents would be wise to depart as well. If they know what's good for them."

Some of those gents did depart. But the unknown runner stayed, along with another man of middling age. Akono nodded to the dealer and the dealer called for all antes as Luca Genovese slid into the seat beside him.

"What are you doing here?" The question came out a bit brisker than he'd planned, but this man removed any urge from Akono to be deploy the fake charmer facade he whipped out for the other patrons.

Luca reached into his pocket and pulled out a couple of leaves to throw onto the ante pile. "Paying my dues to sit in a chair for a game, is what."

"That's plain, but not my question." Akono put his full-on gaze on the smarmy asshole. "Why are you in my club? Checking up on your sister?"

Luca grinned. "Eh, she can handle herself. More like visiting an investment. My sister speaks highly of you."

Luca picked up the two cards dealt to him and snuck a peek.

Akono's gaze never wavered. He did not trust this man. Would never, not with the open threats the younger Genovese had already cast in Akono's direction.

"Is this your way of saying that I've got your father's permission?" He peeked at his own cards then threw some crinkle into the pot. The cards must have been good as the other two players stayed in. "Your bet."

Luca added his own wager. "My father would never give you permission to do anything with Rina, except maybe lick the bottom of her grav boots. No, you've got her buying into this idea you're some upstanding, clean-cut business owner when we know those assignments you keep hiring Morales for show you're hiding things."

Fatch me sideways. "I would caution you that using drugs can over time causes serious health issues." Akono kept his eyes on the dealer, then the cards for the flop. Because he needed to steer clear of the question he wanted to ask, the one about the person who was selling information to the Genoveses.

"I don't mix vice with business. Rumors are you won something big. Something game-changing, enough to make a man richer than my father, and Morales was sent in to retrieve it."

Anger simmered beneath the smirk Akono let surface. He'd kill whoever had let this viper into his nest. *Focus on the dealer, and the new card being revealed.* With the rush of emotion came a dozen questions, concerns and newfound distrust. Goosebumps spread over his flesh. Had Rina fed him bullshit? Was she spying for her brother?

The next card put him in line to win again. So Akono bet big. One player folded, then the runner stayed in. Finally, Luca... "You're playing pretty big for a guy who's about to have extra expenses."

"I play according to how the cards let me. It's a game." And like all games, he'd win the one between himself and the Genoveses. He had to — multiple lives depended on it.

Luca, for all his bluster, didn't have enough intel to launch anything against him. Akono needed to throw Luca and the informant off the scent. Trick them into revealing themselves. Akono had a room full of fancy prizes and trinkets given in exchange for debts — he could try to fake them as Genisys.

The money from tonight's play would help Akono pay Emilio and Toni's fee for fixing the cruiser. *Here's hoping the bill doesn't go up.* Especially if he had to call them in to fix something else.

Luca matched his bet before they turned over their cards. The bastard clapped his hands in celebration. "Wow, looks like Lady Luck found herself someone better to latch on to. I think I'll go again. You always have big winners at the tables, Sweet?"

Akono shook his head. "Not usually. When I'm not playing, the dealers are."

More cards, more betting. *Less talking.*

The next cards went down. Luca bet first this time. "So, no matter what, the house has a chance to win?"

Akono threw in his bet and raised. "Always."

The two gentlemen folded and both left the table. Akono had probably played the hand too high, too fast, but he wanted to beat this sonuvabitch, since getting rid of Luca in the physical sense was out of the question.

The dealer looked at Luca, and Akono asked the question. "Are you in or out?"

"How about in exchange for the cargo Morales is carrying for you, I sign your club back over to you?"

Akono's fingers tensed around his cards. Admitting Emilio and Toni had cargo would give him away — trading such a thing would give away the worth. He'd learned a lot over the years, and like any card game, the goal was to keep the opponents guessing.

"You're as bad as the patrons, feeding into rumors and speculation. Morales hasn't come here since his confrontation with Grecia and I'm in the business of vice. Not running." He set his cards down and looked at Luca straight on. The grease-slicked, black-haired man with eyes devoid of anything stared back.

Whatever Luca saw was enough to get him to throw his cards at the pot. "I'll fold while I am ahead. I'm smart enough to know a good thing when I have it. Until next time, Sweet. Don't pinch the deposit or my sister."

Luca stood up and left the table, heading for the door. Akono watched his progress, to see if the spacehole went straight for Rina. Unexpectedly, she intercepted her brother, a glower of mass fury on her face. *Hell of a show.*

Instead, he took the opportunity to cash in. "Jones, add my winnings to the vault money."

A couple of ladies approached, all sequined dresses and fur stoles.

"Is this table closed?" asked the blonde.

"No." Akono motioned for the woman to take his chair and summoned his best smile, the one that seemed to charm everyone but held little truth to the real him. "You can sit right here and start a game. The dealer will happily accommodate you."

The redhead slid her hand up Sweet's arm. "You look worthy of our time. Will you stay with us?"

The offer, while enticing, was a reminder of how he, they, all his employees at The Sweet Spot were viewed as entertainment. Nothing but pawns to amuse those who had more than them. Something he'd change and no one, not even a strong black-haired beauty with tattoos, could be allowed to stop him.

"Afraid not, ladies. My business calls me away to other matters, but if I take care of things, I'll be back." He didn't wait to hear their groans of disapproval or experience their frowns.

Instead, he glanced over at the door. Luca still stood there, glowering at Rina. Their exchange was terse, their crossed arms and clenched fists telling the story.

He took the opportunity to slip away, up the spiral staircase and down the hall to his office. Zeke followed at a matched pace.

"Stay outside and guard the door," Akono commanded before he went inside the room.

He moved immediately to the desk, checking and searching every crack and crevice. He climbed down on his hands and knees, like a toddler playing on the floor. His efforts only earned him dirt on his suit pants. He stood, half-disappointed, and almost smacked himself in the forehead. *The bug detector.*

Pulling it out of his top desk drawer, he flipped it on and set the frequencies like Sampson, Toni and Emilio's engineer, had shown him. One thing about being in business together, it meant Akono received assistance at times when he didn't want it.

A slow sweep and not long before a double beep came right over the bronze status of Atlas, the weight of Earth-before-the-nuke on his shoulders. Akono pulled the small wired listener out from under the statue and crushed it under his boot heel.

No fatching way would he trust Caterina Genovese with anything more than a bottle of whiskey.

Chapter Seven

Rina enjoyed her new routine. Busy meant she couldn't let her thoughts stray to dead Rose, to the missing people, or become aroused by random thoughts of Sweet. *Depraved* was the best word she could use to describe how she easily moved from death to lust without a blink of an eye.

She'd done her part and reviewed the books every night after closing, stayed out on the floor to observe the operation and ensure that Sweet wasn't funneling flash out another way. So far it seemed everyone was above-board and acting in the best interest of the club, though if the dead bodies were any inclination, something simmered beneath the surface.

If she could only rid herself of her other problem...Luca. Who had showed up at the club unannounced. He acted so smug and pompous, as though he was checking on some investment, when in reality he wasn't doing anything but stirring shit. She needed him to leave things be, let her build rapport.

If Sweet was hiding anything, she couldn't find evidence of it. Though his conversation with Luca had appeared less than entertaining. Her brother had refused to tell her what the hell they'd been talking about. None of her fatching business...she'd prove him wrong. If it happened in this club, it was her business. *My name on the line, my people on the line.*

Tonight would be the first night the Genoveses got their cut. The first deposit of funds over to her father's safe, and she was there to make sure it happened.

"So, you've had a few days to look over things. What do you think?"

Rina refused to look at Sweet as he came to a stop next to her. She stood on the second-floor balcony overlooking the tables, the dance floor...everything. "My opinion hasn't changed. I find the club impressive, the employees competent...except for that spacehole you have for a second, Ant. And no one appears on the take or drugging it up in some corner."

Sure, the comments would only increase Sweet's ego, but she believed in speaking the truth.

"Nothing big and bad to report to your brother?"

"I don't report to him. Besides, my father knows I operate on my own, unbiased. So take your insecurities and shove them somewhere the sun panels don't shine." She let her attitude ring free, full and unashamed.

"Sorry, it's hard not to think the worst when your brother shows up here threatening me and you intercepting him as he left."

She glanced at Sweet then. His crossed arms and the firm set to his face were more guarded than he normally acted toward her. The look of desire in his eyes had been wiped away without a trace, way out of character. "Tell me what's really bothering you, and not some made-up bullshit either."

When he turned those dark eyes on her, the riotous attraction awoke as hungry as a gambler was for flash. *Ridiculous how I can want someone in such a desperate way.* She'd never experienced such a deep-seated need before.

"It's nothing. Don't worry about it."

"Fatch, you say. Lay it out or don't, but standing here being a jerk to me doesn't change things." She held up a hand as if to say *no big deal* and focused back on the party below. "I've missed this type of place. It's been a while, but I've always loved the sounds, the smells... Clubs are in our blood, so my father says."

Sweet scoffed. "You're a good actress. No wonder your father wants you working here."

"Get jacked. It's not an act." The lust burned into a bright ball of anger. "Is that what you think of me?"

"Makes no sense. You're a successful woman, with a rich-as-Neptuner father. Then you disappear from this life, give it up for a tattoo shop. Now you're back. There's a reason and it's got nothing to do with missing club life."

She warred with saying anything, yet the urge to tell someone something struck her hard. After Dominic, she'd kept quiet. Voicing true emotion could get someone killed. But maybe getting personal with Sweet would get him to open up to her.

"My fiancé attempted to kill my father, in the middle of one of our club's celebration affairs. A big to-do and he almost succeeded."

Sweet whistled nice and low. "That's some serious stuff, but nothing rumors haven't already spread."

"Yes, but he had no reason to do it. We were supposed to be married, start a life...we had plans to have a life separate from my father's empire. Suddenly he makes himself a target. I needed to get away. From possible suspicion and to mourn. That type of stuff makes a person distrust themselves and their environment."

"I've never trusted mine and after your brother's visit, I'm more suspicious than ever."

Rina's eyes narrowed. "What did he say?"

Out of her peripheral vision, she watched Sweet relax his arms. "He hinted about knowing things about my business that I have never told anyone. Hinted at having a plant here in the club. Someone is spying on me. I found a bug later that night in my office. The only people who have been in there are my guards, my second, me, you and your brother."

She opened her mouth to respond, but caught sight of a patron, hunched eyebrows and curse words flying at a petite female dealer. "Hold up for a minute. We are not done talking about this."

Her legs moved on instinct, going from stride to full-on sprint in seconds. Everything disappeared and she operated on muscle memory as she flew down the staircase and headed for the gambling area. She registered the sound of Sweet's voice calling out after her, but never bothered to respond. No, she had to reach the table and stop this madness.

She grabbed Curse-Ass's hand. "No touching the dealers. Under any circumstances."

"Oh, and who are you? Just another Arcas twat looking to make some flash."

She twisted, popped and pushed the flustered man by his wrist only. "I'm the one who decides how the rest of your night goes."

He howled in reaction, right as Zeke and Terrance arrived at the table. "What about my stash?"

"Consider it deducted for damages. Take him away, boys."

Sweet marched up, looking pissed, though she would have expected the anger to be directed at the spacehole who'd touched his employee. She side-eyed the table repeatedly, in the hopes he'd play this smart.

"A round of drinks on the house for everyone at the lovely Nicola's table," he announced.

Cheers rang out from the remaining patrons at the table.

Rina nodded. "Good job. I'll just resume my post now."

Sweet bumped up against her and leaned in close, a blend of scents—whiskey, leather and honey, familiar and arousing. "I guess I'll pretend this is still my club."

"It is. My father would say better your problems be solved than worrying who solves them."

"I think it's better to remember the old Earth proverb, beware the animal backed into a corner." He walked away, following the guards dragging the grabby jerk to the door.

She wondered which one of them was the animal. *And which one does he want to be?*

Akono stalked towards the entrance, lengthening his strides to catch up to Zeke and Terrance. "We need his name in the book. Ned?"

The host pulled out a dreaded purple faux-fur monstrosity from underneath the podium. It smacked against the wood and Ned undid the small golden lock with a key from around his neck.

"I didn't mean to grab her. I overreacted," the scared patron said.

A bright light went off as Ned held up the book so the camera could scan for facial features and recognition.

"What's your name?" Akono asked.

A jot of a name in the book was irrevocable, the act banning them from their establishment and all others. Not often did they need to put a name in. Sometimes the threat of such a thing quelled dissent.

Except, tonight Akono wanted to prove a point. Rina's little stunt, her take-charge attitude, aroused and hit some primal urge in him. He liked her being in charge, but he wanted to show himself equally capable. She frustrated his very state of being, telling a tale, protecting his dealers…a puzzle without a solution.

Akono kicked the man in the back of his leg, causing the patron to drop to his knees. "I won't ask again."

"It's Howell, C.J." A couple of fake tears leaked from the idiot's eyes, followed by a sob.

Akono couldn't call up any bit of empathy for this man who'd brought to a focal point how Akono's life, the very fabric of his identity, crumbled in the wake of Rina Genovese and her family's claim to his club, their threats to dismantle what he'd built. It wasn't rational or fair, and he didn't give a fatch. "Write it in the book, Ned."

Ned picked up a solid black pointer and started to write. "The offense?"

"Laying hands on a dealer."

Sobs emerged anew from Howell on the floor, his head bowed to his hands.

"Pick the trash up and kick him out. He's no longer welcome in our establishment. Maybe Geno's will give him a chance, but once this information is loaded into the Arcas gambling system, probably not."

The final tear in the oxygen mask came when Ned closed the cover of the book and locked it back up. Terrance and Zeke hauled the distraught Howell away and Akono sighed. Acting out his vengeance did nothing to ease the swirling confusion Rina presented him with. *Trusting her is a bad idea.*

He took another gander around the club, but failed to spot her.

"You haven't booked someone in a long time. She getting to you?" Ned asked.

Fatching hell. He didn't want to talk about it, especially not with the king of club gossip. "Is she getting to you?"

Redirection seemed the best choice. The topic of their conversation resumed her post on the balcony of the second floor, looking down upon everyone like a queen viewing her subjects.

He didn't want to like her or admire her at all. Except he did. From how she dressed to the way she assessed every situation. She hit the buttons he wanted pressed. Except, everyone had a sob story, the tale of woe and warning a symbolic tie between every person on Callisto. Though, her fight to escape implied she wasn't the type to embrace her demons, not like the rest of them.

"I like her. Seems she has a good handle on what it takes to run a club." Ned shoved the book under the podium and turned his attention back to the entrance, where a group of men were walking in.

"You're entitled to your opinion." Akono headed for the bar, debating a drink or going back to his office. Ned laughed out loud behind him. He was another person who'd known him in his youth and read his moods better than most.

He glanced up at Rina again. And her eyes connected with his. *Craps.* He rubbed at the knot in his chest and decided the bar to be a safer haven than talking to Rina again.

Every event, sentence or word seemed to be a ploy meant to lower his guard so that when her brother showed up to play his games, Akono would be too caught up in her to think straight.

Unless Luca wanted his sister dead, wanted to stir up distrust? Akono signaled Sway, one of his bartenders, and shook his head. He would send himself spinning in circles at the numerous theories he could generate, and there remained another one…one of his employees had betrayed him. *Not possible.*

Sway poured him a glass of his favorite Scotch and brought it over. "Need a pick-me-up, boss? You look tired."

"I need a new life." And that was exactly what he was working toward day by day, hour by hour. The more people spent the crinkle, the more likely he'd get his employees out of here before the Genoveses could discover the truth.

Betrayal would ruin everything, and with Luca pretending he knew something about Genisys, Akono needed to dig into the bottom of the mess, sooner rather than later, because what he'd said before to Rina was true—he'd never trusted his environment. Never allowed himself to get fully invested.

"I heard there was a problem." Ant's booming voice cut over the music and the noise of the crowd with ease.

"You missed it."

"I had to take care of something for Maple."

"Something or someone?" Akono tipped the glass back and took a long swallow of Scotch, its smoky taste burning a trail down his throat. The older woman had mentioned more than once that Ant hung around a few of the girls too much, keeping them from their business.

His second frowned. "Something. She wanted an extra lock on the back door, something only she has the key to. Don't need the girls slippin' out without her knowledge, she said."

An easy excuse. Easily verifiable. Damn, this business had him second guessing everything. "Understandable."

"Why, did that Genovese bitch say something?"

Akono raised one eyebrow. "No, she didn't. Should she?"

"I buried my issues, but I still say we get rid of her sooner than later. Just say the word and I'll get it done."

Ain't gonna happen. "I'll take it under consideration. What other news?"

"Numbers are good. People are drinking, betting, eating and fucking."

The four major food groups, as Akono always boasted. He'd learned the phrase from Tibo, prior owner of the club, who believed that keeping those four things available to people equaled unrivaled profits. Drugs could be left outside the doors.

"Excellent. Then business is good." Akono finished off his drink and set the glass on the bar. Business could have been the best, but he still wanted the things he couldn't have. Including one delicious, sexy, badass woman who watched over his club like an avenging angel.

"When are we done with the Genoveses altogether?"

Akono faced Ant, staring him down. "When the time is right."

No sense in stoking a fight that would divide the club. No sense in telling Ant they would never be rid of them, and confessing more of his plan to anyone at the moment was out of the question. Until he found the person selling him out.

Hours later, the club was closed, the employees deep in cleanup and Akono using the counting machines to add up all the receipts. Terrance and Zeke guarded the door. Ant was over in the brothel to help with cleaning out any lingering patrons.

Akono just had to get past the next little bit, then he'd be home free for another night. Free from the temptation of Rina and her clove scent.

Siren that she was, like Earth stories of old, Rina sat in a chair across from his desk, puffing on her cigarette, which smelled far better than a lot of the tobacco product that came from Earth. She had one dainty leg crossed over the other, dangling in the air. *Bet they're strong enough to grip my waist.*

"How much is the take?" she asked.

"Enough to make your father wonder why he wasn't squeezing me sooner." There were other things he wanted her to squeeze.

"It appears your ladies next door bring in a fair amount too. What tricks have they been taught?" She winked before blowing out a thin puff of smoke into the air.

His dick grew hard, as images of tricks came to him again. Especially the idea of her here, with him, in the office, rough and fast. "All the usual ones, I suppose."

"Really? In my experience, men like something fresh and tight."

Akono laughed. "In mine, all it requires is a hole."

"That may be for some, but others enjoy a more enlightened experience. Like the one from the playroom?"

"Oh, that's tailored for specific clients. Not everyone can handle that type of pleasure. Tends to overload the senses and tap into parts of the person they don't want revealed."

She smiled. "So, it's for people like you who hide yourself away?"

"Or for people who seem to enjoy inflicting pain...like you."

The comment got a rise out of her, literally. She sauntered over to his desk, all hips and curves. He stood up to give himself a little bit of an edge, because the predator in him refused to completely roll over and give himself up.

"Is this your way of saying you're interested?"

He licked his lips. "Interested or not, we can't happen."

The heat banked in her eyes told a different story. One that got harder and harder to deny or push aside with each passing day.

"Why not?"

The question sounded like a dare to him, one he could respond to easily. So he did. He snaked out and reached for her, hauling her against his body. She might beat the shit out of him for this, and he'd like it.

His lips descended upon hers and he expected them to be soft, but not to taste like spice. A hint of spices. He was ready to pull away when she melted against him, no resistance and all in charge. Her hands interlocked behind his neck. She shoved her tongue into his mouth and took control. The kiss went on and on, a dance of desperation, and it appeared she wanted him as much as he wanted her.

A lot of unspoken emotion and words were transferred in that kiss. They were enemies, natural-born by circumstances. They were forbidden, and that made her tongue against his all the more sweet.

Then, as wild and close as it turned, she broke away. Taking two steps back, she held up the money bag. "Thanks for this. I'll make the drop and see you later."

Akono stood momentarily shocked as he watched Rina hustle out the office door as if she couldn't escape fast enough. They weren't done and he sure as hell wouldn't wait until tomorrow to revisit what in the fresh hell had just happened. He shoved out of the chair to go after her.

Chapter Eight

Rina barely made it ten steps out of the front door of The Sweet Spot before a man stepped in front of her, light from the club marquee sign glinting off his big knife.

"I'll take that money bag."

"For the love of cards." It was bad enough she'd given in to kissing Sweet, got lost in kissing him. Now this spacehole wanted her take, and in her haste to get away from Sweet, she'd lost her focus.

"The bag, now."

She looked at the idiot again and immediately recognized him. "Oh, Howell, right? You're the crap-stain that got booked earlier."

"Yeah, and I want what's coming to me."

Rina hefted the flash bag up. "You mean, you want what my family has coming to them?"

"Give it to me and I won't gut you right here."

Oh, he wouldn't be the one doing the gutting. Rina dropped the bag on the ground between her legs. She wanted this fight more than anything...at least as a distraction from reliving the damn kiss with Sweet over and over. "You can have it if you can get it."

The Taser light and click came from behind right after her words and electricity sent her into survival mode as her body started convulsing before she fell to the ground. What happened next, she wasn't too sure, but the crap-stain and his accomplice were jumped by two or three men. The scuffle involved plenty of painful grunts and groans. Even though her shock treatment stopped almost immediately after she fell down, she remained inoperative, still a shivering mess.

She'd suffered Taser treatment before, at the hands of her own brother. The incident came on instant recall. Playing in the backyard. Luca threatening her because he'd been upset that she'd gotten something he hadn't. Then the Taser. She'd learned that even those closest to her couldn't always be trusted.

"Rina? Rina, can you hear me?" Akono's face came into view as he hunched on the ground next to her defeated body.

"I. Can. Hear. You. Don't shhakke mmmeee." Broken words, *for the love of cards.* Everything in her still seized, and hands gripped her shoulders. A pair of them, rubbing up and down her arms. She wanted to rebuke the contact, the help. *First the kiss, now this.* Contact between them seemed a bad omen.

"Let me know when feeling comes back," Akono ordered, before turning his head. "Both of you need to get these two idiots down to the APUP station. I want them charged, immediately."

She started to feel less like a vibrating chair and more human, with Sweet's ministrations to her arms, then her legs. "You can stop that crap and help me stand up."

"Don't you think that's a little fast?"

"They Tased me. I'm still hearty and whole. Besides, seems touching you brings me bad luck." Rina stuck out her hand.

"Quit talking nonsense. That fool would have tried the same crap on whoever walked out with the bag." Sweet grabbed it, helping her to a standing position.

She still shook a little and glanced down at the bag. "Well, they wouldn't have gotten it easily anyway. Not with my deadweight body on top of the damn thing."

"Definitely not the brightest pair. You want to go back inside? Get a drink or something?"

"I'm fine. Or I will be once you stop worrying about me."

"You've just been attacked. I think a little concern is warranted." Akono looked her up and down and she hated the sympathy in his gaze.

Embarrassment pooled in her gut and water gathered in her eyes. She'd be spaced if she started crying in front of this fool. No way would she allow herself to look so weak. They were enemies, only on the same side until she could provide her father with a reason to end things.

"Your concern is noted and ignored. I'll make it fine. Besides, like you said, those guys are idiots."

"Where there's two, there are always more."

She despised how right he was, how the words made sense. And dreaded the next ones.

"I'll accompany you to your father's."

Her jaw nearly dropped open. She expected Sweet to suggest that one of his men walk her the rest of the way. Instead he was offering himself. She shouldn't have been surprised, but maybe she'd expected him to take her sudden departure a little more seriously.

I guess not. She opened her mouth to suggest one of his bodyguards accompany her, but he'd read her mind.

"Don't suggest anyone else. If something happens to you, who do you think your father will blame? I'll have a war on my hands. So if you still plan on walking and making the deposit tonight, then I'll be going with you."

She shook her head. "You talk a lot."

"I'll say all the words necessary to make my point."

She shrugged free of his hands and grabbed the bag from him. "What is the point?"

"You should quit arguing, save the drop for another day and let me take you home. I'll send a message to your brother."

Fatch. "Not necessary either."

"They'll want to know why you didn't show with the drop."

She frowned. "You're assuming I'll go along with your plan."

"My plan ensures your safety."

That was when she really woke up to the difference between Sweet and her family. Her father would have demanded she turn in the money over everything else. Over security and safety, whatever the cost. Making the drop was more important. Sweet appeared to value her life more than that—even when she was his enemy. Someone he shouldn't give a care for.

She wanted to see where all this led. Where empathy and concern got a person. "All right, we'll do things your way."

"Good. Zeke, get a message to Luca that Rina was attacked and I'm taking her home. The drop will be made tomorrow."

"Right away," Zeke said before walking off.

"Terrance, you can head home too. I'll take care of Ms. Genovese."

And she wondered just how much he'd take care of.

Akono was damn glad he'd decided to come after Rina. Glad that Ned had pointed out that going alone was a bad idea, with all this Genovese business. If he'd been alone or even a few minutes later, she might've... *Nope, I'm not going there.*

The idea of her being harmed, in any fashion, bothered him. It irked his practical side that screamed *let her go.* Let her be victim to whatever came her way. Except, reason told another tale. One he hid with the excuse of a would-be war between him and Vincent if Rina came to harm.

Hell, she'd kissed him with a passion he'd never expected. He'd not been the only one spinning the roulette wheel. Except she'd walked away from him. Ran right into danger. He understood her fear, but his paled against desire, which had evolved into a craving to see how deep such a want went. So seeing her Tased and set upon by that dumbass he'd banned had enraged him like no other. But he'd chosen to remain by her side instead of chasing after the assholes.

"Fatching Howell better hope I never see him again."

Rina eyed him as they walked across the street to Yash's place. "He better hope no one sees him again."

"Why are we going to the tattoo parlor?"

"I live there."

He'd expected that she lived in the neighborhood, but not where she worked. "Good, then you have antiseptic materials there."

The problem with Tasers was that they weren't clean. Whether in space or on planet, people tended to die for two big reasons, drugs and infection. Fights with cuts, exposed skin—the bacteria would get in and kill someone before they knew better.

He had his fair share of scars from his own dances with death. They gambled with more than crinkle on this damn moon every day.

"A bit of a worrywart, eh?"

"I've reason to worry."

Rina pulled a key ring from her pocket. It bothered him that she was still shaking a bit, and he wanted to step in and take over. But she'd snap his damn hand off, he was sure of it. She shoved a key into the lock and got the door open a few seconds later.

They stepped through the main entrance and the lights came on, motion activated. The windows were obscured from view with floor-length blackout curtains. *Helpful in deterring thieves.* Even the most dangerous people could become prey to those desperate and hurting.

He followed her in, shutting the door and locking it. She hobbled over to a station with bottles of fluids, cotton swabs and pieces of cloth. Akono took the chance to examine his surroundings, the images of her tattoo artistry displayed on the walls. "You do pretty good work."

"So they say. But I'm not the only one. Yash, the owner—a lot of the walls are covered in his stuff. He's the one who taught me all about skin art." She undid the buttons on her vest, shrugging out of it with a wince.

"Here, let me help you get those cleaned up." He stepped toward her, hands outstretched.

The narrow-eyed gaze she leveled at him froze him in his tracks. "I can take care of it."

He shrugged, moving closer to her once more. "Sure, you have arms that grow extra inches whenever you need them to, enough to reach your back. Quit being hostile and get your rear on the table. I won't bite."

She threw the vest to the floor. "Fine, but let's hurry. I've got a date with my shower. Hopefully, it will help me relax so I can sleep."

"Why would you have trouble sleeping?" Akono started perusing the labels on the bottles of the table. Inks and stabilizers...nothing to help disinfect. He looked at Rina. "Also, where do you hide the cleaners?"

Rina put both hands to the tattoo table and hoisted herself up with a groan of pain. He almost suggested the chair, but he needed access to her back. To her bare skin. *Focus.*

"Antiseptic is in the cabinet under the nebula design." She avoided the question about her lack of sleep, and he let it go. None of his business why she had trouble with anything.

He moved to the cabinet and pointed at the nebula design, the drawing itself nearly jumping from the page. "Did you draw this?"

"On one of those sleepless nights. Yash lets me display my artwork here, a gallery of sorts. He's even convinced a couple of people to buy some of it."

He found the bottle she spoke of, a green solution clearly labeled for use in treating cuts and wounds. "Seems you work pretty well without sleep."

"I've gotten better. Waking from nightmares of guns pointed at you, people you care about gunned down, it's not easy to channel fears into something worth putting on display."

"Can you roll to your side?" he asked, approaching the table.

She did as he requested, showing off the twin bloodstains on the back of her white T-shirt, surrounded by a smattering of black where the fabric had burned from the electricity. He lifted her shirt, and the angry, puffy red entry points stared back at him. They would easily become a problem if not taken care of.

"This may hurt." He poured the disinfectant directly onto the wounds and she hissed, arching back at the pain. He pressed the cotton swatches to them, to soak up a bit of blood, and the pus emerging. *Not pretty in the least.* "I'll make sure Howell pays."

She rolled to her back and stared up at him in confusion. "Why does it matter? He'll be on every list at this point. He won't be able to gamble anywhere. Why care so much?"

"Because attacking you is essentially attacking me. Is it just the nightmares that keep you from sleeping?" He needed to change the topic, move away from the surface she was scratching.

"Lack of sleep has always been an issue with me. Usually I've had someone around to screw senseless during those times, but lately I've been alone."

The words were like a tempter's call to him, to his desire. Jolting him back to life, reviving the same tension that had lit the air before their first kiss. He should be respectful of her injury. Not attempt to take advantage of her in this state. Except he never made a move — she did.

She grabbed him with one hand and pulled him down to her, the kiss as incendiary as the last one, her lips like the key to unlocking a part of him he never let loose, wild and hungry. Their tongues melded in an interpretive dance, one that told a story of what could be between them. *Something hot and wicked.*

Akono became vaguely aware of other noises around them, a banging on the door, shouts from a voice, though they didn't stop him acting in the moment and staying focused on continuing this physical embrace with the beautiful woman he gathered gently in his arms.

The door flew open and a brisk air wafted into the room. Chill bumps emerged on Rina's bare back beneath his hands. *I can keep her warm.*

"Get the hell away from my sister."

Akono pressed a soft kiss to Rina's lips before lifting his head. He stared Luca down, his hooded gaze on Luka's narrowed eyes. "Or what? You'll do worse than plant a bug in my office?"

Everything officially hit chaos. Rina pushed away from Sweet's hold, got up off the table and yanked her T-shirt down. "Well, you did what you said, Sweet. You can go now."

"What he said?" Luca replied as he reached into his jacket pocket.

She stretched for the vest on the floor. "Yes, brother. He promised to get me home safe and treat the exposure from the Taser so I don't die from infection or worse." *For the love of cards.* "I swear on every piece of flash in that collection bag, if you dare try to say you're here because of some misguided idea about my honor, I'll happily start listing my conquests. In detail." No way would she let Sweet be attacked, not after he'd shown more caring for her than her own family ever had.

"I'll leave if you want me to, Rina." Sweet's eyes asked the question he refused to say out loud.

She had a choice to make, except with her brother standing there ready and more than happy to report her current state of existence to their father, she'd rather pick the battle she could win without doing more damage to herself. "I told you I'll be fine. We can talk more tomorrow."

"What she's trying to say is your dick's appointment with her will have to wait."

"One day, Luca, you're going to reap it." Akono walked past her, past Luca and out of the door without a backward glance.

The door where she saw someone else standing, some hulk of a human being. "Who's that?"

Luca ignored her question. "Where is it?"

Rina sighed. *Figures.* She reached for the cash bag on the floor, next to the table. She stared down at the cotton swatches Sweet had used on her back, still lying on the hard plastic cover. Her brother cared about the money. Sweet offered his care for her. She turned and tossed the bag to her brother. "There it all is, what you really came here for."

He caught the bag with ease and opened it up. "I came to make sure you were all right."

Yep, the same way he sits glued to a bag of gold leaf. Counting through it as fast as his little fingers can flip. "And to get the money."

Luca shrugged. "Hey. That goes without saying. It wouldn't have been right to leave you in a vulnerable state with this much flash."

"I'm not vulnerable."

"Uh, dear sister. I beg to differ when I have to bust down the door to see you lip-locked with the scuzz of

Arcas. You heard father at last family dinner. We don't want you sullying yourself."

She picked up her bloody cotton and threw it into the trash. "Surprised you know such big words like sully."

"Don't sass me."

"Too bad. You're going to get more than sass. Father and you know nothing." She shoved the bottle of disinfectant back in the cabinet and slammed the door shut. The nebula painting rattled against the wall. "You should be thanking me. If Sweet is attracted to me, then he'll be putty in my hands, and why the hell did you bug his office?"

Luca stalked over to her, zipping the flash bag as he walked. "Lower your damn voice, and you didn't honestly think I wouldn't use every angle I have to get to the bottom of his operation? You're not the only option."

"So, there's something else going on. What is it?" She ignored the inkling of hurt trying to niggle at her heart. Who cared if they didn't trust her? They weren't trustworthy themselves. Sweet had that part right.

"Can that *inspector* look. You know what you need to and only that. After Dominic, Dad believes it's best this way."

"Right, I get it. But have the courtesy to tell me what the hell I need to be looking for." Though all she'd do was warn Sweet. Anything her father and brother wanted outside of the business couldn't be good.

"I'll leave that decision up to Dad." Luca hoisted the bag onto his shoulder and motioned at the hulking figure outside the door. "Mound is going to stand guard for the rest of the night in case someone else shows up. Wouldn't want to leave you without backup."

"Mound?"

Luca pointed to the huge male specimen still standing outside the door to the parlor.

"I don't need protection." She wanted to shower and lick her wounds in private. The emotional ones.

"Maybe you don't, but the whole kissing-our-enemy thing seems pretty stupid to me. I should at least leave someone here to keep you from making the same mistakes."

She clutched her fists together, hunching her shoulders, and the wounds on her back twinged. "I think you need to go now."

"Calm yourself. I'm not saying anything that isn't true, and we don't need those jerks coming back and thinking they can bust up our business. Who attacked you, anyway?"

Funny, it took you this long to ask. This long to care. "Some spacehole Sweet booked tonight for putting a hand on a dealer."

"His name?"

"Howell. You should be able to find it in the system." All the clubs had access to it, and all the booked names went inside, along with their offenses. The club law, the law of Callisto, said a booked name at one club was a booked name at all of them.

"He enters Geno's, he's dead. End of story." Luca reached out and stroked her cheek. She did her best to stay still, not to flinch at his cold, clammy touch. "Looks like you may get a bit of shiner on your eye. Sure all they did was hit you with a Taser?"

She took a step back. "Yep, that's it. I may have hit the pavement hard, but nothing a little powder and face cream can't cover up. Go home, Luca."

"Fine. I will. Mound will stay outside, so holler if you need him. He'd be a better choice than Sweet."

She clenched her fists. "How about you leave my personal life and business to me and focus more on getting that extra thing you want from Sweet so bad?"

Luca winked at her. "Don't worry, big sis, we've got it covered."

Yep…and it would most likely bite her in the ass when she least expected it. The question was, what angle would Luca play this time, and did she care enough to interfere?

Chapter Nine

"I'm sorry for kissing you. I'm not sorry at all." Since Akono had left Rina in that tattoo parlor, their second kiss had been all he'd thought about. He debated the words out loud, because they were the ones he should say. He ought to apologize for making things confusing between them—except she'd kissed him first. She'd pushed for the second coming of a physical attraction they both seemed unable to deny. Telling lies about it would make things worse.

There were other things to discuss, like how the first pickup had gone since Luca had shown up for the money. How she was feeling, since her brother had barely offered any words of concern. That part sat wrong with him. Sure, he'd been raised by house ladies and gamblers, but where he came from, caring and concern were given freely. It seemed the Genoveses had none of that.

The door opened, and the very focus of his thoughts poked her head in. "Are you in another meeting? I heard voices."

"No, just a little out-loud thought processing. Come on in."

"About kissing me or apologizing for it?"

Fatch. She'd heard him.

"An apology for that first kiss, since it sent you running out of here and right into those spaceholes who attacked you."

She crossed the room and slapped both her palms against his desk top. "How about an apology isn't required, since I kissed you the second time?"

"Do you own a whole closet of these shirts and vests?" Another night, another view of her near perfect breasts behind a black vest and white shirt.

She grinned, and his pants got a little tighter. "Prefer variety?"

"I don't care either way. I think you're aware that whatever you're wearing, you still look good." This whole conversation was a losing hand he had no chance of winning.

She shook her head and took a step back. "I came in here to tell you I don't think something between us is a good idea."

The opposite of what he'd overheard her tell Luca last night. He was supposed to be clay in her hands for her to mold. "That's a different song than you sang to your brother last night?"

"If you believe everything you hear, then you're more gullible than my first, second and third impression of you." She went for a drink, but not the hard stuff. No, she poured a glass of water. "I told him something to play the game, make him think I still support my father's idea of ruining your business."

"That's the big plan. I expected more from the great Vincent Genovese." Though Luca's prying told a different story and the likelihood she was in on it grew dimmer with each conversation they had.

She took a long gulp of water. "Get used to disappointment. Now, back to us. There should be no us."

"Why? There's someone else?"

"No. No one."

"Then what does it matter?"

She plopped down in the office chair and crossed her arms under her cleavage, accenting the look. *Like waving a bag of cocaine in front of an addicted sniffer.* "You've never had a bad luck run, have you?"

"My entire life has been nothing but a case of trouble. With little streaks to get me where I am today."

"Then you might understand that I'm cursed. Those I bring in close to me always suffer. Those who don't suffer right away are held over my head by the very people I call my family. My father has a certain path for me. His expectation surpasses all, and he will destroy anything that may prevent it. I don't want you added to the list of things he needs to remove as an obstacle to my future."

"Who's acceptable in this future?" The idea of anyone touching her gripped him tight, like a hard shot to the gut. Akono didn't want anyone seeing her pale alabaster skin, enfolding her in their touch. No, every fiber of his being cried out in stern objection. She belonged to… *Scary thoughts should be buried deep.*

"Someone from a wealthy background with ties to the Uppers, I'm sure. I've never asked. But Dominic wasn't what he wanted for me and he's dead."

"I'm not any of those things, and I'm not your dead fiancé." Akono picked up the hat on the side of his desk and put it on his head. He needed to be fully armored for this conversation. "And it's ironic that for once you're down with a plan of following their rules."

"Not exactly, but this isn't about me." The words revealed a truth, one he hadn't counted on.

"You're being threatened?"

"People I care about are."

Akono frowned. "If what you say is true, their lives are in danger if you sleep with me?"

"Not exactly, but circumstances and agreements can always change if we're discovered."

He stood up and walked to her, standing over her. "I think you're falling back on this because you're scared. Scared of what being with me might mean. I've felt it, in your touch...your lips. If you feel even a dice-sized amount of what I get when I'm around you, then I'd be afraid too. I am, actually. But the concept of not exploring what could be seems the bigger error. So, before I make my move, is there anything else I should know?"

"My brother and father are planning something to ensure they get this club and someone is feeding them information from the inside."

How cute. She was having a go at being semi-honest. "Last time I checked, I wasn't planning to sleep with your father or brother, and at first I thought that inside person was you."

She scooted to the edge of the seat and rested her elbows on her knees. "I don't know if I trust you."

"Sex doesn't require trust. It requires attraction."

Ant burst through the office door before Rina could respond. "Zeke is prepped for tonight's duties and I can run the delivery if you still need me to, Sweet."

Poor timing. Ant was set to carry the case of crinkle to Toni and Emilio for Akono's cruiser repairs and hopefully figure out if Luca had anyone trailing him. Sweet motioned him over, picked up the case sitting beside his desk and handed it over with a piece of paper from his pocket. "Light the paper on fire and put it in the ashtray before you leave."

"Will do." Ant appeared unaware that Rina was in the room, because the idiot kept prattling. "We'll get rid of those Genoveses. Stuff seems hard now, but you'll solve the problem. You always do."

"Got any more to say on the subject?" Rina smiled and gripped her empty water glass as if ready to throw it the second trouble reared its head. Akono almost laughed. Comical really, how the woman claimed to hate her family, but was always aching for a fight.

"Plenty, but no time to explain them all." Ant read the paper, scanning the words multiple times.

"Don't strain yourself," Rina said.

His majordomo frowned. "Shut up, space whore."

Anger tightened in Akono's chest at Ant's derogatory phrase. He would have scolded him, but it gave away too much. He needed to show less preference to her, less caring and concern. He needed to be loyal to his people. *Even if one of them is betraying me.*

"Ant. I won't tell you again. Keep things civil or it will cost you."

The lit paper fluttered in front of his eyes as it fell into the ashtray. "You'd really choose her?"

"I'm not choosing. There's no choice in being polite until there's a reason not to be."

Ant hoisted the case and pressed it close to his chest. "Her presence should be enough reason, but whatever. I'll be back."

Sweet nodded at Ant, and the person he trusted with enough crinkle to buy his way off this moon and more walked out of his office, shutting the door behind him.

"Got a deal going?"

He expected the question and waited to respond as he pushed his chair back and stood. "Let's say, like you, my life isn't going to be this club forever. You made a good point—with your family involved, it's only a matter of time, right?"

"Yes. Did you ever think it might be Ant who's selling you out?" She stood and they moved to his office door together.

"Never." The word launched out of his mouth faster than a roulette wheel could spin. "We've been friends since we were kids. Grew up the same way, fought the same fights. Starved together, rose together."

"Except you're the owner and he's still a pawn. My father played chess and he may be a bastard, but he was right about one thing…"

Her voice trailed off as they both reached for the handle at the same time, their hands touching. Sparks wound their way up his arm, wild and promising. He glanced at her and those deep golden eyes connected on his. "What one thing?"

"Even a pawn can defeat a king."

"That's what I aim to do. Will you try to stop me?"

She gave him a grin as he turned the knob with her hand crushed underneath his. "Either way—me or them, you'll get fucked."

He yanked the door open and she stumbled against him. But he'd make the mistake of letting go of the door handle, so the contact between their bodies was brief and too short for what he'd hoped to convey. "I'd rather it be you."

Those last bits of conversation would be stuck in his head all night and the internal debate continued — should he or shouldn't he sacrifice himself on the sexual altar of Caterina Genovese?

* * * *

The night droned on and on. Rina had a hard time concentrating on the bullshit from the drunks, the druggies and the handsy bastard who wanted to do almost everything but make an insertion without paying Maple's girls.

She kicked the bastard to his knees. "Your name is going in the book before I'm done with you."

"She said it was free." The dude had stood about her height before she'd brought him down, mangy-looking as though he'd been in space too long and the ship didn't have showers.

"I would charge you double since you stink so bad." The words filtered down from the second floor, where Maple's girl, Bluebell, stood arms on her hips.

Filthy, because that was what he was, jumped up and pumped both fists in the air. "You're barely worth anything. Should have cut you, made you a bit more like me."

Rina slipped up underneath, getting close enough to the fool that she almost gagged before she laid down two fists, one to the gut and another across his jaw. Filthy crumpled to the floor. Terrance walked in from the hallway entrance and she snapped her fingers. "This is the one. Might want gloves for hauling him, and a face mask. Don't understand why this one was allowed upstairs to begin with."

Terrance made a face and slowed his pace down. "Should he be booked?"

"Yes."

"What's happening? Dash came to get me in the kitchen, hollering about Bluebell being in trouble with some stinky man." Maple's words were loud enough to crash any additional response Rina might have had.

Terrance had already donned gloves and was starting to lift the bastard, who was still out cold.

"Maple, everything is fine. Nothing Terrance and I can't handle." Rina offered the morsel as the older woman stared at Sweet's guard as if he'd invented gambling, their savior and help, which was perfectly fine with her.

"She knocked him out, Mai-Mai. He threatened me, my body and Rina avenged my honor." Bluebell's higher-pitched tones were spoken from the second floor, loud enough so anyone paying half-attention would know what had happened.

The older woman turned and stared at her with newfound admiration. "Well, any hero deserves a few minutes of rest. Ms. Rina, you'll take a seat in the parlor."

"Ma'am, I have to get back over—"

Maple had already reached her side, hooking an arm around Rina's shoulders and guiding her gently to the main sitting room. "I won't accept any reason for an answer. Those knuckles are already swelling. You might be busted up. We'll get something for that right away."

Rina took a seat and the adrenaline started to wear off. Sweet would be pissed, though for all the wrong reasons. She thought his little display of protectiveness, his honesty about wanting her, cute, though ill-advised.

He followed her progress around the club all night, keeping their little back and forth from fading away. She'd ridden high on those sexually frustrated emotions and had fed it with even more trouble when Dash had come running her way, begging for help for poor Bluebell. Any type of physical action was as good as the pain of a needle in flesh. *You're fatching self-destructive.*

The bruising on her knuckles, burst blood vessels underneath the skin, spoke of her love of violence. She'd landed both punches with glee and enthusiasm, though her hands would be useless in an hour or so. She would probably need a shoulder bag to carry the money to her father's.

All that mattered for the moment was that she'd won the fight. A few moments later, Maple swished up to her with two small bags, the woman's long dress sweeping the floor and damn near mesmerizing with its shimmering gold and black.

"Here you go, honey. You didn't have to do that to the fool, though I'm glad you did. Let's ice those poor fists down. These packs have some healing gel in them. Don't know what it's called, but when my gals get bruised, this clears it up in a day or two."

"How long?" She couldn't remain immobile all night. The club would be closing soon and she should get back over there and check in with Ned.

"Oh, an hour or two at most. You can sit right here, and I'll have the gals bring something to eat or drink —"

"I have to assist in closing down the club."

Maple shook her head. "No, I already sent my boy to tell Sweet what happened and that you'll be resting here until the deposit is ready. He won't dare defy his Mai-Mai."

The genuine smile on the older woman's face implied fond memories between her and the man who owned The Sweet Spot. A part of her wanted the same type of moments, the compassion she'd never received growing up.

"Then do it." Because trying to escape this woman would be a challenge, and deep down, she enjoyed the fawning over her. Like her own mother used to before her death. The last time anyone had spent this much time worrying over her had been the previous night, when Sweet had cared for her after those would-be robbers had attacked her.

The woman sat in a chair beside Rina, in all her shimmering finery, the tops of her bosoms on display, and played mom to her, gently directing her which way to hold her hands and applying the packs, wrapping tape around to seal them.

"You're working so hard for us. The girls and I thank you. You go above and beyond in ways we'd never expect from a Genovese."

Them... The gals gathering in the main room to cast looks of appreciation her way were people Rina shouldn't be working so hard for at all. She should be more hands off, sitting back and letting things unfold. Allow chaos to ensue so she could give her father and brother an excuse to move in.

Her previous emotional high fell fast now. The consequences of her eagerness to fight Filthy came worming their way in, like an unwanted guest at a twenty-one table. Even if the packs helped, they weren't going to heal her hands overnight. She wouldn't be able to tattoo clients tomorrow with swollen knuckles. *Dry humped.*

"Where is she?" Sweet's voice echoed through the room as he wound his way through the gathering throng of women.

"Over here, Sweet." Maple replied.

Sweet emerged on the other side of the group and came to a stop in front of her. "What happened?"

Maple's sweet countenance turned to a frown. "What a stupid question. My boy told you what occurred and I'm taking care of Rina. You had no reason to march over here all upset and concerned."

Akono sighed in frustration. "Mai-Mai, I just —"

"No, take that 'men have a right to be concerned' double-standard swill elsewhere. We, as women, are more than capable of handling things without male interference. In other words, continue with your business. Rina will come to you when she's done here."

The grown man, a man she found to be the one providing direction, not taking it, turned on his heel and left the room. Rina almost laughed but stopped herself from doing so. She needed to ensure the women didn't lose any respect for Sweet.

"I can't believe you talked to him like that?"

"Oh, I always have. I've known him since he was running around with nothing but a covering for his ass. His mother and I were friends. When she passed, I tried to keep an eye on him, though I didn't do the best job."

"From what I can tell, he's become a good man."

Maple's countenance beamed. "Yes, he has. I'm proud of all he's accomplished and more than a little disappointed your family is trying to take it away from him."

Those words stuck with Rina for the rest of her time in Maple's, causing her to turn down the offers of food and drink. The Genoveses took enough from these people on a daily basis, the guilt of it clogging her throat and making it impossible to speak. She removed the packs and put them to the side. Her hands were still useless, but didn't look too bad.

She marched to Sweet's office, determination renewed to get the money bag, make the deposit and get as far away from these people as possible. Sticking around where she continued to contribute to their downfall would plague her. She opened the door to find Sweet talking quietly with Ant.

The pair looked at her as she entered, Ant's eyes full of contempt and Sweet's with anger. Good, their aggravation with her made things all the easier. "Is the deposit ready?"

"Ant, leave us." The only words out of Sweet's mouth until his second departed. Once the door closed, Sweet lit in. "You know, I have a full contingent of men to dole out violence when it's required."

"Oh, I'm sorry… You wanted me to wait for backup. Not normally a problem, unless I see one of your gals with a black eye and the man who did the deed threatening to cut her up. Situations like that deserve immediate punishment."

"That may be, but you put yourself on someone else's radar again."

Rina took a few steps closer, arms crossed because if she opened them, they were liable to fly. "Since he got his ass beat by me this time, maybe he'll think twice about attacking me for revenge."

Sweet slammed his palm on the table, causing his hat to rattle and fall off his head to the floor. "Shit…true

Genovese through and through. Always resorting to getting in the thick of the violence and itching for a fight."

Instead of continuing the argument, he sat back down and finished his work on the books, separating the takes between the two bags. Rina approached slowly, watching every movement and seeing nothing worrisome. Sweet was true to his division. When finished, he swiveled the book around. "Take a look. So you'll know the numbers are accurate."

She did, running the tip of her index finger down the intake column. The numbers were solid, and the bag... She hefted it in her hand, doing her best to stop herself from wincing, and the crinkle shifted inside. "Seems about right. I'll head out to my father's immediately."

"No fatching way. You won't be going alone."

"I'm happy to bust up these hands a little more if a fight appears. I can still toss a punch."

Sweet shook his head. "You're no match against Tasers or pistols. I'm coming with you."

Chapter Ten

Akono sent up silent prayers as they made the trek to Vincent Genovese's deposit drop. Rina didn't try to argue with him, they didn't run into anyone trying to kill them, and the streets seemed more jovial, with patrons happily moving to and fro in small groups. Arcas, the city that never slept, and if Akono had wanted, he could have kept his place open longer hours, like Geno's. He would have made more money, but there was safety in having down time.

Instead of heading to the main club of the Genovese empire, they turned away from the commercial streets and onto the private home streets. Behemoths of living space, monuments to old Earth-before-the-nuke homes. Mansions, he remembered Maple calling them. He couldn't imagine living in something like this, something with so many rooms.

"Where are we going?" he asked while they passed some marvel with six giant columns and more windows than he thought possible.

"My childhood home."

"I thought deposits were made at the club?"

Rina chuckled. "Shows how much you know. And here I thought you'd done your research on all things Genovese. Father only accepts deposits at home, where everything is under far better security and control. He doesn't have your fancy tube system to keep things locked up nice and tidy."

Akono found it interesting how, even sitting at the top, Rina's father trusted no one.

They approached the gates. They had bodyguards on both sides, who immediately put their hands to their side pieces.

"Stow your eagerness to shoot someone, boys. It's just me."

The taller one took a step forward. "Who do you have with you?"

"A business partner of my father's. We're bringing in a deposit." She held up the bag of flash and Akono caught the look of pain on her face from the effort.

The ready excuse and her look didn't help matters. Instead it earned them a double frown from both guards. Suddenly pulling his gun didn't sound like a bad plan.

"Your father isn't home this evening." The stockier of the two took a step towards them.

"Then we'll wait until he shows up. Seriously, Jones, I've had a rough night busting up a dude who liked to hurt women. If you don't let me pass, I'm liable to take out the rest of my anger on you."

"No offense, Ms. Rina. We are just doing—"

She lowered the bag and rolled her eyes, every single ounce of rich bitch. "Your job. I get it, after the mess six months ago. Trust me. I wouldn't break my father's rules."

The guards let them pass, Jones muttering something about hating house detail.

Now past the guards, Akono took in the splendor of the Genovese stronghold. Beautiful marble walls, a pair of heavy solid wood doors that could be covered by a sliding metal gate that was rolled up above it. A big solid gold filigree spread across the floor from the entrance to a massive staircase that would take people to rooms, to the second floor, to a million and one possibilities.

"Doing okay over there?" Rina's question made Akono stumble over his feet for a brief second.

"Fine, just…"

"Overwhelmed. Dad had it designed to cause that reaction in the richest of men. He likes it when they enter and are speechless. Guess it proves you're not immune."

"To what?" He didn't look at her, taking in the paintings. The sceneries and imagery from Earth. Mountains, forests and a dozen other things he'd never seen. His life consisted of artificial city light half the year and never-ending nights.

"To the things flash can bring. Follow me, Sweet. Before that painting sucks you into it." She chuckled, grabbing him by the hand.

He let her drag him, stumbling to keep up where she led him, down a side hallway past rooms more opulent than the main entrance. Until they passed another staircase. "Where does that go?"

"A private set of steps to the family wing. The front leads to a host of guest rooms we never use and is designed to give possible intruders false hope." She held the bag out to him. "You can make the deposit."

Interesting. "You'd trust me to do that?"

She winked at him. "You're not going anywhere, not with a chance like this. To see things no mere mortal gets to see. Walk past that staircase. It goes down to the vault. Open that cabinet, place the bag inside and close the door."

He did as she directed, their fingers brushing against one another as he grabbed the bag, latent desire stirring and rumbling within him. He dropped the bag in and slammed the door shut. Whirring sounds followed by a sudden whoosh confirmed the deposit had successfully gone to its destination.

"What next?"

"Let's grab a drink." She wandered across the hall and passed the threshold of what appeared to be a parlor, like the brothel had, but this more masculine. All leather furniture, a roaring fireplace and a bar inlaid into a back wall, which Rina sauntered towards.

"Whiskey?"

Akono shrugged. "Whatever you want to pour works."

A massive portrait sat above the fireplace. A woman, older, and who looked a lot like Rina. "Who's the beauty?"

She walked back to him with two glasses of what he prayed was top-quality whiskey. "My mother, once upon a time."

"Where is she now?"

Rina held out his glass and he accepted it. "Dead and buried, like all the people I've loved. She got killed in an attack on my father's life. The bullet got her instead."

"How old were you when she died?"

"I was twelve."

Akono took a sip of his drink. "Old enough to remember, then."

She chugged hers. "And to be angry, pissed off and with no one to talk to about it. Because to show emotion is weak and to care about someone so much that losing them kills your drive to be greedy is unacceptable to a Genovese."

He moved closer to the mantel, trying to imagine what this type of loss did to someone. He'd been barely four when his mother had died. So many things had happened since then that it was damn near impossible to remember anything about her. He only knew what she looked like from an old holo-image Maple had given him.

"So, what did you do?" He ran his fingers along the cold black marble mantel. It felt as desolate as space.

"I learned to shut things out. To pretend it didn't matter. To believe in only relying on oneself. Then someone made me open up again. Made me care and think I could get out of this place. That person almost killed my father."

Akono turned to face her. She stood mere feet from him, staring into her empty glass. "Does your father matter so much?"

"He's my father. He's ruthless and horrible, but am I one to judge him? Do you care about the people who work for you?"

The sobering truth sat right there with her words and the realization hit him hard. If he lost Maple, Ned, the boys… "They matter. They're my family, except they don't threaten me to get what they want."

"Well, watch out, because sometimes people who say they love you will also do things to hurt you in the name of that love. If you're not ready when it happens, you'll be crippled, and I don't think you can afford to let yourself be so exposed."

Voices echoed around them and Rina's eyes went wide. Footsteps could be heard tramping down the hallway. Akono was ready for the confrontation, but it appeared Rina wasn't. She grabbed Akono by the arm and dragged him to a wardrobe set in the far wall.

"What—"

"Shut up and follow my lead," she whispered harshly. She eased the wardrobe door open and motioned for him to get inside.

"This is not—" His murmured words were cut off as she shoved him into the wardrobe and his arms flailed until his now empty glass caught on a heavy coat. He grabbed hold and pulled himself up as all light was extinguished. Akono worried that if he moved, it might make too much noise, but he had to adjust himself in the limited space and tried to be as quiet as possible pushing the coat out of his way.

He came into contact with a body, a feminine one, judging from the way his free hand framed the hips and buttocks.

"Watch your hand." Rina's whisper sounded harsh and low. Akono froze, still connected to her, letting the heat of her body soak into his palms through her clothes. *If I'm dying tonight, it will be with the memory of her ass in my hand.*

The sounds of male voices were plainly audible from beyond the door. Akono recognized Luca's first.

"Father, the numbers are down a bit, but that was to be expected with Rina not working as many hours in the shop. Yash says he's given her permission to sleep in as needed. You know how he likes to pretend like he really gives a crap."

"That may be, but try explaining that to Tuatha's man. She's not going to accept poor numbers, no matter the excuse." The second voice had to be Rina's father, Vincent.

Glasses clinked, liquid poured and a sigh came. "When should we —"

"May I present Tuatha's emissary, Jacques." This from Jones, the guard from the gate. Akono wouldn't mistake that growly grumble of a voice anywhere.

There were footsteps, right outside the wardrobe they were hiding in. Jacques' words came out loud and crystal clear. "Well, Vincent? Care to share why body numbers have dropped?"

Rina's body tensed beneath his and for the first time since he'd met her, Akono truly believed she had no clue how awful her father's business exploits were.

Dry humped! What could be worse than bringing Sweet to her childhood home? Being cooped up in a wardrobe with him while her father conducted business. Neither one of them should be hearing what occurred in the room beyond, because each word condemned the man she kept trying to make excuses for.

She leaned forward, pressing against the closed doors, her curiosity refusing to abate. The word *bodies* and in relation to her work at the parlor, then this Jacques character showing up? She was reduced to her spying days as a teenager, when she'd wanted to know everything about what her father worked on.

Vincent spoke first. She could tell because her father never minced words. "We've seen a slight dip. Nothing we can't make up this next month. Though, we are having some trouble with people reporting missing persons."

The Jacques dude laughed. At least she assumed as much, since the voice was a little higher-pitched. "I'd think you more inventive. Just recruit the family members as well. They'd be honored to serve. Now, how is the other product moving?"

"Dominic, my sister's ill-fated fiancé, ruined half the last shipment. We need a refill, and I've made arrangements for product to arrive within the next couple of weeks." Hearing the name of her ex-fiancé spoken from her brother's mouth had her grinding her teeth.

If she could get any more tense, she'd snap, all hunched shoulders and rigid frame. What the hell had Dominic found, her family's penchant for killing people and collecting bodies? To kill people for fuel purposes was probably the most illegal crime next to bringing drugs and booze to the Uppers. Callisto played gatekeeper to those sins and Jupiter's Body Collection Service were the only ones making money off the dead. *Obviously not.*

"We're aware. Just know this is the last shipment for at least a full cycle year."

"We understand," Luca replied. "And they only need one dose to do the job, though two helps us spread word of the product. It's a marvel, really."

"Are you taking precautions against discovery?"

"Of course, and we have contingencies upon contingencies. We won't make the mistakes of previous clients. We'll deliver the numbers promised and assume Tuatha will honor her compensation promises?" This from her father.

The message was clear. Her father had some experimental drug and was killing people with it. *Recruiting them, ha!* That was their common phrase for taking someone out. The question was how they were doing it, because just distributing drugs wouldn't meet any type of big number.

"She will compensate when the collection centers report is sent. Your word isn't good enough."

Rina sucked in a breath, and Sweet took full possession of her, wrapping his arms around her body. He provided a stable surface to lean against, because all hell might just break loose in a minute. No one called Vincent Genovese a liar.

"Don't give away our hiding spot," he whispered.

Vincent continued talking and shockingly didn't attack on principle alone. "The numbers should show plenty. We're affecting street scum, idiots seeking tattoos or mindless pleasure. We're even infiltrating competitive markets."

Fatching hell. The girls at Sweet's place. Maybe the missing brother, the missing people on the rise was a direct result of her father's new business venture. Body collecting. Except a conversation heard through a wardrobe wouldn't be enough.

"Excellent, I'll pass on the news to Tuatha. I'll leave you to your whiskey, gentlemen."

The goodbyes were brief, then Tuatha's agent was gone. She tried to break free of Sweet's hold on her. To get away from the heat of his body. Then a glass clinked against the bottom of the wardrobe.

She shoved Sweet to the side and reached for the back-panel doorknob—it took a little bit of shoving, but she got it open. Light flooded the wardrobe and she scrambled out of there, dragging Sweet with her.

"What is this place?" He spoke softly, thank goodness.

"It's a private entertaining parlor that my father and brother use for encounters." She shut the door as quietly as she could and pressed her ear to it, but heard nothing. "We've got minutes."

Swiveling on her heel, she faced Sweet, who stared at the bed across the room. She usually avoided this den of sin, but at the moment it might provide the perfect solution. "We don't have time to make it all the way over there."

He glanced at her. "We're about to have a world of trouble knocking down the door, but it's tempting. I think we could make it."

"Never with all these clothes."

Sweet chuckled. "Fine, what's our cover?"

Thank goodness he understood the consequences if they were caught overhearing a private meeting... If he'd caught what the meeting was about, she couldn't ask, not right now.

She pressed both hands against his suit-covered chest and pushed him backward. He took a couple of steps back, and one more shove brought him plopping onto the couch. She straddled him, leaning down to whisper in his ear, "Our cover is this."

Then she pressed her lips to his.

Chapter Eleven

Rina was the embodiment of sensuality in his arms, her lips and tongue caressing and stroking him as if she planned to consume him completely. Her efforts took away coherent thought and replaced the worry of being caught with something much more sinful.

Akono decided to play up the opportunity. *Got to make it look real, right?* Except being real with her, in this fashion, was no hardship. "I could have had us both naked in that bed in under a minute," he mumbled while he moved his hands up and down her arms, before reaching between them to access the buttons on her vest.

He pulled up the edge of her shirt to get his hands on her bare skin. It wasn't a stretch to let his fingers trail a path to her breasts and tweak her hard nipples. The worst part was that he couldn't see them, wouldn't be able to see them in the dim light. Getting her naked was his new personal goal, under full lighting, where he could map every inch of her flesh.

Her hand had started an adventure of her own when a door slammed open. Akono froze, his tongue caught between Rina's teeth and her hand gripping his cock.

"Saints alive! Damn it, Rina!" Luca's voice couldn't kill Akono's hard-on at that moment.

Rina eased her hold on him in both places and climbed off him leisurely. He enjoyed watching her smile as she faced him and pulled her shirt back down before buttoning her vest. Akono clamped his lips shut and willed his hard cock to recede.

He couldn't see Luca standing near the door. Rina's fine form blocked him. *Thank goodness.* Because he didn't need the idiot seeing him in this aroused state and he'd be liable to tell Luca to shut the door and fatch off.

"It's one thing to be entertaining him in his establishment, but bringing him to our family home and doing this? It's no better than a space whore, Rina." Luca's words had Akono clenching his fists. He'd be damned if Luca would get many more attempts to call Rina names. Or anyone else, for that matter. With her brains, aptitude for empathy and her sensual nature, she deserved respect.

"Sorry." She adopted a not-guilty-couldn't-care-less smile, turned and shrugged. "I didn't expect either of you back here so soon."

Akono stood. No need to stay in the weaker position, in case Luca decided to draw and fire. Akono straightened his jacket, zipped his pants and picked up the hat Rina had knocked off somehow during their rapid make-out session.

Luca stepped to the side and looked at Akono with enough disgust to make a Neptuner proud. "Is he turning you into some woman for his brothel?"

No more. Attraction and desire were fickle emotions, easily converted to anger and rage. His attraction to Rina was worth more than this, though, more than insults and bullshit.

"I'm tired of you implying I'm anything less than a gentleman, Luca. If you want, we can settle this right now, but have no doubts Rina is her own woman. She takes what she wants, not the other way around. So if anyone's becoming a whore, it's me. But if you insult her one more time, my fists are going to meet your face."

Akon glanced at Rina, who surprisingly stood quiet, her eyes wide. He put the hat on his head and continued, still staring at the woman who was a better poker player than he'd ever guessed. "Rina invited me here when I refused to let her come alone. Fool that I was, I believed the drop would be made at Geno's. Instead, I got treated to an opportunity to see the famed Genovese stronghold. Naturally this sensual setting you've put together in here set the mood."

Rina blushed. Whether it was real or not, he had no clue. Except it worked—Luca's face was red with anger, and the idiot cracked his knuckles. "She's not yours."

"She's not anyone's." Akono responded with a cocked eyebrow in her direction, and she pursed her lips. Saying nice things about her was easy, though he doubted she'd believe the honesty he leveled, because they were supposed to be acting, playing their roles of two people interested in screwing, not overhearing a conversation about mass murder.

"I'm going to set a new mood for the evening, one with your face mangled. Maybe she'd keep her damn hands off you, half-breed." Luca was sliding a pair of plated knuckles on, the ones that electrified right up and made a person's insides and face burn.

Rina launched for Luca first, but Akono grabbed for her, pulling her close. "He's not worth the effort."

"That's what she said about you, Sweet."

Akono didn't care now. He let Rina go and went at Luca himself, stopping short as the elder Genovese came into view.

"Enough, Luca. Put those damn knuckles away and stop acting like a heathen in our house. Guests, whether wanted or not, should be treated how we wish to be treated."

Akono tried to steel his face and hide the shock at the words emerging from Vincent Genovese. The same person who so casually discussed the deaths of innocents without a second thought. Who deliberately wanted to put The Sweet Spot out of business. "Your home is very impressive, Mr. Genovese."

"I take it you learned what you wanted, then?"

Dread pooled low, a sneaky snake coiling around his belly. "I didn't know there was a lesson in coming here."

"He escorted me, Father. After the incident last night, and a run-in with another harassing patron tonight, he thought it best I had company on the delivery. Of course I accepted. Wouldn't want the delivery jeopardized." Rina stepped up beside Akono, their shoulders bumping against each other. She did an amazing job of appearing as calm as possible.

"So the delivery is safe?" Her father's raised eyebrow showed his skepticism.

Akono wished he'd armed himself with more than one gun before coming here, though it wouldn't take much to rush Luca and grab the pistol in his jacket holster.

"It's safe. We dropped it before coming in here."

Luca scoffed. "So a little chivalry and you think that's a perfect excuse to fuck him?"

"Luca! Keep your crude tongue still," the elder Genovese hissed, half-raising a hand, and the younger flinched.

Akono tried to keep his face dispassionate. "I appreciate your hospitality, but I believe it's time to take my leave."

"I'd prefer you both join me for a drink first."

So much for good luck. If he'd had any, it had abandoned him the minute his lips had touched Rina's.

The four of them exited the sin den, Rina's father and Sweet leading the way. She wasn't sure what her father was angling at or if he suspected them of overhearing anything.

"You have no shame," Luca hissed as he fell into step beside her, the knuckles tucked away in his coat pockets.

"I never knew a Genovese needed shame. You and Father certainly don't demonstrate any."

"What do you mean by that?" Luca leaned in close, the alcohol on his breath stale and musty.

Rina rolled her eyes. "I mean the dozens of women you've paraded in and out of this house over the years. Women you paid more than a fair share to. So while you're trying to make me feel guilty, I suggest turning that guilt on yourself."

The study loomed before them, crackling fire roaring, and her father encouraging Sweet to take a seat in one of the heavy leather chairs. Those chairs had swallowed up bigger men in years past, made them cower among her father's prowess, and she'd watched it happen.

Heat flushed her face and the hairs on her neck stood on end. All of this from the way her father was attempting to intimidate Sweet. Like he did to everyone. Hell if she'd let Daddy dear get his hooks into Sweet by setting him up to confess to being present to hear his crimes. *I hope he's stronger than he looks.*

"Rina, pour the drinks," her father called out.

"Sure," Rina growled, marching over to the bar. The number of glasses underneath revealed more than she wanted them to. Regardless, she grabbed three and poured a fresh round.

"So, is her story true? You chose to escort my daughter as protection?"

Thankfully, she could look right at Sweet as she brought the glasses over to her father and Luca, who'd already taken a seat across from her would-be protector.

"Yes, sir." Sweet's confident tone gave her newfound optimism and a fresh wave of emotion filled her, the same way it had when Sweet had defended her against Luca. Every time he took action on her behalf, she wanted to be pissed, but found herself enjoying his efforts too much.

Everyone took their drinks and sipped from them without prompting. Sweet's answer didn't lower the amount of tension in the room. Her father sat back in leisurely pose, but he was never one to get his hands dirty. *You hire people for that...* Her father fell back on that excuse for almost everything.

Which was why Luca scooting himself forward to the edge of his chair bothered her. "Why would you do something so stupid?"

Rina frowned at her brother, who offered a shrug in return for his question. "It's not dumb to want to offer protection."

Her father tsked her. "It is to go yourself. If someone truly wanted to take Sweet out of the competition, it would be easy to do so on the way to our home. Better to let an underling, someone he trusts, do the escorting. Unless he trusts no one, an equally troublesome idea. Which makes me believe the motives here are not as pure or coincidental as you both keep trying to make them appear."

Fatching superstitious fools.

"You're right." Rina took a deep breath and let it out, anything to quell the fluttering in her chest. The swarms, like buzzes of electricity, similar to the feeling when she'd gotten shocked, vibrated within her, made worse by the three sets of eyes trained on her with varying degrees of suspicion.

"I wanted to impress Sweet. Seduce him. A poor choice on my part, but rich surroundings with the hint of being caught made me weak." As she spoke, she focused completely on her father, ensuring that her emotions went straight to him, and surprisingly it wasn't hard to lie. *Goddess, half of it isn't a lie.* She wanted Sweet naked and at her mercy, but not in this house. Nowhere near this tainted place.

As a child, she'd found lying to Vincent Genovese the greatest sin and she'd often told the truth for fear of his wrath. There was nothing more important than truth telling, except in this case now...she'd discovered that Vincent lied whenever he chose, whenever it pleased him.

"She has a point, Dad." Luca agreeing with her was also a bit gag-worthy, but right now she'd take whatever got her and Sweet out of this house. "I'm guilty of doing the same stupid stuff. It makes the sex more exciting."

"Indeed, though disrespectful it may be," her father replied. Then he turned his emerging frown on Sweet. "Do you stand by this assessment? My daughter brought you here for a good screwing?"

Sweet polished off his drink and visibly swallowed. "Yes. Though I'll admit my first concern was ensuring her safety. After we arrived, I found out about her ulterior motives."

"I find it interesting you are so concerned with my daughter's safety. Tonight and last night, from what I hear, you helped her when she was being attacked by a patron you had to book."

Rina shouldn't have been interested in Sweet's reaction at all, but she was.

"Why wouldn't I want to keep the daughter of my business partner alive? If I didn't, you would have the perfect excuse to make a move on me, which implies you might be trying to endanger her for a chance to kill me. Also, what better way to prove my commitment to this newfound partnership than by ensuring your representative's safety?"

The fluttering in her heart, the part of her hoping this thing between him, as he put it, held a future, sputtered and died at his cold, analytical delivery. How this was all another motive. Her whole life was filled with games and angles.

Sure, something more between them besides this damning attraction and sexual tension was probably not in the cards, but that didn't stop her from wanting it. They had a connection, something she hadn't experienced since her friendship and later relationship with Dominic, though what she'd shared with her previous fiancé was a fraction of what she'd experienced thus far.

"Touché." Her father held his glass up in silent congratulations, something he wouldn't do for just anyone, before he downed the rest.

Luca smirked. "This one isn't as dumb as he looks, Rina."

"I tried to tell you that at the last family dinner, but you didn't believe me then. Funny, but before the Dominic debacle, my word meant something." All right, so all the old hurts were coming out tonight. *On top of a mountain of lies and bullshit.*

"Yes, Caterina, and I apologize for not listening to you then. Since the deposit is made, we'll let Sweet get back to his business. You're welcome to stay the night here."

She shook her head. "No, I have an early opening at the parlor in the morning."

Her father stood, and everyone else followed suit. Even though he was a murderer, the man still commanded the actions of everyone in the room. "Then, let me kindly ask if Sweet can escort you back to your place."

"I'd always intended to, sir."

She tried to keep her bullshit under control, though she wanted to tell all three of them to fatch off. To leave her be. Except leaving this house now, with what she knew — her life, whatever meager existence she served, was over.

"Maybe try getting some sleep tonight, Rina. Sweet can keep his damn hands off her." Her brother nudged her with his shoulder, giving her that grin that always creeped her out.

Sweet growled. "One day you're going to get your ass kicked for not minding your own business."

"Oh? I doubt that."

Vincent clucked his tongue. "Luca, no need to follow them like some dog protecting his master. Your sister is fully capable of leaving on her own. Though I recommend you both take a hover cycle instead of going back on foot. The late hour makes the club losers more desperate."

Rina frowned, thankful her expression was hidden from them both. "Thank you. We'll do that."

They'd just crossed the threshold on the way out and the hover cycle was pulled up under the entrance by one of her father's goons. "Miss Genovese. Your father said do not worry about returning it, as it's yours."

Sweet's jaw almost touched marble, it hung so low. "This is—"

"No speaking until we get out of here." Rina held up a finger, pushing it against Sweet's lips. *Damn those lips.* "Where do I take you?"

"Your place will work...for now." He still glanced at the cycle. The most expensive thing she'd ever owned and a distinct part of her life taken away from her when she'd run.

She sighed before she grabbed hold of the handlebars and wrapped her legs around this fine piece of machinery. "Hop on. I'm driving."

Sweet raised an eyebrow at her, but slid on behind her. Him wrapping his arms around her waist brought them close, his dick rock-hard against her back. She kept her mouth shut, though she wanted to ask what made him hard—her or the cycle.

They zipped around the streets with ease, the time it took to venture back to the tattoo parlor cut in half compared to their earlier walk. She rolled into the alley behind the buildings. No way did they need to showcase their position to anyone watching them, and she didn't trust her father and brother not to get paranoid all over again.

Rina brought the hover cycle to a halt near the back door and they both clambered off. She pointed to a tarp stuffed up against the wall. "Grab that."

Sweet did as she asked, though he held the offending thing far away from her. "Please tell me you don't plan on covering up that fine piece of technology with this stinking thing?"

"Oh yes. That stinking thing will deter someone from making the mistake of stealing this fine piece of tech."

He frowned. "That's a Cannenhiem."

"Your eyes are still working, thank goodness. Now throw it to me if you're so worried about your clothes."

"It's not a horrible thing to want to keep your clothes clean. Or prevent beautiful things from being defaced." Akono tossed her the dropcloth and she spread it over the cycle.

Then she headed for the back door of the tattoo parlor, but when she looked back over her shoulder, Akono was still standing near the bike. "Are you coming in?"

"I don't know if I should."

She chuckled at the irony. He'd walked into her father's house without hesitation. Being invited back into her place made him stall. "I've never known you to be the hesitant type."

There was a wariness to him, one she hadn't noticed before. "I'm warring between self-preservation and this stupid urge to see if what happened in your father's house is going to turn into something more."

"It's definitely more, but I'm not talking about it in the open. I'd rather be behind closed doors in an environment I can defend myself in." He brought up *them* as if he hadn't excused away all his kind words and efforts like a shot of whiskey when talking to her father.

They made it inside and she locked the back door, noticing how Akono inspected the rest of the place, ensuring the front door was still secure.

"When you're done, head upstairs." She trudged up to her place and through the door. The vest she ditched. She turned when she heard footsteps on the stairs, her high alert setting still pulsing within her. There was an undercurrent of adrenaline, latent but present. The anger toward her family, the sense of unfulfillment after letting Sweet put his hands on her, and his easy dismissal. Lord, he'd put his hands on her.

Amid all this mess, she'd been unable to fully enjoy him, and looking at him now, it seemed he faced a similar problem. "I'm not sure my father letting us go doesn't mean he's still not suspicious."

"Did you really mean everything back there, in that room?"

They spoke at the same time. Completely different thoughts.

"You have a one-track mind, and weren't you the one who told my father you were just protecting your own self-interests?" She chuckled, shaking her head before she toed her boots off.

"I was playing the role you wanted me to. We wanted to get out of there alive, right? That was the goal." Sweet set his hat on the little table by the door and shrugged out of his coat. They matched, black vests and white shirts, except he had a tie.

"Yes, but... Sorry, for a second your acting was really good and I wanted to believe I was more than just a safeguard."

He marched over to her, the full focus of his whiskey-colored eyes bearing down. "Truth, I spoke it. And if you need more evidence, it's right here."

Rina gasped as Sweet grabbed her hand and brought it to his crotch. The hard length of him pulsed beneath her hold. She squeezed gently.

He groaned. "I'm harder than a rock and having your body pressed up against me on that cycle didn't help. I should be running away, but I find that even if your father ordered a hit on me, I'd still want to be with you. In a biblical sense."

She licked her lips and let those words soak into her very being. Pair the desire with the remnants of almost being killed, and her body soared to life. Though she still had to ask, had to attempt to be the voice of reason. "Shouldn't we discuss this other thing?"

"It's going to be there in the morning, but if I'm going to die, I'd rather know what you taste like."

"Let's see if you feel the same way once I get you tied up."

Chapter Twelve

Akono swallowed hard before he tugged on the edge of his button-down shirt collar. For the first time in a long damn time he regretted dressing to the nines every night. "Are you sure?"

"I like how you're into consent, but you suggested this. Surprised you're anxious to back out now." Of course she'd say that as she started to unlace her boots, sitting on the edge of her bed.

The studio place above the tattoo parlor had a wide-open floor plan and, outside of the small kitchen area with breakfast bar, the random chair, and end table with lamp, the majority of the area was taken up by a big bed.

"I'm not backing out, merely giving you a chance to change your mind. I mean, we could have died."

She glanced up at him and chuckled. "Kind of what I mentioned already, but I think we were talking about two different things in the alley."

Yes and no. Truth being he wanted to forget what had happened at Vincent Genovese's house. At least for tonight. The only thing analyzing those overheard conversations could do was stir up trouble in a big way. One that was liable to put them both on a hit list, if they weren't on one already.

No, he'd rather get lost in her hair. The long ponytail stopping mid-back. He shrugged out of his suit jacket, tossing it at the chair and missing completely. *Craps.*

The action brought a fresh smile to a barefoot Rina, who was working her way to the buttons on her pants.

"Stop." Akono hoped his voice didn't sound as growly to her as it did to him.

"I thought we agreed I'd be the one directing your downfall, since I'm turning you into one of my whores?"

His dick strained against the front of his pants at how she threw his words back at him. "Happy to let you be in charge, but may I undress you?"

She sighed, rolling her eyes. "Since you asked so nicely, but hurry. These clothes are stifling after tonight."

Or most likely from the heat. He felt it coming up the stairs and it only grew, a wild burst of energy crackling between them. He slipped out of his fancy shoes as he neared her, followed by loosening a few buttons on his shirt and tugging it over his head. By the time he reached her, he was in only a white cotton tank and his suit pants.

His hands came toward her first. Starting at her arms, she shivered at first contact. He basked in the knowledge that she experienced a similar reaction to his. A slide up to the shoulders, down alongside her breasts, spanning her waist, to finally pick up where she halted.

Fingers on the clasp around her pants, he paused. "Direct me."

"Undo the button and get these damn things off me. Make sure you leave the panties on. I've got plans for those and don't want them discarded."

Blood pounded in his ears as he did as she directed. He went with the pants, crouching down and letting her lean over his shoulders to lift each leg out.

She was all silk and fire. He wanted to explore everything, his hands retracing their way up each leg, massaging and kneading.

"Stand up."

Akono released his hold and did as directed. Their eyes met and he saw the blaze there. It matched the heat on her skin.

"Have you ever been restrained before during sex?"

The blunt question took him a bit out of the moment. "Once."

"You'll need to give me more detail than that." She shucked her T-shirt and her breasts were covered with just a thin strip of cloth.

All moisture fled his mouth at the appearance of her creamy white skin. He longed to put his hand against it, to see dark mix with light. Though he was probably far more innocent than she'd ever been. And he'd never wanted to be corrupted as much as he wanted it now.

For all his bluster, Akono hadn't fought many fist fights or battles. He preferred his wits to action. If someone told him he'd have to fight to the death to touch the bounty being displayed before him...he'd demand a weapon.

"Akono, stay focused. Did you enjoy being tied up?"

"Yes. Tie me up." Anything if he'd get rewarded with her body.

She laughed. "I don't think you're even hearing what I am saying."

"It's your breasts. They're amazing, and I'm trying to guess the color of your nipples. Pale pink? Dark, like your hair, like cocoa powder. Or as red as a rosebud."

She closed the small gap between them, her hands going to his pants. "I would have unveiled my breasts sooner if you'd told me they'd render you incapable of concentrating."

Cool air hit his dick and he jumped to attention as Rina slid his pants and underwear down. His ass was bared to the room, made worse when she wrapped a hand around him. He groaned, loud enough that it had to echo against the walls. "Goddess, bless."

"Religious?"

"I wouldn't—" He cut off with a gasp as the warm heat of Rina's mouth enveloped him.

She surrounded him in a pleasurable caress, like sliding into a cocoon of blankets. Except this particular blanket was wet, and swirling a tongue around…

"Fatch me."

A corresponding chuckle made him shake, reaching out for any source of stability. Instead, he put his hands to his hips, because anything else would only cause him to fall forward. And for a few minutes, he got lost in the sensation of Rina. The best damn woman he'd ever had, one who enjoyed herself. It made the experience unreal and he vowed silently to return the favor, multiple times, if she'd let him.

The idea of letting this go too far stirred up guilt. He'd been told growing up that a woman's pleasure came first. This certainly wasn't the way to go about it.

"Rina…oh, aces. I mean, this feels amazing, but what about you?"

She dragged him out of her mouth slowly, his dick leaking precum. "Oh, I'm getting mine. I'll take it in multiple ways. In case you aren't aware, this brings me happiness."

Her mouth might have been talking, but her hand took over while she did. Her gaze focused on his face, watching. She'd become a study in what made him gasp, tense up and finally...she stopped.

She stood up, releasing her hold on him. His dick arched of its own volition, as though the damn thing had grown a brain and would go after her at any cost. "I want you on the bed now, and I'm going to restrain you."

"What else?" He climbed onto the bed and sprawled on his back. Ready and willing.

"If you were more familiar with this, I'd spread you out and claim you. Instead, I'll think we'll stick with penetration."

Every inch of his skin tingled at her words. This woman could possibly make him come by merely discussing sexual appetites, urges and actions. Maybe one day he'd get the opportunity to find out, but therein lay the problem. After tonight, would this continue? Would they even—

"No, sir. You don't get to wander off with thinking," she said before jumping onto the mattress.

Her long legs straddled his body and she leaned down and kissed him. This was what had been missing. Their bodies pressed together, tongues tangling.

The smell of her, the closeness and warmth from her skin. While the kiss dragged on, she pried his hands away from tracing lazy circles along her ribcage and up to the headboard. He felt heat from cloth around his wrists, the material soft and embracing. Instinctively he should have been scared, but he only found peace in being able to let someone else call the shots.

She sat back, rubbing her clit against his cock. "Try to pull your arms down. See if that damn breast strap holds. I've never tied up anyone with it."

He glanced down at her breasts, free and swaying. Bountiful things, tipped with dark brown, hard-as-stone nipples. He struggled against the binding. Somehow, in the moment of her lips on his, he'd lost track of her baring another part of herself.

"I think they'll hold, but my sanity won't without those beautiful nipples in my mouth."

She pulled farther away, slipping backward to remove those panties, and that was when he about lost it. A patch of hair covered her mound, uncommon in a place where woman preformed impeccable grooming, often leaving them bare. Something about that last little mystery drove him wild. He needed a closer look, but the damn bindings prevented it.

"I'll let you have those, if I get what I want."

He looked in her square in the eye, allowing the rush of emotion to wash over him. "What do you want?"

She climbed back on top of him, notching her pussy entrance to the tip of his cock. "All of you, inside me."

Then she slid home.

Rina had meant to drag things out, to torture them both by holding off as long as possible, but she needed the quickness of this.

At least, that was the lie she repeated to herself as she plunged down onto Sweet's long, thick dick. A reward worth getting early.

Without his hands to use for guiding, she was able to set the pace and he urged her on. His chants of 'show me', 'take me', and the continued enthusiasm for her type of sex proved how dumb and dangerous this idea of sleeping with Sweet was.

Too late to stop now, as she climbed toward relief for the ache in her core, the tingling inside paired with the desperate need to orgasm. To free herself from the building pressure. She didn't want to stop. Didn't want to lose the look of dazed bliss in Sweet's eyes.

He appeared drugged. caught up in whatever this thing was between them. "Lean down. Your breasts."

Rina smiled and complied.

Sweet locked his lips around one bud and sucked it hard into his mouth.

Sensation shot off her nerve endings and she wanted more. "More."

"I can't. The ties."

She glanced at his restrained hands and undid the fabric knot, in between gasps and shivers, because the damn tease refused to let up.

Freeing him quickly became a mistake—he wandered to her breasts, pulling her closer to him. She enjoyed that part—it made her feel worshipped and wanted.

"Aces and eights."

He reached up touching the tattoos on her neck. "No eights there."

She opened her mouth to respond, but never got the chance as Sweet picked her up and switched positions. Her back pressed against the soft mattress, sinking in.

Sweet leaned down next to her neck, trailing his tongue along her skin. "You taste like candy. Imagine what's between your legs."

"Don't want to know. Not tonight. Just fuck me."

His eyes bored into hers, a connection she didn't want forming there. A caring look. *Madness, here lies ruin.*

"You don't like a man between your legs?" He kept up the pace, pumping inside her.

A situation she could use to her advantage. She clenched her muscles, refusing to let him pull out.

He groaned. "Goddess bless."

"I want you to take us both over the edge or we won't be going anywhere."

His eyes narrowed on hers. "What about after that?"

"I'll tie you down and beat you until you're wearing marks from me, almost as permanent as a tattoo. At least you'd feel me for days."

He flexed within her, his cock growing harder, if possible. That in and of itself was a miracle. "Sounds like bliss."

She relaxed at his words and he was able to pull back. "Would you really enjoy that?"

He leaned down and nipped at her lip, before licking the same spot. "You're not the only one with a taste for sexual adventure. I wasn't joking when I showed you that room."

Then he plowed forward, knocking the air and shock right out of her. And she finally surrendered. To the thoughts, the feelings he evoked in her. She scraped her nails down his back, relishing how he cried out her name.

Her reward, a faster pace. She bit him on the arm, almost breaking the skin, and he roared, adding more force to each forward stroke.

When their eyes met, she uttered the words, "I'm going to come."

And she would, when he did. She'd practiced the art of control long enough to know not to lose it. Except he didn't keep going.

No, he pulled back, and she tried to keep him there but wasn't fast enough. He stopped everything, backing away. It shouldn't have mattered, but it did. Maybe he had changed his mind.

"What are you doing?"

"Slowing things down." He scooted to the edge of the bed.

She sat up and moved toward him, crawling on all fours. "There is no reason for that."

"Really, there is. I want this, but I'm not looking to get kicked out of here five minutes after we're done and I can tell this isn't your first round of poker."

She sat back on her knees and reached for his shoulder. "What are you talking about?"

"I'm talking about orchestrated. You're controlled, locked in, and I'm drowning in it. Anyone ever tell you you're too much?"

Rina laughed. "Really? I've been told I'm more familiar with the opposite."

She trailed her fingers down Sweet's shoulder, between moments where she gently gripped the muscles. For a man growing up on the rough sides of things, he certainly possessed a lack of scars. Though sometimes scars remained on the inside, not the outside.

"My fiancé refused to indulge my darker interests. Preferred to bring in a third to get the job done. He was my best friend, but he was weak in areas where I needed strength."

Sweet grabbed her hand, encircling it with his. Her eyes naturally flew up to his, meeting his gaze. "I would never trade up an opportunity to be beneath, above or a part of you."

This was supposed to be blowing off steam and adrenaline from surviving her father, but those words created an idea that things meant something more. He wanted more.

"How about you not squander that opportunity now?"

He tugged her close. Their lips met. Action, instead of words. She enjoyed that, how things deepened between them. *Fast.*

That was when she got lost, the control he spoke of disappearing as he played her lips with tongue and teeth. *Sweet. In person and in every movement.* Once second she was kneeling next to him and the next, she was flat on her back as Sweet pressed kisses down her neck, the valley between her breasts, her stomach and finally between her legs.

She would have objected, but when the first touch of his tongue stroked her core, she gave in. Nothing could have prepared her for Sweet's mastery with his mouth. The man started slow, licking his way through a litany of phrases that she cried out.

She'd never been a quiet person during the act. But rarely had she ever been this loud. No, her control was shredded, worn thin by months of grief, then her world tipping on its axis.

"It's okay," Sweet mumbled. "Set yourself free."

So she did, relaxing into the sensation, letting nature take its course instead of trying to control when she would come undone. Everything got brighter, which was when he latched on to her, sucking hard, nipping at the sensitive part of her with his teeth.

She screamed, a guttural, unnatural sound only a wild thing might emit.

When he lifted his head, the sheen of her orgasm resting on his lips, he smiled. "You can call me Akono."

Then he entered her, arching his back as he drove her right back to the top of the place where white light existed. Where *she* no longer existed as this harsh creature, if the way he stared at her said anything. He whispered her name, *Rina*, like some sort of religious prayer, more valuable than flash and reminding her how the power she held was equal to the power he had.

Magic. It was the only word she had to express what occurred as they both came at the same time, shakes wracking both their bodies. He collapsed on top of her, extending his elbows to keep his full weight off her. She basked in this closeness, more than she should've and nearly wept when he pressed a soft kiss to her temple. One wasn't enough. He trailed those soft caresses until he reached her lips.

She let him enjoy one full kiss, tasting the rise of desire all over again, fresh and dangerous. It seemed that once wasn't enough for her body to be sated — the wild animal inside her demanded more.

"Sweet."

"Thought we already discussed this...Akono." He rolled over with a sigh, then picked up one of her hands and pressed it to his chest. "You can call me Akono. It won't kill me."

"Akono." She whispered the name, testing it out as she traced the muscles on his upper body. "We should take a step back."

"Happy to oblige, but are you sure that's what you want? Your hands are telling a different story."

She smiled and stilled her movements before separating her connection to him entirely. "What we did just now, that was..."

"The best sex of your life? Not enough? Perfect?"

"Wow, let's not get away from ourselves here."

He smiled back, a genuine grin that gave him a more youthful look than the fake half-smiles he gave at the club. "Just speaking the thoughts running rampant in my mind."

Rina hesitated, her own truthful confession dying a guilty death on the edge of her tongue. Instead she went with another truth, even if it was dangerous. "It's definitely not enough. But I need a few minutes to recover."

He beamed, brighter than before. Rina almost regretted the words, but then, when had she experienced any of this excitement in the last couple of years?

"Totally understandable." Akono lay next to her and sighed.

"What's on your mind?"

"Do you ever dream of getting away?"

Shock rippled within her, with a hint of mistrust. She'd told no one except Dominic of her childhood dream, the one where she escaped this damn planet for somewhere greener, bluer, with fewer secrets and hidden bullshit. "Doesn't everyone?"

Akono propped himself on his side, facing her. She couldn't help but notice that his cock lay between them, semi-hard. "Be serious. I want to know."

She rolled to face him. They were a portrait in opposites. Her pale skin, long hair. His dark brown skin and short cropped hair. Her soft parts, his hard parts. *Delicious.*

She decided to give in to the fantasy fully, take the risk. He'd taken plenty for her. "I dreamed of moving off-world, to somewhere with open skies and tons of creative inspiration. To explore my art, be it canvas or skin, and be my own person. Not the daughter of a mass murdering nightclub-empire owner."

A faint sympathy entered his eyes. "If I told you there might be a way to make those dreams come true, what would you say?"

She scoffed. "I'd say don't talk crazy. It will only get you killed."

Chapter Thirteen

Rina rolled the hover cycle to a stop in the main drive of her father's house. Her brother stood right outside the front door, glowering at her. Two days had passed since she'd overheard her father and Luca discussing how they planned to kill hundreds, how they'd already killed more than that.

Disgust coiled low in her belly, paired with a twinge of nausea. She wouldn't have felt that way walking into Sweet's…Akono's. The fondness of his name — a secret she got to keep.

Also two days since she'd woken to an empty bed. Akono had left a note about seeing her that evening, and she'd chosen to stay far away, working hard in the shop and trying to uncover where her father might be hiding this drug. A good excuse to not have to face Akono and the fact that an entire night of adventurous sex had done nothing to quell her body's interest in or craving for him.

She'd gotten almost nowhere in the research. The lists she'd produced had included suppliers for the tattoo parlor, but she couldn't believe that Yash had anything to do with her father's insane plans. He believed in protecting those less fortunate, not destroying them.

"Did you get your fill of him?" Luca's words echoed among the marble columns.

"Fatch off, Luca. My private life is none of your business." She climbed off the bike and propped the kickstand down.

"We'll see about that."

Rina flipped up her middle finger and marched past her little brother, heading straight for the dining room, where her father sat in his seat at the head of the table. "I can't stay long. Too many people wanting tattoos at the shops. Yash could barely spare me, it's been so busy."

"What are your intentions with the street scum?" No additional references about whom he spoke of were needed from her father.

She seethed inside, doing her damned best to keep her facial expression calm and collected. "I'm exploiting the attraction, looking for loopholes. I'm making him think this is a long-term arrangement, then I'll pull the rug out from under him."

Those words must have been the right ones, because her sick, twisted father smiled at her. "Impressive. And to hear your brother tell it, I was going to have to deal with another Dominic situation. But I know where your loyalties truly lie."

Luca scowled, walking past her and taking his seat, at her father's side. Like a den of Mars vipers. *Stay too long and I'll surely be bitten and damaged.* "She could be lying."

"And you could be jealous. Poor Luca—everyone makes him feel small." Rina gripped the back of the chair in front of her, squeezing the wood tight.

Vincent shook his head and chuckled. "Grown and still fighting like when you were children. Luca, your sister has too much pride in herself to lie. She wouldn't betray me in such a manner. Just as she couldn't predict Dominic would lose his mind. You could learn a thing or two from how she runs her own schemes and business."

Rina smiled wide, enjoying the momentary frustration and reddening on Luca's face.

She'd never predicted her visit would yield this tiny victory.

Except Luca always had a good comeback. "I don't play with trash to get my job done. I can do it without rolling in refuse."

The hard ball of anger bowled around inside her again, gaining strength and the urge to burst forth, maybe knock Luca off his prejudiced high horse. While Luca thought himself at the top of some castle in the sky, their father had come from nothing and made his fortune through ingenuity, but now she started to wonder if Daddy dear had made it to the top by more dubious means.

She'd never discover more details playing the sidelines. "If you like the work I'm doing, then I'd like to talk about next steps. I'm ready to come back."

Two sets of eyes bored into her, one in surprise and the other in rage.

"I thought you were done with our business, dear sister?" If Luca had needles for eyes, she'd be overdosing right now.

"No, I was only taking a break. Besides, as oldest and heir, it's only right that I ensure you don't run this enterprise right into the ground." Her mother would have smacked her for the lies she let spill from her mouth. In truth, she'd do just about anything to get closer to discovering what her father had planned. She needed to know, in order to stop him.

Vincent steepled his hands, the tips of his fingers resting against his chin. "I'm happy to see you come back to the fold, but let's wait until this Sweet Spot business is finished. Then we'll talk."

Rina balled her fists. "What about now? Surely I can do more than watch over some books and deposits at Sweet's. If you want a takeover timetable, that won't be a problem."

Luca snorted. "She's too busy with painting tattoos that she can't meet today, but eager as a space station traveler to get in the thick of it. Which is it?"

"It's whatever I want it to be. I can be an artist and the background of an entire empire. You think great kings of old only did one thing. Great queens?" She took a step toward Luca, standing tall and straight. He might be able to pull a gun faster than her, and even had more of a mean streak than she did, but in the end of it all, she wasn't scared of him.

"Enough, you two. You've been doing good work at the parlor, from what Yash says. The work at Sweet's as well. You show the initiative. Yet I don't want to push you too fast. You keep doing what you're doing."

She whirled on her father, years of pent-up frustration exploding without a second thought. "You don't trust me? After everything?"

Her father shoved his chair back, standing with a speed she'd never have suspected of the older man. He came to her and, for a moment, she fell prey to memories of her childhood. Of a doting father who'd encouraged her tutoring in all things business as well as weapons. He'd never held her back, and prided on showing her off to everyone who came around. He indulged every ask, every preference, even her desire to marry Dominic, who her father had found all right, but never believed the young man to be good enough for his heir.

"I think your head gets clouded sometimes." Vincent touched her hand and she let herself absorb this one fleeting moment of contact without reality. That craving for something new, like the open maw of a black hole, eager to attach to anything in the hope it would be filled.

She topped his hand with her other one. "I can handle this."

Vincent Genovese's sympathy and caring were brief. He broke the hold. "We all get clouded, Caterina. A reminder we are still fallible, after all. I can't risk you again, and I won't. Just finish the job with Sweet. There will be plenty to do after that."

"All right." She left it at that, turned and walked out of the door, expecting Luca to come running after her any minute.

Except he didn't.

And she left more confused than before. Because for the last two days she'd believed her father to be the scum of the earth, but now she wondered if his head was suffering the same way.

The clouds would only lead to more gray space, a space where Akono might be put on a target list and she'd have to suffer losing someone else she cared about. A notion she wasn't sure she could accept.

* * * *

Two days since he'd seen her, left her sleeping in her bed, and Akono still debated on his decision to leave, since she was avoiding the club completely. Akono glanced at his watch again. She should have showed up an hour ago. He could only pray she'd appear.

"Did you hear what I said, Sweet?" Toni's face in the holo-screen was front and center. Had he really thought she might be a match for him at one point? Her ever-changing hair was currently a bright shade of red piled in a mass of curls.

"Yeah, the cruiser."

Emilio butted in, scooting in beside Toni. "Yeah, it's going to take another week or so, but then we're good to go. We brought on some extra hands, people who won't ask questions and like flash."

Akono frowned and glanced again at the door. "You need more leaf to pay them?"

"No!" both Emilio and Toni replied, their faces screwed in matching expressions of disgust.

"Good. What about Genisys?" *When the hell will Rina get here?* It had taken everything in him to stop himself from walking across the street yesterday and begging her to do what she would with him. He'd become pathetic, but for the first time in a long time, he found someone who saw him. Though he couldn't put himself out there again, not with her. He needed Rina to come to him.

"Sweet? What the hell?" Toni's admonishing tone brought his focus back.

"Hmm?" He looked at the holo-screen, at Emilio's arms around Toni. Akono craved the same closeness displayed in front of him. Experiencing a moment's worth of it with Rina in her bed after they'd orgasmed twice had made him desire more. More of the feeling of her in his arms, her hair tickling his skin.

"Why are you distracted?" Toni asked.

"Because he's thinking about a woman."

Akono raked his hand over his face and groaned. The last thing he needed was for the two of them to start in on him. "No, that's not the case."

Emilio grinned. "Then what were we talking about?"

"Genisys, if she's safe."

Toni's jaw dropped open. "You're not listening to anything we've said. Of course she is. Tests confirm it. Things are in motion. Have you thought about your passenger list, the papers and documentation you'll need? If not, Doc says he may have someone who could help."

Shit. He hadn't focused on those details yet. No, he and his dick had been too wrapped up in other things. "That would be good."

"Who is she?" Toni's eyes narrowed as if she meant to closely inspect his person for evidence.

A knock at the door gave Akono all the excuse he needed. "I'm sorry, we have to cut this short."

He leaned forward to press the button to end the transmission.

"I'm not done talking about this, Sweet," Toni parroted back.

Akono had no hesitation before ending the call and saying, "Come in."

He prayed it would be Rina strutting into his office, her usual uniform in place, and looking sheepish, maybe embarrassed for not having come sooner, the reason she'd bothered to knock this time. Maybe they'd even have time to take a moment to themselves.

But instead of the woman haunting his dreams, Ant marched in, his serious expression not blending well with his bright blue tie and the blue weave in his braids. "We've got pups."

Akono shoved out of his chair and grabbed his hat from the desk. "How many?"

"A group of five. Demanding to search the place — a hot tip about housing illegal weapons on-site."

"Fatch. Where are they now?" Pups were the scum of the universe, at least that was how most people felt. The Allied Planetary Union Patrol, the long version of their title. The short version…spaceholes. People called them pups for short, as if they were puppies constantly chasing a tail. The only problem was, most lowers and sinner moon folk had never had a puppy, Akono included.

"Ned has kept them at the main entrance, telling them the establishment is co-owned by Vincent Genovese and sent me to grab you."

They strode out of the door, Akono in front with Ant and Zeke to the rear. Akono hoped the purposeful, thunderous strides they made left an impression as they headed for the front entrance. As mentioned, five APUPs dressed in their all-black tactical uniforms stood heavily armed.

One of them was in a serious conversation with Ned, evidenced by the host's tight-lipped frown and podium-clenching hands. "And who exactly informed you about illegal happenings on our premises?"

The very question Sweet wanted answered. Someone had put The Sweet Spot on the APUP's hit list, because all the clubs committed questionable actions. 'Illegal weapons' was the worst charge a club could get hit with.

"We are not at liberty to reveal information about our sources."

"And you would doubt the word of Vincent Genovese's partners?" Sweet asked as he came to a halt in front of the podium.

The pup looked at him with one eyebrow raised. "No one's word, business owner or otherwise, influences what we do for our government. We've been given an order. If you still plan to stay open this evening, you'll let us finish our business."

Akono nodded at Ned. "Let them pass, but scan each one. I want to know when they leave as well."

The APUPs waited while Ned took out the book and scanned each of them. The scan confirmed that they were law enforcement and it was a club's right to get more confirmation than a quick look at a badge.

They filed past, jostling by Ant and Zeke and several of the others. Akono nodded to Ant and that led to each of his men pairing off with one or two APUPs to follow their progress through the club. No way would he trust these fools alone, never in his place, since they had probably been dispatched by the very people he was supposed to consider his partners.

He watched the group trek around his club, the few patrons remaining either ignoring them or taking their presence as a signal for them to leave. This would put a damper on their numbers for tonight, numbers he desperately needed if he was going to get everyone out of there.

"What the hell is going on here?" Rina's question rang out loud and crystal clear behind him.

He whirled on his heels. "Your brother felt like upping the pissing contest, obviously. Your family's dirty ties to parliament are showing but aren't providing any entertainment value. Convenient how you weren't here ten minutes ago."

She halted in her progress. While she wore her usual uniform, her hair was wild, strands sticking out every which way from her updo. "I just came from my father's."

"So you knew?" Akono stalked closer to her and kept his next words to a harsh whisper. "I guess all that talk the other night meant nothing. You used me."

The accusation in Akono's voice hit her like a fist to the gut. She'd left her father's arguing with herself over who deserved her focus, her caring. She'd arrived at The Sweet Spot, the place that reminded her of the people working inside, of the man who understood her like no one else did. Then this.

"Where are they?"

Akono pointed at the bar. "The head of the group is over there looking at my booze stores and questioning if I'm hiding anything."

She cracked her knuckles. "Give me ten minutes."

"No, Rina." He reached out to stop her and she shrugged him away.

Her footsteps thundered in her ears as she headed for the APUPs at the bar. He truly believed she'd known this was coming and she'd had no clue. Her visit with her father might have been used as a decoy, to get her away from the club, and in the hopes the APUPs could execute this search before she got back. Thank goodness she'd left early, refusing to stay to eat.

"They'll just cause more problems if we bother them," he called out at her.

Fatch. Not on her watch. If there was one thing she could do, it had to be this.

"Excuse me? Who are you?" She let swagger carry her, channeling every last bit of the Genovese better-than-thou attitude that pulsed through her veins.

The pup-in-charge stopped poring over bottles of inventory and popping open cabinets to look at her. Beady eyes connected to her own and she steeled her gaze. No looking away, no intimidation. "I'm Copenhagen."

"Well, you're done here."

The beady fatcher hopped over the bar like it was nothing, big weapon in hand. "Do you work for the APU?"

"No, I am Caterina Genovese. My father co-owns this establishment and you're trespassing on a government-sanctioned club," she intoned as best she could, emphasizing the points.

"I don't care who the owner is. We investigate every claim." The bastard stood toe-to-toe with her and he had a couple of inches on her. But she'd taken down bigger jerks in her time as a club manager. She cocked her head back, connecting gazes with him once more. A battle of wills, one she'd win.

"Copenhagen. I'm sure you know the Genovese reputation. I'd hate for your precarious position and the honor received to be stripped away. Especially if you're aware of my father's work with Tuatha."

The name from the meeting, one she had no clue what it truly meant. Only that the name had to hold some sort of power, if her father would kowtow to it. Hopefully, it meant something to the APUPs as well.

"Excuse me?" Copenhagen blinked, the firm set to his lips and grip on his gun relaxing.

"My father's business is closely linked to Tuatha, and I imagine you don't want to interfere."

Her words worked, Copenhagen stepped back and whistled to his other men with earshot. "Gather the crew. I think the tip was bogus. We leave immediately."

Rina watched as the secondary sent a message into an earpiece and within under a minute the other APUPs reappeared, forming a single-file line towards the door. Shock and fear radiated within her at how a single name could evoke such an immediate transformation.

Even worse, her father had cultivated a business relationship with this person and had agreed to kill innocent people. Did Tuatha hold anything over her family, other secrets Rina wasn't aware of?

"What the hell did you say?" Akono stood next to her, his anger still palpable, lingering like a bad smell.

"I mentioned the business with my family."

His attitude towards her made it difficult to believe he wouldn't use this information against her. Best to keep the Tuatha news to herself for the moment.

"I told them the same thing."

"Sometimes it takes a woman's touch."

Ant stalked over. "They didn't touch anything, boss. I watched my guy like a hawk and made sure he didn't plant any bugs in your office either."

"Good job for playing guard dog, but you don't win points by not taking action." Rina didn't trust this guy. He still struck a wrong note with her.

"Don't even start cutting into him. This whole thing is your damn family's fault."

Rina glanced around the crowd that was starting to file in again, now that the pups were gone. "How about we take this argument somewhere private?"

Not to mention she wanted to keep the revelations about her family from becoming public knowledge until she could prove them. Akono had still avoided talking about the dead body situation. Even now, she wasn't sure she wanted to tackle a conversation when she didn't have all the answers besides a piss-poor confession, a missing person and two dead girls who'd worked in The Sweet Spot House.

"Fine, follow me." Akono turned and headed for the stairs.

"What if the APUP squad comes back?" Ant asked.

Rina frowned, following Akono a few steps behind him. She wanted to tell Ant to stop being an idiot, watch over the club and report if any changes occurred. The idiot hadn't needed hand-holding before, but now he was acting incapable.

"Manage the club and let me know if they come back. I'm going to wrap up this business arrangement once and for all."

Those words should have made her nervous, but no matter how frustrated he was with her, seeing him again reminded her of all the things they'd done together. She trailed after him, envisioning his naked body, those lean muscles working hard, bringing them both to pleasure. At the time, he'd seemed like a steady port in the storm surrounding her life, though her true feelings were conflicted.

Akono represented everything she'd run from. The club scene, the gambling, the living a life with constant risk. Sure, she'd come back to protect Yash and his family, but she'd always planned on finding a way out.

They'd barely crossed the threshold to his office before he turned on her. "So, speak. Got a reason why your brother unleashed those APUPs on the club? Are they going to war with me?"

Rina turned and shut the door, snapping the lock into place. "Not that I know of."

"Then just fatching tell me something. Because nothing makes sense. Unless they know we slept together."

She chuckled, facing him once more. "They definitely do not know that, because it's none of their business who I'm sleeping with. Though we didn't do much sleeping."

He caught her meaning, the anger melting from his face, though fire blazed in his eyes. How easily anger could turn to desire, how both fueled adrenaline. She'd been in this type of head space before with him and she couldn't help herself.

"You disappeared for nearly two days." He took two steps backward and she saw her chance. No distance would be allowed.

She closed the gap. "I was trying to figure out what I wanted."

He visibly swallowed, halting with the edge of his desk directly at his back. "If this is a means to distract me, it would have worked better if you had shown up sooner."

"Trust me, the pups, my father, my brother... I've decided whatever happens with them doesn't matter with the right now, the between us. I've tried to fight. After two days I thought I had things under control, but being this close to you proves me wrong. So, no ulterior motives besides you and me exploring more of this thing." Rina reached up and removed his hat, setting it down on the desk. "Between us."

She wouldn't be able to remember later who brought their lips in first. All that mattered was that they were kissing, exploring each other with tongues, teeth and lips at a pace bordering on desperation.

Seconds turned to minutes before Akono started moving away, downward, pressing kisses to her neck, prying her shirt from her collarbone.

"Tell me what you want, and I'll do it," he said in between movements.

Her whole body heated and came alive beneath his touch. This was what she wanted, to be honest, the chance to feel alive after so long being dead, but he required more direction. They would take this as far as she dared and she swore she'd take everything.

"I want you on your knees."

Chapter Fourteen

The smell of clove and tobacco brought Akono out of a dead sleep, jolting him awake to find Rina sitting across from the bed in a chair, staring at him. A thin trail of smoke drifted up from her cigarette, the lit end sparking red as she took a drag.

"Good morning." The words should have evoked happiness, but coming from her they were weary, worn-out. The opposite of her displayed enthusiasm from last night. They'd come here for a safe space to unleash their desire, engaging in whatever she wanted. He was a fool for her.

He rubbed his eyes with his free hand, propping his head up with the other. "What's wrong?"

Beauty in the form of her alabaster skin and dark hair. She was like some fairytale, all twisted…if the tattoos were any indication. He'd trailed his tongue along each card etched on her neck, then nipped them. She'd cried out, aces and jacks her words of choice, before she'd tied him to her bed, made him beg.

"Nothing." She glanced away, out of the window. Daylight didn't reach Callisto this time of the year, a perpetual nighttime only chased away by the reflectors, satellite simulations that bounced illumination from Jupiter onto the moon. Fake, dull light. It reminded Akono of the sunsets his mother had talked about and shown him in picture books.

Though there was enough to give him some sort of visual in the unlit room, enough to see her.

"You slept well." She took another drag and leaned back into her chair.

"Have you been up all night?"

Rina shrugged. "Most of it."

Akono sat up and reached for her, just a touch. One thing he was still having a problem with, even when he believed she might have played some role in the APUPs being at his place. Damn him. He'd wanted to touch her then. This incessant need rivaled his desire for food, for drink. It smacked of more than a mere obsession. "Tell me what's wrong."

"That conversation we overheard. I tried to find out more information. That's why I was late to the club, why I was dining with my brother and father to begin with."

He'd done his damnedest to forget, as she'd directed a few nights prior. Better to be alive than dead, but she was obviously willing to risk things. "We don't have to talk about it. Tell me about your tattoos instead."

"We should talk about it. The future is going to involve this."

He clasped her free hand between both of his. "Give me this, five more solar minutes. Tell me about the cards."

"The cards symbolize my birth, my mother's passing, Dominic's passing and my twenty-fifth birthday...the day I left my father's house." She lifted her hand, turning it so she didn't break his hold on her, but enough to show the infinity circle on her wrist. "That's a reminder that the past can repeat itself. I've got to learn to flow with things instead of fighting against them all the time."

Akono traced the never-ending circle with the tip of his index finger and watched as chill bumps emerged over her skin. "Your story is deep and vast, like the universe. I find it inspiring how you carve your lessons into your skin."

He pressed a kiss to the tattoo next, scooting to the edge of the bed, half-tempted to pull her to him. Cigarette and all.

Except, she didn't let him. No, she removed her hand from his grasp and put her cigarette out in the ashtray. "Five minutes is up. We need to talk about what's being planned."

Akono fell back against the pillows and let his business mode take over. "Did you learn anything from them?"

"No. They won't say anything to me or agree to bring me in on what they're working on. I think we heard enough the other night, but I... I need it confirmed. If what they're saying is true, then that means they're spreading this crap via clubs, and tattoos—"

"Your father is the reason my ladies are overdosing?" He'd failed to put two and two together. "Drugs in the tattoos, by putting it in the ink."

"I believe so. If my interpretation is correct, but I can't believe my boss or any other tattoo artist would do this willingly."

"I'm going to kill the fatching bastard."

She stood up and leaned over him, blocking out his view of the piss-yellow ceiling. "Now wait a second, I've got no legit proof. Nothing to truly tie anyone to anything. Just a dead body at your place who happened to get a tattoo in the downstairs establishment, and a missing person."

Excuses. Seemed she liked to get close to him whenever she wanted to distract or cover for her brother and her father. "Your story and actions change pretty quick when I mention getting rid of them."

"I never —"

"It's implied." Akono rolled away and rose from the bed to pick up his discarded clothing. Time to get dressed, to do anything that might stop this seed of pain growing in his chest. He'd do anything for her. Anything, if he hadn't proven it already.

Last night, like a fool, he'd abandoned the club, after things had got started in his office. Both of them naked on uncomfortable furniture wouldn't have worked. They'd been at her place in under an hour, with express direction for everyone to handle things and only send Zeke to get him in an emergency. Zeke, blessedly, had never showed up.

"You have to understand. After my fiancé, Dominic...I can't just run to some snap decision. I need proof."

Akono chuckled. "You sound like the APUPs. When my mother was killed, they said the same thing. No witnesses, no weapon, no proof. But sometimes, the truth is all too present in words and actions. The same john who always saw her, who'd left her battered and bloody, and he's not at fault. Your brother and father have more blood on their hands than that man ever got out of my mama."

Facing away from her, snapping those buttons into place, he was spared whatever look she leveled at him. Whether frustration or pity, he wanted none of it. He wanted her to treat him, treat the people in his life with as much consideration as she'd give her own damn family.

With the last button on his shirt in place, he pulled on the jacket, forgoing the tie. No, he stuffed that sinful red thing into his pocket. Even when he was angry at her, looking at the tie sent him right back to having been bound with it. "If they don't have the blood on their hands, they intend to put it there. What we heard verifies that," Akono said.

When he turned to face her, she was dressed too. No more naked exposed skin for him to ogle, breasts tucked away, and he should be happy he didn't have to face her without clothes. She felled him like the poison her family peddled.

"I can't make a decision until I know something for sure. Would you willingly condemn someone you believe to be your family over a mistake?"

"I would if they were killing innocents. How can you still defend them?"

A crash and bang sounded beneath them, rattling the already less-than-rock-solid walls.

"Oy! Calm down," the cranky voice of her boss hollered out.

It seemed their conversation would need to halt. He reached for his belt, the last piece, holding his gun and knife. "I'll go down first."

The hell he would. She'd be damned if he got downstairs before her. "Now hold up, this conversation isn't over."

He wasn't listening to her, but then again, why should she suspect he would? He'd called her a liar and believed she was defending her family, when she wanted more than just conspiracy and possible rumors. She wanted to discover the truth.

She'd thought Akono's level-headed business mind would be able to understand, but she'd underestimated male pride. Some mythical thing that made him believe she somehow owed loyalty to him, when in fact the only thing he was due at the moment was a swift kick to the ass. As soon as pride kicked in, her whole planned conversation fell to the wayside.

Unfortunately, his hasty departure and her lack of boots kept her from chasing him down. Working in a tattoo shop had taught her the big lesson of never running around barefoot. She had to scramble to the other side of the room to grab her boots, as they were next to the couch where she'd ditched them last night. By the time she'd slipped into them and cinched them tight, Akono was already out of the door. She was beyond pissed, scrambling after him, and barely remembered at the last minute to grab her knife from on top of the little table by the door.

She hop-skipped down the stairs, two at a time, until she came to a halt because of Akono's outstretched hand, the index finger of the other poised against his lips.

The voices, Yash and the dearly idiotic Ant, filtered back to them.

"Did you pass along my message from last night?" Ant's deep bass came in crystal clear.

Her boss' baritone sounded more cautious. "I did. Why are you here? We don't open for a while and I don't need Rina hearing you."

"I told you, I'm here for Akono. Zeke reported he came here with that Genovese woman, the bitch."

Rina clenched her fists, everything in her screaming to fight, to launch around the corner and take on everyone. She had just as much pride and respect for herself as them, as Akono. And damn it, but she was tired of being treated as lesser and considered worthy of derogatory terms.

"I wouldn't call her that. Remember who's paying you. And, if he is up there with her, that would be news to me. Why not wait till he comes back?" Her boss simultaneously stood up for her and revealed Akono's mole. *Funny how Akono believed I've been selling secrets.*

"We need him. The more time he spends with that woman, the more she poisons him, and the plan is about to be set in motion."

She shared a quick glance with Akono, who rolled his eyes and stepped out, one hand on his gun as he made his presence known. "Really? And this whole time you've been the one informing on me, planting bugs in my fatching office."

Rina came off the stairs and turned, seeing Yash and Ant for the first time. Her boss, seated on the stool in front of his station, seemed neither concerned nor bothered by her discovery of them. Ant seemed to relish her appearance, his lip curled in disgust at her entrance.

"Nothing to say?" she asked.

"Nothing to you. Your family may think you're worth something, but to me you're more worthless than a brothel whore."

Anger fused down her spine, mixing with the words Akono had already imparted. Either way, she looked like some guilty party, unworthy and unwanted. In reality, she was found wanting because of her sex. "Interesting how men are always trying to make it seem like women will be the ones to betray them. Seems like you men have that part all figured out without us. What about you, Yash? Any reason you're trading in information and not just tattoos?"

Her boss looked pitying, his entire form deflating like a balloon losing air. "It's pretty self-evident. My shop doesn't stand by me alone. The Genoveses helped me get this started. A favor is the least I can do in return."

Foolish barely scratched the surface of her emotions. One word followed by hundreds more—anger, betrayal... She reached for her knife and pulled it out. "Were you in on Luca's plan too?"

"No—"

"Enough with this crap." Akono moved forward, hands at his hips. "I don't care about the reasoning or the need for it. Informing on me is something I can't forgive."

"You misheard." Ant moved his hands to his waist.

Rina reached for Akono's arm. "Wait. I want to know. I got roped into this mess because Luca told me he'd kill Yash and his family if I didn't. I took on this whole fake fucking role to save lives. Instead, this is another lie?"

Yash chuckled and shook his head, reaching under his stool. "Got too much of a soft spot, girlie. Always have, and that's how they know where to apply pressure. Except they aren't inking you with an image. No, Luca's sketched puppet strings."

She caught a flash of metal where Yash positioned his hands, going for a weapon. Her pulse pounded in her ears, the air in the room tense, adding to the tightness in her chest. There were so many questions she still wanted to ask, but there was no time for that as Ant attempted to draw down on them first. Attempted, because Akono shot him before Ant had even fully pulled his weapon out.

Ant cried out and grabbed his right leg, and Rina's boss scooted in front of him, a pistol of his own trained on Akono. "Now, we don't have to continue this. Keep this up, we're all going to die."

Akono aimed at him. "Dying right here and now is preferable to continuing with the lies."

Ant pushed up onto his good leg and drew a knife, which was when Rina decided to charge in, her knife hefted in her left hand. She held on to it with courage and determination, ready to slide it into his ribs. Lord knew she wanted Ant dead on the ground. She slipped around Akono, but realized all too soon that Ant was coming around Yash and going for her lover.

Panic locked onto her, even as she pulled her momentum and brought the knife down on Yash's gun-wielding hand. The slow motion of the room erupted in fury as Yash let out an inhuman howl. Ant hesitated and Akono fired another shot at him. The bullet missed its mark and Ant fell to the floor with a yelp, sliding past Akono and moving for the back door.

"Stop him." Instinct propelled those words as Yash, all one hundred and fifty pounds of him, plowed into her. Air whooshed out of her lungs and she hit the floor with a hard thud, mainly on her back. She was smart enough to tuck her head.

"I'll kill you, bitch. Take away my creative force, the instrument…" Yash grabbed for her head and banged it once against the floor. She tried to summon a need to fight, but she'd been betrayed and the words Yash mumbled as he elbowed her in the gut devastated her even more. Outside of this, she could only think about Akono. *Is he safe? Who cares if I live?* If he suffered injuries, she'd never forgive herself.

"Hey! Stop hitting her." The sound of heavy footsteps and Akono's voice kindled newfound hope inside her, starting out small, but speeding up, growing like a big card game pot.

She'd blocked a few punches and was using her arms to protect her face, but now she sought an opening. "Better do as he says or you won't get any revenge."

"What does it matter? I'm dead whether he kills me or not." Yash pulled his fist back and that was when Rina burst forward, shoving a hard punch right in his solar plexus. Yash fell off her.

Immediately, Akono was at her side, offering her an arm. "I would have shot him. I still can."

"No," she replied with a shake of her head. On her feet once more, she kicked at her old boss. "We need information."

"Fine. We do it your way, but don't think I'll allow him to live after what he's done."

She glanced at him and winked. "Never thought otherwise."

While he might have had some issues with crappy masculinity, she did believe that on some level he liked her. Maybe he didn't respect every part of her and what she was capable of, but she'd probe some of that now. "I handle the questions then?"

"All yours." Akono held out her knife to her and she took it, looking around for something to wipe it off with.

"What about Ant?" The jerk could ruin everything, tell her brother what was happening, if they didn't stop him.

Akono frowned. "Got out the back door and off into the alley. Too much potential to bring APUPs to our door if I fired a shot, so I held back."

Frustrating, and an additional problem they'd need to solve. She decided to focus all her concentration on Yash and ignore the growing headache she had. "We're ready for story time, Yash. You tell us what we want to know, you live."

"Bad pop culture. They do that stuff in bad old Earth pop culture." He spat on the floor at her feet.

Thank goodness for grav boots. "I don't care. You'll die no matter what, but who's going to suffer with you?"

"I'm not telling you anything. I'm as good as dead anyway. At least I'll go down not being a snitch." He lay back on the floor, accepted his fate. The stubborn bastard, except…

"Is this what your wife would want?" Rina crouched down next to him and used his pants to wipe off her knife. She'd known this man since childhood. He'd been a fixture with her family and an opportunity for her to escape her own. His wife had been a maid in her family's home and Yash a previous enforcer. Sure, he had a lot of loyalty to the Genoveses, but her father always said everything had a price.

"She'd want whatever I thought best. I'm not betraying your father, Rina. Not today or tomorrow."

"Even if he's using your place to kill innocents?"

Yash shrugged. "What do I care if a few fools die?"

"Fools the same age as your children? You're marking them to die and don't care."

"You make it sound like I had a choice. The one who ran out of here a scared alley cat was feeding information to your father about the club, about some side projects Sweet has. Including one about Genisys. So far Ant didn't uncover much. That's where you came in, Rina, a distraction meant to keep Sweet occupied so Ant could search for more info. The whole club angle worked out for him, in a big way. Too bad the informant never really found anything. At least not yet."

Rina leaned in closer this time, enough to reach out and connect his face with one of her fists. "I don't care about devices or Sweet's business. I want to know about the drugs, about the ink."

He clammed up, until Akono cocked his gun and pointed it at his head. "Tell the lady what she wants to know."

"Fine. It's a drug. Some potent shit, the sellers call it Kiss Kiss. It was manufactured by some East cartel on Earth. They designed it to be a one hit and that's it. We don't get as rich off addiction as we do death."

The tip of the truth hovered on the surface. The horrible truth. "You're telling me you're deliberately killing people and turning them over to fuel reclamation?"

"Don't look at me like that. You know there's no money in life, only death. Besides, overpopulation is an issue Earth-before-the-nuke had. We can weed out that problem now."

"But people don't reproduce like they once did. There are laws." Rina was familiar with those laws, operations performed on teenagers limiting their ability to have babies, especially on the upper planets. On the lowers, sterilization. It was a pick-and-choose world they lived in. Whatever overpopulation jargon someone sold was a bunch of crap anyway. Everything was designed to exact control.

Akono butted the barrel of the gun against Yash's head. "Those are some bullshit lies and you know it."

Yash's shoulders shook in fear. "It's not bullshit if there's a basis in truth. You get how much crinkle for a body — bones are worth at least a half-pound in leaves. That could feed a family for months. We make a quarter of that off a person looking for a tattoo. Do the math."

She glanced at Akono and his horrified expression mirrored her own. "How do you get the product?"

"It's pre-mixed, into the ink."

Rina moved over to the bottles. "All of them."

"Only the classic tattoo shop purple. It clearly defines everything for us and the bodies. The reclamation centers then know who to assign the quotas to."

"There are more?"

Yash laughed. "For someone as deep into this world as you both are, you're both a bit naive. Your father has financed more than one tattoo shop over the years. He's not just a club owner. He has his hands in everything."

Sure, she'd been aware her father ran his money like a bank, financing operations for others when he thought it wise. But more tattoo shops? That sounded surprising.

"Each shop uses a different color ink to mark their product. This way we can get reimbursed properly."

Rina exchanged glances with Sweet. They were finally getting somewhere, though the confession was almost as horrifying as the crime. "The man searching for his brother, Sweet's girls…they were all planned."

"I don't plan them. They select their own colors, don't they? If their design contains purple, then it's meant to be. Right?"

Unbelievable. *Fatch.* This was pure insanity, concocted by someone who believed people deserved death over life, and here sat another man who bought into it. She was starting to believe that everyone on Callisto might be off their rockers. Making eye contact with Akono, she nodded.

He leaned down as she stood, and put the barrel to Yash's head. "This is for Lily and Rose."

Then he pulled the trigger. She'd be lying if a small piece of sadness didn't latch on to her. Inside, she wept for the man she'd believed Yash to be, for the fact that his children would have to live without him, and that they might not survive if their mother couldn't get work. Or maybe he would just never come home. Why explain to his loved ones how horrible he'd become? The man had been corrupt to the core, his appreciation for human life gone.

"I'll get someone over here to clean up this mess. Better to let Luca and your father think Yash has disappeared."

"I like that plan."

"Do you get it now? Do you see what they are capable of?"

Rina did understand, but having some of the truth left room for her to want more. "What's Genisys?"

Chapter Fifteen

Twelve hours. To some, that might have been a long time, but for him it was short, considering he'd shot his best friend, a person he'd grown up with. He and Ant had kept watch over each other's backs for a long time. Except pulling the trigger had turned out to be easier than expected. The idea of someone hurting Rina... He glanced over at her now, curled up in one of his office chairs and poring over a file of information. A file he'd provided.

The parlor owner's body was gone and Akono had instructed Ned and Zeke to stay on high alert. He'd put feelers out to let everyone they trusted know that they were looking for Ant. He expected Luca and his mountain of muscle to come stalking in at any moment. Not only had he warned the front door, but Maple as well. She needed to ensure the girls didn't come in with anyone unwanted.

Plus, every employee had received a mandatory check for tattoos, with future direction to forgo getting inked by order of management for their own protection. So far, no one had balked at his decree. No, they'd seemed aligned, though he could tell Zeke, Maple and Ned had wanted to ask questions. He'd promised answers, later. If they survived tonight.

"So, this thing…Genisys. It can create a planet?"

Akono moved from behind his desk and sat in the chair next to her. He wanted to be close to her, to remind himself she was safe. It still bothered him, and that depth of feeling wasn't going away like it had with other women in the past. Nope, it lingered.

"Yes, it can create a planet from nothing. All the data in the file is from initial tests, which led me to believe the thing works."

She sat up a bit straighter, folding the file shut. "How did you get it?"

"The same way I received the majority of things I own. Someone bet it." Though he'd known about the device long before he'd gambled for it. He'd set things up to drive the scientist to his door, not the Genoveses'.

"He could have gambled anywhere and you brought him here." She truly was smarter than anyone gave her credit for and his lingering doubts about her loyalty had disappeared when he'd seen her charge at Ant in the hopes of stopping his attack.

"Then you know the whole of it."

She sat up and tossed the file on to his desk. "Not really. Why are you doing this?"

He wanted to lay it all out there, but that niggling need to protect himself bubbled up and out before he could stop it. "You're familiar with the infamous Emilio Morales. It was his idea, his and Toni's, not mine. I mean, the government controls enough, and him being a runner and all, their business is sketchy. It'd be nice to have a place away from government purview."

She scoffed. "Oh yeah, no doubt. But once this thing develops, it will be plenty noticeable."

"They've got a plan for that. I'm just helping them populate the place with a group of good hardworking individuals who want to make something of themselves, live a bit freer."

She patted his hand. "You're sweet, Akono. Your last name fits your nature, but we all know freedom is an illusion. How do you plan on keeping people protected? How will they get goods?"

"We're still working on all that, but believe me, I've asked the same questions." He'd pondered them for years. This wasn't some harebrained scheme he'd concocted in a shine-lined haze.

No, he'd spent solar years coming up with the ins and outs. How he'd keep a colony sustained, how they'd make cash and avoid the place becoming just another den of sin. He wanted his damn Utopia, one where space ships weren't needed because no one wanted to leave.

"I'm not nearly as kind-hearted as you think."

She grinned. "Oh, I know, and I'm not as dumb as some think. You can try to pin the mastermind of this plan on someone else, but I think I've learned you're the one calling the shots, Mr. 'Have-You-Ever-Thought-About-Escaping'. Also, I wanted to say thank you. Don't think I said that earlier—we were dealing with so much."

He flipped his hand up and embraced hers, tracing her fingers with his. "No thanks necessary. I told you I protect the people who work for me. Do you think we'll have to deal with your brother tonight?"

The words were there, hovering in the background. The ones he should have said, but instead he'd gone the

Landra Graf

easy route. Besides, admitting any depth of emotion could be viewed as weak. He needed to be strong.

"Nice way to change the topic, but we can talk about the situation, though. I trusted the wrong people." The censure in her voice spoke volumes.

He wanted to reassure her, but lying did nothing for anyone. "You made the mistake I did, put your trust in someone you've known from childhood. You're not the only fool in this room tonight."

"A unique way of looking at it." She squeezed his hand gently in return. Touching her, sharing this moment, reminded him of how they were alike. "But, truly, I should have known better. The people who work for my family on some level have to be rotten like spoiled meat in order to continue to associate with us. As for my brother, his arrival could happen, depending on what Ant tells him. Paranoia is his middle name, but he might not risk making a move with you being here. Staying at the club is our safest bet."

"You can't go back to your place." He'd never told her about the bedroom he kept behind a hidden door, how before her he'd never left on a regular basis anyway. Not with the constant threat of someone trying to make a move.

She pulled her hand away and rolled her eyes. "I'm not sleeping with the house women and if I don't sleep there, where will I? Not like I can walk back into my father's place either."

Fear snaked through him, a fear for her safety. "I've got a room here. I'll go with you to get some things and we can stay—"

"You like this, don't you? Me in a position of mercy. If I didn't know you better, I'd say my brother is right."

She moved out of the chair and came to sit on his lap. "You're trying to make me yours."

He thrust his hips forward a bit, to let her experience exactly who was at whose mercy. This was supposed to be all serious. She was upset about her boss and instead she'd gotten him harder than a rock. "I think you have the parties mixed up."

"I'll stay with you, but we still have to figure out a way to make the drops, keep up pretenses. Do you really want to bring war down on the people who live here?" Rina leaned in and nipped his earlobe.

"I really can't have this conversation with you here. On top of me."

"Earlier, we didn't get to finish our conversation...about me and defending my family." She moved from the ear to pressing kisses on his neck. The heat from her lips, then her tongue against his skin drove him crazy.

"I rushed to judge. Stupid pride tends to make men say dumb things. I acted like one of those." He deserved an award for still being able to speak and articulate the right words. Because he had acted rashly, immediately believing the worst of her because she didn't advocate for him. Since he'd put a bullet in his best friend, she'd attempted to protect him and they'd both found trust in each other where there was none in the people they'd relied on the most.

"You're right, though, that's what I want to tell you." She leaned back, still in his lap, but there were no more kisses.

He wanted to tell her they could talk about it later. Beg her to just continue having her way with him. But he found the patience to listen. "Go on."

"I wanted to hide from the truth, but when it's people you grew up with, people you cared for, it's easy to shy away from the difficult stuff. Having Yash line it out for me changes things. And—"

Akono held up a finger to her lips. "Come with me, away from here and this horror."

She shook her head and tried to pull back. "We have to fix it."

"And we will, but leave with me. That escape you keep talking about? Let's do it together." He kissed her and felt when she finally gave in. No resistance, her arms around his neck.

This was something he refused to give up. The satisfied, bone-deep need to have her close to him. He wanted it now, tomorrow...always. He'd already put himself on the line inviting her away. Already flayed open his chest when he'd all but said that she had him at her mercy. When she finally broke the connection between them, he almost said the words that mirrored his emotional state, except he held back because the look in her eyes, the one where she stared at the door to his office, told a different story.

Rina opened her mouth and Akono pressed a quick kiss to her lips before she could speak. "No, don't answer yet. Think about it some more, but consider this. We'd be going to a place where you could make your own mark, free from expectation and reputation. Somewhere you could truly be you."

"What about the club? My father's mass murder plans?"

Akono wanted to say 'screw it' to everything, but they couldn't. *A man is culpable if he sees evil and does nothing about it.* Tibo had said those words more than once, though it seemed it was harder to follow such sage advice. "We'll stop him."

Rina smiled, overwhelmed by Akono's offer. He'd thrown it at her like it was nothing. Like it was no big deal. To her, it meant everything. No one on Callisto offered something like this for free. A person would have to sell everything they owned or trade their body in return for a free pass to another world.

He offered it to her, asking for nothing in return, a once-in-a-lifetime chance. And the little piece of her heart still holding out soared. However he wanted to act, a part of him cared about her.

The only caveat was the details. She wasn't sure about all of them. Sure, he'd supplied the information about the device and even pointed out the fact that most of this inventive strategy came from people he knew. He was financing the adventure, providing money...but a deeper *meaning* lay there. A meaning he didn't fully trust her with.

Why would they? Why would anyone, when your father kills people by the thousands?

Then he offered the impossible. Agreeing to go after her father and brother. They deserved to pay. "We'll need a plan."

A knock came at the door. They both glanced over and she failed to keep the tension out of her body. She'd downplayed her thoughts about her brother, but what he would do if Ant had told him about the confrontation at the shop?

Rina scrambled off Akono's lap. "You'd better get that."

"I will, but are you okay? My offer didn't freak you out?"

"No."

Akono smiled. "Then you'll consider going?"

She nodded, even though what was the point? Yash hadn't been the only one to tattoo purple ink on people's skin. The dead girl with the butterfly had been Rina's fault. There was that truth that had been rattling in her brain all day. She was as guilty as Luca, as Yash and Ant. If her brother stood with any type of force against them, she'd leave with him. Do whatever she could to keep Sweet and the people here safe.

Maple's voice echoed behind her. "I know we talked earlier, but this cryptic crap is not going to cut it."

There in a nutshell, the older woman's voice reminded Rina of the damage. Running to another planet, even one not under Allied Planetary rule, didn't change things. Wouldn't change them once the truth fully came out about her relation to murderers. Her inability to detect them.

Akono did a poor job of blocking the older woman from entering the room, and she turned her gaze on Rina. "Girl, are you sure you are feeling all right? You look pale and out of sorts."

Realizing you're a killer all over again will do that to a girl.

"I'm fine, Maple. It's been a long couple of days and I'll admit all this double-job detail is not helping me sleep."

Dressed to the nines, Maple patted her hand and sat down in the chair Akono had previously occupied. "Indeed, we're all burning the midnight oil lately. Which brings me to the reason I'm in here…what the hell is going on, Sweet? And don't give me the half-baked concerned-for-security crap. Ant betrayed us, but shouldn't we suspect foul play—"

"You said it yourself, Maple. Always watch out for Ant. Tibo said similar things. He had a greedy part of him and I believed loyalty would keep him from acting on it." The words came out sure and swift as Sweet leaned back against his desk. He didn't look at Maple though. His focus lay on his hat as he traced the brim.

Akono imagined he wasn't the only one in this room carrying guilt. Ant had been bought, by her brother and father. *How?*

"Why?"

"Because of me." Rina let those words hit the air before Sweet could pass off another excuse.

"Not true. Don't listen to her. Ant chose his own path. I don't think he likes the direction I'm taking things, wants to be the person in charge. Whatever loyalty he had was more fickle than luck at a card table."

Rina crossed the short distance between them and got right in Akono's face. "Really? We don't know that."

"You're so quick to take the blame for everything. You going to take the blame for the poisoned tattoo ink, too?" Akono stood straight, his full attention on her and not that damned hat, though he gripped the pinstripe gray thing in his hands.

She ripped the hat from him and threw it on the floor. "It's true though. Really look at this. From the moment I walked across your threshold a month ago, I've brought nothing but disaster to you and your business. Even your workers. Two dead and I played a part, even unwillingly."

Akono grabbed her by the shoulders, gripping her tight. "Fatch it all, woman. You'll do anything, say anything to leave yourself stranded with these wolves."

194

"I think I might go check on the girls and make sure those extra security measures are in place." Maple rose wide-eyed from her chair and left the room.

Rina sighed. "Don't forgive me, old woman."

"Honey, sounds like you need forgiveness from yourself far sooner before you need it from me. Akono, don't let her out of here angry. People make too many mistakes when angry. Don't think I've forgotten about this. We're going to talk more. Soon."

The door opened, the sounds of the club wafting in — the jazz music, the din of a crowd, clinking of glasses…the world continuing on half a dozen steps away. Then the door shut and all noise cut off and, leaving the pair of them with nothing but heavy breathing.

"You're not guilty of anything except caring about people who don't deserve it."

She sighed. "Even if that's true, my father won't let me go. Won't let me escape. Vincent Genovese doesn't believe in losing the things he believes are his, unless it's to the Goddess of Death."

And she'd be damned if he used Sweet against her too. The tug of war in her heart played out again, between pain and elation, gnawing at her with every passing moment as he stared at her.

"He won't do a damn thing to you."

"It's not me I'm worried about."

He pulled her against him, wrapping his arms around her body. His heartbeat merged with hers as if he could make them one person. A heart filled with love. The word bounced around her mind, trying to find the route to escape. She'd thought she held this emotion for Dominic, but in retrospect she shared more with Sweet.

"Instead of worrying about what they could do, let's find a way to stop them. Then there's nothing holding us back."

The idea sounded fabulous, but completely flawed. "How do you stop the unstoppable?"

"The same way you create a planet from nothing. Ingenuity."

"Fine. Then we'll figure out what they're up to and come up with a plan." Simple enough, and maybe during the time they did that, she could figure out how to stop loving him. Not to protect her heart, but to protect him.

Chapter Sixteen

Whoever had told him being tied up was a bad thing had been damn wrong. In the last week, he'd spent more hours in his club bedroom than planned, wrapped in ropes or bindings at the mercy of Rina and her sexual appetites. When not engaged in making them orgasm as much as they could without pushing them to pure exhaustion, they'd been busy hatching plans.

The first three days had been the initial planning stages. Since then, they'd been working to get all the pieces moving. From the government investigator Akono had contacted, to searching for Ant with no luck. They'd even set up a new drop method, having Zeke deliver the funds to the Genoveses'. No one talked to the lowly delivery boy who passed off the bag to Vincent's muscle guarding the doors of his home.

"You're telling us you want to take everyone?" This from Zeke.

His office currently held his closest employees — Maple, Zeke, Ned, Eights and Rina. After all the planning, they were ready to start implementing. But he needed this group to make it happen. "I'm telling you there's a place on the cruiser for everyone employed by me."

"What about some of the folks with families? I know these girls got siblings, younger ones and older ones. Think people are going to be eager to leave family behind?"

Sure, he'd considered it, and debated on how the offer would emerge. "Yes. For some the familial bond may be too strong to break."

"For others it may be easy," Rina chimed in, stepping up to stand beside him. "So that's why we're asking you to gauge your workers, the ones you've been alongside for years. Dealers, the bar staff, the waitresses. See who might be interested in an off-world opportunity. Formulate a list, in your head — anything written down is too risky. Then bring those lists to our next meeting. There may be room for a few extra bodies, families and the like if others are not interested."

Maple shook her head. "I can't believe this. A cruiser to take us to another world. Forgive me, Sweet, but this sounds a bit too good to be true to these old ears."

"Believe me. I know how crazy it sounds, and that's why I wanted you here for this." Akono pressed the button and the holo-image popped up from his screen.

"Oh wow," Emilio stood there, hands on his hips, surveying his audience. "You said I would have to do a little public speaking, but I didn't expect this many."

Damn runner. The man's ego had no bounds

Sweet growled. "If Toni would prefer, she can do the speaking."

Emilio held up his hands in mock protest. "No. I've got this. Besides, Toni is off-ship right now."

"Let's get to it then. Time is crinkle."

Emilio clapped his hands together, the sound reverberating throughout the room. "All right. The ship I'm standing on is your cruiser. I can't take you touring around, but behind me is the main pilot deck. My team has been working round the clock to get everything operational. I can say that the ionic showers work and there are thirty-four functioning cabins — this is minus six crew cabins that are double bunked. Functional galley, twin turbo trolling motors and a class A slip drive with double fuel canisters." He sang the last bit, reminding Akono of an old Earth song, one his mother used to sing in the colder months when others celebrated the pagan Yule holiday.

"Any questions?" Akono asked.

Silence reigned in the room.

"Your people appear overwhelmed and they haven't even seen the thing in person."

Thanks for stating the obvious, Emilio, you ass.

"There are also four shuttles. We're preparing to have two of them available at the surface to transport at all times."

"All times? When does that start?" This from Ned, who had been the quietest of the bunch so far. It had bothered Akono, because usually his host always had a wide variety of comments to make in any given situation. The flamboyant and whimsical Ned had sported this more subdued attitude the moment Akono had told him Ant had betrayed them.

"An exact day hasn't been determined, but soon. We need to secure additional funds, plenty of crinkle to help support things as we get our home running."

Ned frowned. "Infrastructure on this planet?"

"We'll dismantle the cruiser for that when we arrive, and keep the shuttles for short-range transport and working with traders." The answers rolled off Akono's tongue with ease, but doubt crept in.

"You're asking us to give up everything. Everything, our comforts and the like, to go play colonist?"

"Colonist on your terms," Rina added.

Akono sighed. Earth's history, his people's history here on Callisto — there was some bad blood there.

"Excuse me, Miss Rina, but I don't see how this concerns you. We're going to lose everything. You can choose to stay or go with ease and make your way anywhere. And the hell if I'm roughing it on some unproven planet." Ned stood up and made his way to the door.

Akono tensed. He'd expected some resistance to his idea, but not this.

"If there are no more questions about the cruiser, I'm gonna go," Emilio announced to the room and immediately ended the holo-transmission.

The others stayed put and Akono motioned to Rina to step up.

"Do what?" she mouthed.

He shrugged. Hell if he knew the right move here, but he needed to go after Ned. Needed to gauge how his host's attitude could spectacularly blow up everything they were planning. "Ned, hold up."

His purple-clad friend had already walked out of the office door, and Akono followed, shutting it behind him. "Seriously, slow down now."

Ned whirled on him. "This is your big scheme, the thing you've been cryptically mentioning for months?"

Akono nodded. "It's an opportunity to escape this place."

A place that held nothing but death and destruction for them all in the end, to see their bodies sent to reclamation to fuel government ships. In the long run, that type of future held no appeal to Akono.

Ned shook his head. "That's assuming the majority of us feel like you, but for a man like me, Callisto is paradise."

Akono had forgotten Ned hadn't been born here. He'd come here as a child, abandoned barely past ten years for having been caught kissing another boy. Going to a new place, one where every part of him might be on display due to a lower population, would be worrisome. "No one is saying you have to go."

"But everyone here, or the majority, will want to. You're not just taking away your family to a better place — you're going to leave the rest of us with nothing to protect ourselves."

The anguish on Ned's face filleted Akono. All those points were good. They made sense and he would need to add this to his list of problems. "I don't have an answer right now, but I hear your concerns. Give me time to think of a solution."

Ned nodded. "All right, and I am sorry. It's not up to you to provide for everyone. The fact you're trying to means something."

"Does that mean we can still count on your help, on your secrecy?"

Ned gasped and flipped his tie. "I'm shocked to think you'd believe otherwise."

"After Ant, I can't be too sure."

"Did he really... No, never mind. I don't want to know. I want to remember him as he was to us. A brother and loyal friend. I'll let you reassure the others. I wouldn't ruin a good future for them, no matter the cost."

Akono clasped Ned by the elbow and nodded, then turned on his heel and re-entered his office.

Rina stood in the center of the group, bombarded by questions. An angel, haloed by a light glow from the neon sign against his back wall. The twinge of need and want arose anew, with the words he'd held back saying to her. Each moment they shared contained this urgency filled with the unspoken. Except he refused to use the situation in which they were depending on each other, in which she depended on him, as a platform to tell her what he wanted beyond this. There would be time for those heartfelt confessions once they were en route to Genisys.

"How much stuff can we bring?"

"Do we pack food as well as personal belongings?"

Rina sighed and looked over at him. "All excellent questions, but those will be answered soon enough. Right now, we have something more important that you need to be concerned with. Flash."

So, she hadn't gotten to this part yet. The part where they were going to ask everyone to keep working.

"I thought you said we were going to a Utaupa. Don't need flash somewhere like that."

Akono stepped forward. "It's pronounced Utopia, and we will until we get everything up and running, housing and irrigation, animal stock. There are lots of little things that we'll need to get launched. I can't get everything on the front end, so we'll need as much flash as we can get hold of."

He stopped next to Rina, bumping up against her. The action infused him with resolve and determination.

This task didn't seem so large with her next to him, though the reminder of how she'd replaced his best friend sat right below the surface. He and Ant had never experienced a type of relationship like this, however.

She put a hand on his arm. "We need to win the house, as much as we can. Upsell everything. Encourage higher bets, more drink, a taste of flesh. Let's have them spend every last cent here before they leave, but have so much fun doing it they won't miss the heavy feeling to their pockets."

The three remaining nodded in agreement.

Eights spoke up, though. "What about Ned?"

"He'll help however he can, though he might not go with us. We can trust him," Akono said.

Zeke scoffed. "Like you trusted Ant."

Rina tensed beside him and he flexed his arm beneath her hand. "Like we trust you, Zeke. I trust everyone until you give me a reason to think otherwise. Now we get back to work. When I have more info, I'll let you know."

Zeke, Maple and Eights left without another word. Akono couldn't decide if they were excited by the prospect of escaping Callisto or overwhelmed by what was to come.

"They're excited, trust me." The fact that Rina sensed what bothered him should have been another sign he was in too deep, but it just reminded him of how much he wanted her on the cruiser with him.

"Thank you for covering for me while I talked to Ned. Now that we've got that out of the way, we need to talk about this plan of your father's."

She circled to face him, breaking their connection. "It's foolproof. I had Zeke help me load all the ink onto the transport you've rented. You've confirmed Emilio and his crew will help."

Akono nodded in agreement. That was why Toni hadn't been there earlier — she'd been meeting someone for the paperwork that would give her, Emilio and the rest of the crew the jobs of wait staff with the catering company. "The details are all placed, but I'm still worried."

Rina shook her head. "Trust this. I've got them scrambling with the anonymous report about the tattoo shop being broken into, Yash missing and all the product gone. Their attention is distracted, but my father will still keep up appearances."

She stepped in closer, closing the small gap between them. Her body pressed against him effectively cut off all worry, replacing it with something far more dangerous at the moment.

"If you're trying to distract me, it's working."

She smoothed the lapels of his jacket. "I just like touching you. Too bad we have to actually do work tonight. I could — "

"Boss?" Zeke cracked open the office door.

"What's up?"

"We caught Ant."

His eyes widened. "Where do you have him?"

"In the holding room down the hall. He got brought up via the back entrance."

"I'll be right there."

The door shut and he put his focus back on the woman sliding away from him. "We might find out some new information."

She'd taken two steps backward. "Let's hope so. You need to find out what he told my brother. I'll do the rounds and keep up appearances. Is that investigator coming, Miles?"

"She said she'd be here."

That was the only part of the plan not shored up. They needed support from the police, and not the force on Callisto, but the one who reported directly to parliament. Parliamentary investigators, a level up. They investigated reported crimes and were typically far less corrupt.

"We can only hope."

She was nearly out of reach and Akono grabbed for her. Her body fitted against him and he took her lips fiercely. They were almost to the end of their game plan. The party would be held within a few days. There were words he still hadn't said, fearing her reaction.

She pulled back first. "Quit kissing me like it's the last one."

"Tell me you'll be on the cruiser with me."

"We'll see," she replied with a grin.

Rina found her strength back on the club floor, amid the roulette wheel, the pop of champagne bottles and the cheers from the tables. The energy in the club was frenzied. Akono's people were doing what exactly had been asked of them. *Surprising how fast word spread amid the dealers and wait staff.*

Usually there would be someone grumbling or angry about a loss, but not tonight. No, patrons were happy to lose, or at least enjoying the losing. She moved from table to table, ready to mitigate, but her services weren't required.

Leaving her time to think, to let her mind wander to what Akono was building towards. She loved him, though she feared voicing those words like bad luck at a cards table. She cared about the people who worked for him. To see him succeed at this would be a miracle in and of itself. But this was about more than escaping Callisto for some utopia planet. This whole plan centered around bringing her father down.

For the last week, she had tried to imagine leaving everything behind, but if things played out the way she hoped, the Genovese throne would be empty. Vultures would swoop in. She couldn't help but think how she might turn the tables, create something good out of something so evil. If she were in charge...

"Rina?" Terrance brought her back to the present, away from the interesting daydream that hovered.

"Something wrong?"

Terrance shook his head. "No, but Ned wanted me to send you up his way. Something about a guest."

"Keep an eye on the tables?" She didn't bother waiting on a response from him before she took off. Any type of action would be good at the moment, because ultimately her insides churned the way a roulette wheel spun. Where her final decision would land, she wouldn't know until the last possible moment.

The host with the most, Ned, his bright purple attire a beacon for her, stood smiling, greeting a decent-sized crowd coming through the doors, his mood a far cry from the disapproval he'd voiced earlier.

"We're pulling in extra tonight."

Ned chuckled. "Well, a couple of our more creative employees are out there on the streets, trying to drive traffic in the door. There may be some rumors shuttling around that Emilio Morales was spotted. That he might return to the club."

No surprise there. It would be the perfect way to get a few extra folks to come to the club, in the hopes of seeing some sort of drama unfold. She sent up silent prayers to the Goddess for less drama than they'd like.

"Any problems? Terrance said you wanted to see me."

Ned never looked at her, just greeted and smiled at the incoming patrons. When a lull came in the traffic, he turned his attention to his book, noting the numbers, and initialing in any big names. "Do they really have Ant in a holding room?"

"They do." Another one of many things she'd tried to avoid thinking about. She wanted to go with Akono, but her presence would get him nowhere with his friend.

Ned greeted another group, then looked at her again. "Also, I want to know, are you really on our side?"

"Yes, I am. I want to see everyone get out of here if they want to, and see that people get more than their fair share."

Ned nodded. "All right. I mean, I trust Akono's judgment, even if I don't want to. There's a Loyda Miles here to see you. Came in about five minutes ago. I sent her to the bar and signaled the bartender to give her a free drink. Looks pretty fancy, definitely Upper."

She nodded. "Thanks. Oh, and, Ned...I'm sorry. I know you grew up with Ant."

"It's fine. Just don't hurt Akono. I can't take losing another friend, especially one who's done more for me than anyone else ever has."

Those words thunked around, like the roulette ball on the wheel, clanging against the spokes. Her intention would never be to hurt Akono, but she had to make sure no one could get to him.

Rina skirted around the sides of the dance floor and eating area, attempting to be invisible and out of the way. She succeeded in reaching the bar. Loyda stuck out like a sore thumb. The woman, who was a bit on the shorter side of things, wore a maroon-colored dress that clung to her and showcased every last curve. A cascade of dark brown curls in a fabulous updo made it look like her hair spilled artfully with wisps hanging in front of her face. She wore a fancy pair of heels which added some extra inches.

Where her attire announced to everyone she was from the upper planets, her eyes were constantly assessing. Following people around her, behind her, and even monitoring Eights and her bartenders on how drinks were being made. Her stature itself cried out investigator. Being dressed to the nines meant nothing if a woman failed to own the whole package.

Rina thought about tapping the woman on the shoulder, but decided the risk was too great and tapped the bar instead. "Ms. Miles, we have a spot open for you at the roulette table. Apologies for you having to wait."

The inspector didn't miss a beat. "Fabulous, and call me Loyda."

"Follow me, Loyda."

Rina led the way to the gambling area, right for the roulette table. She signaled to the dealers to ensure they received space and people moved around accordingly. The inspector stood on her right side as bidding and betting opened.

Flash flew, and the inspector pulled out her own bills, dropping them on the word red. "Got to start out small, build up a little pot."

Rina found the inspector's enthusiasm surprising. "Is roulette your favorite?"

The other woman swiped her ponytail over one shoulder, revealing a wicked-looking patch of scar tissue. "Not my usual preference. No, I like something with a little more return value. Play too long at the wheel and you lose, much faster than with card poker."

Final bets were called. With a new player, people didn't bet as much. They wanted to see what would happen first.

"Isn't the risk sometimes worth the reward?"

Loyda shrugged as the ball slowed to a stop and landed on red. "When you win once or twice, it gives a false impression."

The inspector divided her winnings out, pocketing some then dividing the rest between black and a couple of numbers.

"What's with all the division?"

Loyda smiled. "My parents always taught me to leave a gambling establishment with what you arrived with, and hedge your bets whenever you can. I'm not going to commit to something unless I know it's a for-sure deal. Someone can get burned easily if they think otherwise."

Rina liked her and could see why Akono admired her. She was forthright and circumspect at the same time. *Easy to read between the lines with this one.* "How do you know Sweet?"

She'd never speak it out loud, but jealousy tinted her veins. The woman next to her came from wealth and prestige—anyone with eyes could appreciate this type of lady and a smart man like Sweet would try for more.

The clink of the ball on the wheel began anew, and Loyda stayed quiet. The rest of the group standing around the table kept their eyes intently focused on the wheel.

"We met after that shootout between the runner, Morales, and Grecia. I showed up hoping for a way to get to Grecia. Unfortunately, that never happened."

Of course not, since Emilio Morales and his woman had killed the big-time cartel leader. The details were still not very clear, but plenty of stories had made their rounds across Callisto. Everything from that they'd killed over thirty men to that Toni's father, leader of a gang on Mars, had died at Morales' hands too. Tall tales, ones that inspired some sort of idea that the pair were heroes of the less fortunate.

Rina knew better. "Yeah, you're a little late to bag that one."

The ball dropped into the red, red number five.

Loyda smacked the side of the velvet-topped table with her palm. "Glad I held that initial investment back." The inspector turned away from the table and leaned closer to Rina, bumping their shoulders. "Word is you have something even bigger for me than a cartel leader with deep pockets."

"I do. Follow me." Rina's instinct was to take her to Maple's. Or at least head that way. If anyone watched, they would see two women headed to seek pleasure elsewhere. Except at the top of the stairs, she took her to the right and decided to go for Sweet's office.

They'd barely made it through the door before Loyda spoke again. "So, a Genovese in a competitor's stronghold. Seems like a trap."

"You've got me at a disadvantage." Rina crossed the room on a path for Sweet's desk, trying to decide whether she should go for a gun or a drink.

"Any inspector worth their weight in crinkle has kept up on your family. You're the biggest deal on Callisto.

Your father has his hands spread out like wires embedded in a ship and he's the central processor."

In the end she decided on the drink. Rina poured from Akono's decanter, splashing whiskey liberally into a glass. Reminders of her father's dire warnings presented themselves unbidden. *APUPs are dangerous. Some are greedy and they'll say anything, do anything to get you to confess.* Those were her bedtime stories. Tales of how the only ones she could trust were family.

"So, then, this is the big break you've been waiting for?" Rina turned the glass in her hand. She didn't bother offering one to the inspector.

"Truthfully, a big arrest would be nice, but I'm told you might know why reclamation center numbers are the highest they've been since the center opened." Loyda made her way slowly around the room, taking in the variety of items, from the paintings to some sporting-type shirt with a set of numbers on the front.

Akono had large quantities of memorabilia from a place long abandoned in the hopes the elite and richest of the human race would find more success in other parts of their solar system.

But things aren't better in the here and now. "I know why they've increased. There's a drug."

Loyda faced her, the frown on the woman's face formidable. "Tell me something I don't know."

"This drug, it kills fast. Within days. What you don't know is that my father is supplying the drug in his clubs and via tattoo artists all over Callisto without discrimination, targeting debtors, people stupid enough to like a certain color and those unfortunate enough to just enjoy doing drugs."

"Now the plot thickens." Loyda wasn't smiling, though, not like Rina's brother would at such pure torture.

"My brother, being my father's right hand at the moment, is also involved."

Loyda stepped next to Rina, took the glass right out of her hand and downed the rest. "And you?"

"I had no clue, until a week or so ago. Sweet and I might have overheard some things."

The woman slowly exhaled and looked at the glass longingly. "That's good shit. I guess it speaks to either your smarts or the fact this is a ruse, since you're still alive. How are you proposing I catch him? Your father isn't known for having his hands deep in the muck. Typically, he leaves that up to peons."

Yes, her father was good at keeping his hands clean, but his arrogance would be his downfall. "In two nights, there's a big party. To celebrate his current achievements, which includes those reclamation numbers. Supposedly even his parliament contact will be there."

Loyda coughed. "Excuse me? Parliament? There's no way they are involved."

"That's not what I heard. I specifically heard a name...Tuatha."

If Loyda recognized the name, she gave nothing away, but her next words shattered Rina's last shred of doubt that this situation was just a small piece of a much bigger problem.

"What's your plan?"

"You might need another drink."

Loyda extended the glass and Rina took it, marching back to the decanter and filling not only Loyda's but also another glass for herself.

She launched into her plan as she headed back to the inspector. "I may have located tainted tattoo ink and arranged for it to be moved to my father's vault in his house."

"Sneaking in can't be easy." Loyda accepted her glass.

"Yes, but without the drug on his property, you can't exactly arrest him or hold him guilty. That's why the vault. There are only three people with access to it."

"How do you know he won't suspect you?"

"I don't, but it's a risk I'm willing to take." Rina threw back her drink, every last drop. It burned in her throat the way fear burned her veins. She'd had trouble sleeping with this plot rolling around in her head. Akono had helped with that a little.

"Tell me more about how you're getting this ink in there."

Hell, no. Rina had put herself out there enough. Technically, Loyda could have her arrested right here and now, simply for knowing about the drugs, but the woman was smarter than her father gave most law enforcers credit for. Loyda found merit in using Rina's lure to a much bigger prize.

"I'd tell you, but that puts my associates at risk. You understand I'm taking a huge chance even trusting you with this."

Loyda scoffed. "You know your father is considered a pillar of Callisto. Parliament cites him as the reason for success and control on this moon."

"I know, but reputation can be earned by way of fear and pain as much as financial success."

Loyda drained the rest of her whiskey and set the glass down on the side table near Akono's chairs. "Why are you trusting me?"

"Because Sweet trusts you. He believes you operate with some sort of moral compass, or at the very least, integrity."

The woman took another look around the room, her expression neutral, and Rina had to quell the worry sifting around her body like cards in a shuffling machine. "Fine, two nights from now I raid the Genovese main house, but one hint that this is some sort of ambush and I'll lock you up faster than you can flip twenty-one."

"Agreed."

They shook hands, and she tried to toss away the little pea-sized amount of guilt she felt for selling her family out.

"Now, do you mind showing me a way out of here that avoids the front door? I don't want to draw extra attention to this meeting, if anyone is watching."

Rina nodded. "Follow me."

They went down the back stairs, a set she'd only learn about recently and one she was sure Akono's team had brought Ant up. The holding room stood at the end of the hall. No noise could be heard. Trudging down the staircase, Rina found a similarity between Loyda and Rina's father, in the secrecy of the investigator's departure. Paranoia appeared to run rampant among the APUPs as much as the club owners and sin dealers.

They made it to the back door safe and sound, no one on guard with Zeke in the holding room and Terrance out front. Rina would need to get someone back here sooner rather than later.

Loyda pushed the heavy metal thing open and turned to face Rina once more. "Thank you. I appreciate the opportunity to do business."

Rina didn't offer anything back. The right words weren't there because she'd officially set in motion the thing that could bring her family's reign on Callisto crashing straight to the ground.

Unless you want to pick up the pieces. Oh, the offer tempted like no other, but would anyone see this as a way to set things right? Would Loyda and other APUPs get the impression she was overthorwing Daddy for a shot at the throne?

A creak behind her sent her turning with fists raised, but something heavy hit her first and it was lights out.

Akono…

Chapter Seventeen

"We're going to try one more time, then I start using more than these brass knuckles. What did you tell them, Ant?" Akono stood over this shell of a man who had been his best friend. His hair hung matted and ratty, his skin jaundiced with bags under his eyes. He looked nothing like Akono's friend of old.

"I told them no more than what I saw. Beat me if you gotta." Ant lifted his bowed head and stared at Akono with determination. A false bravado that fell flat when Akono lifted his hand. Ant visibly shuddered at his blood dripping from the brass knuckles Akono wore. The cut over Ant's right eye and the bloodied lip were the only outward injuries. That didn't even compare to the internal bleeding.

"You know this is going to get worse. Just tell me and it will be over."

Another shudder. "No, I've already suffered enough. What you're doing is no more than I deserve."

Akono released his hold on the idiot, stepping back. He'd been at this for more than an hour. From nice talking, to slaps, to punching, to the brass. Idiot should have passed out already, but judging from his teeth and the dilated state of his eyes, the number of drugs coursing Ant's system probably rivaled the colors of the rainbow.

"Then why not talk? You betrayed us once. Earn your way back now," Akono mused out loud, rotating away and staring at the room decor. Hooks extended from the walls. He could mount the bastard up there, really put him through some pain and suffering. Akono had never considered himself to be a sadist, *but if people keep lying to me…*

A gurgled whisper came from behind him.

He pivoted on his heel. "Say that again."

Ant spat blood onto the floor, then cleared his throat. "A cure."

Fatch me, it worked. "Cure for what?"

"This damn drug. Kiss Kiss."

"When did they give it to you?"

"Two days ago."

Cure or no, Ant had a day, maybe hours left. *To lie or not to lie.*

Akono stepped back and leaned against the wall, the possibility of the drug transferring side-effects to him all too real. He kept his hands to his sides and attempted to rein in the revulsion at the tainted brass knuckles on his hands.

"I'll give you the cure in exchange for information."

"They said the same thing, but I don't believe them. Why should I trust you?"

Akono shrugged. "You can't, but you're running out of time and I'm probably the last shot you have at living past today. The only person who probably gives a shit if you live or not. So tell me what information you gave them and I'll make sure you get what you need."

"Fine," Ant replied with a cough. "I was supposed to be setting everything up for Luca's plan. He wanted whatever you had Emilio working on, the location and everything. Of course I never found it. Then he wanted to take you out."

Akono's fists clenched. "Does he know we killed Yash?"

The dude shook his head, droplets of blood spattering the floor. Good thing Akono planned to burn this place to the damn ground before he left. "Luca thinks he might be dead, but isn't sure. He's going to grab that sister of his, too."

"Why would he grab her?"

Ant smiled. "To kill the bitch, I hope. Though I think Luca wants her for other reasons."

Akono threw the brass knuckles at the door and Zeke jumped to attention. The younger man had started to become less than attentive as the interrogation wore on.

"Need something, boss?"

"Find Rina." His heart sped up at the idea that Luca had used this piece of dead crap as a distraction.

"You knew she wouldn't be left alone. Genoveses keep what's theirs." Ant looked happier than ever at this part of his confession. The metal door slamming shut echoed off the walls, a death knell.

"Ant, what did I do to deserve this? What did anyone here do? You chose them over us, what we were working towards."

"You wanted to get rid of everything we worked for and on top of that, you chose her. Like Luca said you would. I didn't believe it at first, but you feel for her. Giving up everything we worked for, for some unproven future elsewhere and a warm pink center to sink your dick in."

Akono's fist flew, the crunch of Ant's nose echoing in the room. "Don't talk about her like she's nothing."

"We were more than something too. Rising from the ground up. I might not be here to see it, but imagine my laughter when Luca gets started. He's got you both swinging on his chain, like a pair of dice in a sling, and you're too blind to see it. He knows Yash is probably dead. Figured you were in on it, but that's okay. There's already enough information planted to tie Rina to the drug. She'll go down for the disappearances—besides, she worked in the tat shop. Knows all the other tattoo shops. Then they'll tie things back to here."

Fatch it all to the center of the sun. "Then it's me and her teaming up to take on the rest of the world."

"Exactly. In the next forty-eight hours, you'll both be arrested and sent to the ring's jail, if they don't decide on auto-reclamation." Ant laughed at those words before the coughing began and more blood spilled.

The worst part being that Akono could do no worse to Ant than the what the drug ravaging his body did.

Akono saw the door start to creak open. Zeke opened it. "No sign of Rina. Even Maple says—"

"Maple says get the hell out of my way." The door swung open to reveal his would-be mother in all her crowning glory, looking like she'd run a short sprint. Her sequined headband had slipped too far back on her head, tendrils wisping around her face. "Someone spotted the back door cracked. We think she might have been taken, and I know for certain she's not in the club or on my side of the roof."

Ant chortled again, a guttural unnatural sounding thing. "Luca wondered if you thought you'd win. He wanted me to tell you...once from the streets...always trash."

Each word brought a new twitch to his body, until Ant finally stopped moving and slumped back, a thin trail of blood coursing down his chin. Eyes wide open. The sight almost made Akono gag.

"Sweet, baby...you're never been trash." Maple reached for him, and he held up a hand to block her.

He took a couple of steps back to be safe. "No, don't touch me. Fatching bastard was on that drug, Kiss Kiss. Got no clue if the stuff is communicable with bodily fluids. I need a new set of clothes, shoes, the works. Bring that down here, with water, soap and a scrubber."

Maple eyed him up and down, nodding. "Well, Zeke, don't just stand there. He said do something. Hop to it."

Zeke ran off, scrambling out of the room.

"You scared the devil out of him."

Maple gave a single nod. "As he should be. I heard most of what Ant said. Bad blood running in that boy from childhood. Sorry you had to suffer for it. Can we believe him, though?"

"I don't see why we wouldn't. Rina's been taken, so Ant spoke some version of the truth. All the cards are getting laid out. We've passed the river and flop. Now it's time to put together our best hand." One that got them out of here alive. Akono glanced down at his ruined suit, the blood a reminder that the possibility of this plan coming to fruition was slim.

"Sweet, what is the plan?"

Akono glanced up and almost broke. The older woman clutched her headband in her hands, wringing it to the point her knuckles were near white against her brown skin. "We get the hell out of here."

"But what about Rina?"

What about her, indeed.

* * * *

The first thing she noticed was the smell, dust and age. Along with the scent of fresh rain. Everything always smelled like rain. *At home.*

Hands at her hair and the sickening scent of anise. Luca's favorite candies were anise-scented. She tried to stay relaxed as the memories of being hit at The Sweet Spot back door came rushing to the forefront, but her heart refused to abate. Danger sat next to her, touching her.

Bile rose up the back of her throat and she swallowed it back, choosing that moment to open her eyes and push up with her hands. Up and away.

"What the hell am I doing here?"

Luca frowned; his hand pausing in mid-air. "I'd think you'd be happy to be back home. In your own room, among your things. Away from that trash."

"Sweet is a man, like you, and not even close to trash." Rina scooted again, getting closer to the far side of the bed. *Just keep him talking.*

"Yes, I'm afraid I know exactly how much of a man he is, if your squeals and moans were any indication from that night in your apartment."

All of her backward motion halted and her jaw dropped open. She'd suspected her brother had issues, but this confirmed it.

Luca flashed a big smile. "Sure, Sweet got a little paranoid about his place and I never found where he sleeps, but you never bothered to check yours. I also like how you tried to defend us. I took that into consideration when thinking about my plans for you, but Sweet is still going to die."

She fisted the comforter underneath her, but the growl escaped anyway. "Over my dead body."

"It's difficult to lose your fatch toy, I imagine. He made you scream a lot more than Dominic ever did."

Her stomach churned at the words, the confession laid bare. She'd suspected her brother of listening in on her activities, keep track of her movements, but him hearing her sexual exploits? "Jealous, much? I get it, the ladies aren't willing to give it up to a man who can't get up."

"Oh, I do more than get up. I've ruined women taking their mouths as I listen to the recordings. They play you in every way possible."

I'm going to throw up. Disgust merely scratched the surface of describing the riot inside her. If anything, the words gave her the motivation to move, and move she did. Up off the bed and straight to the dresser. She'd shoot him, right dead. Then fight her way out of the house.

"I wouldn't bother digging for your knives or guns. I clean swept this room so you wouldn't get any crazy ideas."

She was up to her elbows in her underwear drawer and pulled back immediately, shaking her arms at the visual of Luca putting his hands on her undergarments — or any garments, for that matter.

"Father is waiting on us." Luca stood from her bed and walked slowly toward her. "He has his hopes pinned on some nice family dinner. Most likely...the last one."

He picked up a chunk of her hair and slid it between his fingers. She assumed they had figured everything out, at least everything that had occurred in the tattoo parlor. She'd found new happiness in agreeing to stay with Akono over the last week. Keeping their important conversations away from possible prying eyes.

They'd given enough away. *Let this bastard think he has control.* "I'm to be punished for your sins, then?"

"Tsk. Tsk. Dear sister, you have a problem of wanting people to die for the loss of your fiancé. We're only doing what's right by bringing you to justice." His hand moved from her hair to her arm, gripping her tight. She froze, letting the words play out. The story unfolded before her, and they had all the pieces lined up.

"This is the story we will tell and the one that will be believed. A perfect scapegoat you turned out to be, and your lover too. The only reason father agreed to keep you alive."

Run. Flee. Rina yanked away from him and turned to face the door. The handle wouldn't budge. "No one will believe such a story."

"That's what crazy people say. Don't you remember those Alice Tales? One step away from chasing a white rabbit...or did you already chase it?"

Rina's back came flush against the thick wood, reminding her of how she'd run away after Dominic. How she could easily look guilty for every part of this plot. "You've made your point."

There was no getting out of this room without Luca, who dangled a key on a string. Sadistic mischief glinted in his eyes. *A spark of the devil inside.* "I'm in control."

She nodded. "Yes, Luca. You and father have played a spectacular game. Can we go down?"

"Ah aah. You haven't asked about Sweet." The key rocked back and forth like a finger waving goodbye.

If I do, it might be real. Except her brother wouldn't let her out of this room. A caged warrior, and she tried to prepare to lash out. To fight back. Now wasn't her moment, but she had to find one.

"What happens to Akono?"

Luca laughed as he snatched the key up into his hands and headed in her direction. She side-stepped and he stuck the key into the lock. A twist, a turn, a tug and the door came open.

Then he swiveled to face her, the anise overwhelming her senses as it punctuated each word. "If everything goes as planned, he'll be dead in an accidental shootout during apprehension by APUPs tomorrow night. Your accomplice killed when he refused to be taken in. Like tragic poetry."

She squeezed her eyes shut and tried not to breath. *It's not real.* They had trusted Loyda, believed in the woman and most likely sealed their fates.

Luca leaned in closer, forcing her to open her eyes and stay on guard. "It's real, Rina. This whole thing is. Your reign finally ends, and mine begins. All is as it should be."

Only it likely meant another person she loved would be killed.

Chapter Eighteen

Every damn candle was lit on every sconce the entire way down the stairs and in the dining room hallway. Her father had enlightened the house, as he termed it. It was most likely a test for the coming party in a few days' time, but it fatching well appeared like she was being led to her trial. Where she'd be judged by her father and her brother for only one crime...betrayal.

"I'm not fit for dinner, Luca. I need to go back upstairs and change."

Luca slowed his steps beside her. "By all means, let's change."

Her stomach curdled. "I can do it by myself."

"I have explicit instructions to make sure you're not alone, that you're surrounded by a familiar face at all times. Most of the staff has the evening off, to rest before heavy party preparations begin tomorrow."

"Never mind." She continued walking down another set of steps, and another. Memories assailed her.

When Luca had tried to shove her down the stairs, when she'd shoved back. Dominic kissing her at the very bottom, for the first time, right after they'd ducked inside from a surprise rainstorm, after the first days of winter night.

Then there was the entrance to the study, where she'd dragged Akono. She wondered whether if they hadn't come that night or had just dropped the money and left, maybe things wouldn't be as they were now.

You wouldn't have a fatching clue your brother and father were mass murderers and were framing you for their crimes.

A few more stairs, and they reached the bottom, turning to the right and into the large dining room. The entire behemoth chandelier was lit. A holdover from some famous Earth castle, where the hallways were lined with mirrors. The damn thing had been a special gift from some rich parliament chap for her father's generosity. No doubt a payoff. Normally they used the wall lights, but tonight no…he showcased the wealth.

"Ah, Luca was able to rouse you. Come sit. We've got some new things to try tonight. A goat soup, some root potato dish and a cocoa dessert concoction. The menu is ever-changing as we try to find the perfect items to serve for tomorrow."

She took her normal seat, tucked in her napkin, and stared at the empty red-tinted plate in front of her. "You'll serve dinner on these?"

They were hideous, but the plates matched the bowls, matched the glasses.

"Is something wrong with them? They bleed." Her father reached to clasp her hand and squeezed it. Hard and tight, pushing down on the pressure point between her index finger and thumb, the one he'd taught her to grab for every time. "Like my heart, Caterina."

"My heart bleeds too. For all those who've lost their lives in your bargain with some Upper devil."

A single servant brought out the meal, a tray with a tureen and two platters. The three dishes her father had mentioned.

"Leave them on the table and be gone. We'll serve ourselves." Her father's coarse words surprisingly didn't rattle the younger man, who placed each item with care and departed. No glance at her or anyone. *He's smart.*

Once they were alone again, Luca set to fixing his own plate. Her father frowned. "You don't eat until we all have some. Since you're in such a rush, get your ass out of the chair and serve your sister and myself first."

Luca growled, but followed the command. At least her father exercised some sort of control, but for how long?

Then Vincent Genovese turned his infamous heartless gaze back to her. "I'm afraid those recordings your brother played for me are quite damning. You've betrayed our family, in the worst possible ways. Your mother, if she were still alive, would love to laugh at me in this moment."

Luca poured the soup carelessly from the ladle into their father's bowl.

"You damned fool," her father growled as he snatched his napkin off his lap, holding it up to wipe the splatter of soup on his wrist.

"I'm not a servant, Father. I don't serve food." Luca moved on, added the root appetizer to their father's plate and a scoop of the cocoa-whipped dessert to a smaller plate.

"Maybe I should shove you into the kitchens so you get some practice."

Rina ignored the theatrics and focused on her father. "Let's get back to the point. Why would she laugh at you? What are you talking about?"

"I'm talking about how I trusted your mother, to my regret, and she bore me a daughter who wasn't mine. She had a tendency to seek attention from others when she felt she wasn't getting what she needed at home. I agreed to let the slight pass if she would give me a child of my own."

On one hand, the news hit her like a hover cycle plowing into a wall. Her father wasn't really her own flesh and blood.

"I foolishly believed I could teach the weakness out of you. Raise you to the same standard of conduct as your brother, but time and again you sought out the gutter."

The shock dissipated into a slow, simmering fury. "People with less aren't trash."

"That" — Vincent dropped his fork and pointed a finger at her — "the type of attitude you just displayed — is exactly what I'm talking about. Your mother had similar beliefs. Damn woman would have given everything I worked for away to beggars, if given the chance."

Rina bit her tongue, because he expected a retort. Luca, the bastard, finished putting the vegetables on her plate, deliberately brushing against her shoulder. She elbowed him out of the way, enjoying the *oomph* he let out as she connected bone with his soft stomach.

"You're gonna pay for that," he whispered.

"Quit messing around and sit the fatch down. I'm ready to eat."

Luca did as told, a regular puppet on a string, clothed by her father's own hatred and bias — he'd worn them for years. When her brother finally resumed his seat, her fa — *no, Vincent* — waved his hand to signal that they could begin eating.

Rina picked up her fork and decided to do her own digging. "The least you can do is tell me what happened to Dominic."

"Ah, yes." Vincent sipped a spoonful of soup. "The fiancé, he was a complication. He kept your focus, but once he found out about our body business and Kiss Kiss, he had to go. I'd hoped his betrayal would have helped you regain your dedication to the family, but instead you pulled away."

The truth hurt as much as the past months of speculation, and was further proof that association with her was damning. "Then why bother waiting so long to get rid of me?"

Vincent took another spoonful of soup. "Eat. It's good. Almost fit for a king."

She rolled her eyes and took a mouthful, to keep him on topic and not concerned with the fact that she wanted to get the silverware knife off the table and into her pants pocket.

"See, not so bad, following some rules. I've always stressed the importance of patience and I make sure all the people who serve me, even my children, serve my purpose and mine alone. You're going to try to bring the government down on my head, I'm sure. But we'll fix that."

A bite of root vegetables next, and Rina followed suit, stuffing her mouth to keep her expression as neutral as possible. *Give nothing, but take everything...* wasn't that a lesson her father had used over the years as well?

Vincent continued with his monologue between bites. "The authorities are going to find all the evidence they need at the tattoo parlor, along with records to show you purchased the drugs and disseminated them among the other tattoo parlors across Arcas and the other major Callisto cities. Enough to prove you planned to kill hundreds. Not even counting the dealers that Luca and I single-handedly routed."

She set her spoon down, because the ridiculous was super strong in the room and she couldn't eat another bite. "What dealers?"

Luca chuckled. "Those men you hired to steal the drug in places you couldn't gain access to without arousing suspicion."

"Yes." Her father shook his head, a fake impersonation of someone so sad. "They unfortunately preferred to take their own lives than face a Saturn ring jail. Those jails are no joke, as your gutter-trash lover will soon discover."

Fear spread, like alcohol in her veins, but instead of a heady buzz, she sat sapped of energy. They'd made all the plans and her would-be father and demented half-brother had anticipated everything.

"By this time in two days, we'll be celebrating restoring Callisto to lawful order. No more drugs killing people or would-be club owners attempting a coup on the richest of us."

She despised them, and pushed at the food on her plate. Her appetite melted away, replaced with a churning sea of disgust. "What about after that? You're telling me you're done?"

Vincent and Luca shared a look before they broke out in shared laughter. Her brother spoke first. "Who said we were done?"

"Rina, I only wish you were smarter and more loyal. Sure, your brother is a bit weak when it comes to his vices, but he knows who holds the cards. If he wants to hold any in the future, he plays the game. That's what this whole thing is, a game. And I hold the best hand."

I'm fatched.

* * * *

Akono barely slept but found the stomach to eat some bread and a little stew. Something Maple had cooked up especially for him. But the morning dawned with no updates on Rina, and Zeke pulling him off guard shift.

"You look like hell, boss."

"Thank you. Just what I want to hear. Is coffee ready at the bar?" He'd need something to fortify his body after the lack of sleep.

"Yes," Zeke replied, hesitating.

"If you have something to say, please do."

"Nothing, boss."

"He's trying to think of something positive," Ned said from his spot at the podium. The host had spent most of the wee hours of the morning standing watch with Akono, though Ned looked a bit more put together. Anything less would have been unprofessional.

"We don't need words of encouragement. Last night was about our preservation. Today continues as planned, maybe a bit elevated." Akono left it at that and went for the bar. A cup of coffee and one of the cook's pastries called his name.

Eights walked over to him and put a small pad on the bar. "Holo-communication for you. Maple said it was important."

The older woman had been running point, taking care of the books, the people and the host of minor issues that had popped up. Things Rina would have covered for him. *Rina*...damn, he'd failed her and this might be the answer.

"Thank you, Eights." He pressed the green button on the screen and Loyda's face appeared. "Miles, what do I owe the pleasure?"

"You look like shit."

He sipped his coffee and just nodded. "So, I've heard, but that can't be why you rang."

The inspector had her hair pulled back, her face free of makeup, and looked far too plain to be a daughter of parliament diplomats. "I called to warn you. Word in the local pup office is that you and your club are a front for Rina and the drug killing everyone. They plan to move on you and Rina tomorrow. Right now they're waiting for backup from another unit in Calypso."

The second largest city on Callisto and one that had an equal APUP force.

Fatch. "Rina's been taken. Right after she met with you someone hurt her or — "

"I'll check into it and send a message if I hear anything about where she's being held, though you can guess who took her, I'm sure. Miles out." The inspector had a knack for moving fast, and Akono didn't appreciate experiencing it firsthand.

He finished off his cup of coffee and signaled Eights for a refill. He glanced around at the current Sweet Spot, his creation a far cry from the paint-peeling walls and smoke-infused surfaces he'd inherited years before. *All the hard work lost.*

"It's worth it." Emilio's deep bass voice cut through Akono's wandering gaze.

"You don't even know what I'm thinking."

Toni and Lee were chatting with Ned and Zeke at the front door, but the steel-nuggeted Emilio Morales swaggered over to him like it didn't matter. They hadn't been face-to-face in person since Emilio's confrontation with Grecia here in this club. They'd talked plenty since then, a budding business relationship turning successful after Akono had reached out to Emilio and Toni following their wedding.

"You'd be surprised by my intuitive nature, as Toni calls it." He glanced back at his wife.

She offered a good retort. "Don't be a jackass, E."

Akono's eyebrow perked. "Nicknames? One year of marital bliss has changed things."

"All for the good. Speaking of, Sweet, where's your girl? And don't try to deny it. Could see those eyes between you two saying all sorts of things on that holo-vid when I was showing off the cruiser."

Akono's heart panged. It wanted the one it had no way to get to…yet. "Instead of talking about things that distract, let's get to the task at hand."

Emilio tipped his chin in acknowledgement. "You're the boss…for now."

"This is the last of it," Ned called out as he rolled the last barrel into position by the podium. Irony, that the host would put the final explosive barrel right next to the place he spent the most time.

"Great. Have Maple and the small group left?" Akono asked Lee as she strolled in, coming to a stop next to Ned. While the rest of them got the club ready for the blowup, Lee had been tasked with getting the younger and older folks to the cruiser first, Maple and her wide array of luggage being one issue.

Thankfully, the older woman had taken Lee's advice instead of turning stubborn.

"They're secured on the cruiser. We're ready for the next groups to arrive later this evening and tomorrow."

They'd worked all day and into the next one. Removing items, rigging the building and setting up the removal of Akono and his people from the life they'd built. Almost everyone had agreed to go, either today or tomorrow morning. The few remaining on the moon would complete the last stages of his and Rina's plan, with a couple of adjustments.

Two shuttles were docked in Arcas, one from the cruiser and one from Emilio and Toni's ship, *Gina*.

"Excellent."

"Yes, I agree. Free drinks all around," Emilio announced to the room. There were no patrons present for the moment. That had been an interesting part of the last couple days, the number of people they'd turned away at the front door. Akono hadn't really taken the time to think of how many visitors the club got on a regular basis. The fact they were shut down due to a 'flooding incident' would hopefully reduce concerns. He needed the authorities here at the right moment.

"Fine, pour the drinks." He slid back on the barstool and glanced at his time piece. The smell of clove hit his nostrils, and he glanced over his shoulders searching for her.

No Rina, just Ned.

"When did you start smoking?"

Ned laughed. "I've always smoked. Just never when on duty. Rina turned me on to these clove cigarettes though. Good stuff."

"Where is she?" Toni asked, sliding up on the stool next to him.

"Someone grabbed her. Better make mine a double, Emilio."

Emilio had already taken up position behind the bar and was lining glasses up on the wooden top. "Sure thing. Pick your poison."

"Anything not cheap. I've paid for that expensive shit. I want to drink it."

Toni shook her head and sighed. "You're giving him too much leeway. And you still haven't answered my question."

He cleared his throat in a poor attempt to get rid of the lump there. "She was ambushed the night before you came, which pushed up the timeline. I'll give you two guesses as to who took her."

"The evil brother and father duo?"

He nodded.

"What's up with families these days?" Toni sighed and took a sip of water that Emilio had poured. Her family had driven her to drink. A habit designed to help her escape had turned into a life-damaging one, which was how she'd met Emilio. Thereafter, she'd stayed sober.

"I wouldn't know. I've never had to deal with one." The pain and the pleasure of those words was equal to the burn of his first swallow of whiskey. "Seems you're coping well, though."

"Enough about me. When do we rescue your girl?"

Emilio slapped his hand on the bar. "We're not rescuing the girl. Zeke told me all about her while we were setting things up. She's the daughter of the enemy. Can't be trusted."

Toni snaked her hand out and grasped her husband's. "I wasn't trustworthy at the start either. No one is perfect, but if you love them, they're worth bending a bit for."

Akono nursed his whiskey and let those words rattle around. *Trustworthy. Love.* Two things that went hand in hand. He couldn't put one before the other. "Emilio is right. It would be risky and we're assuming she's still alive."

"I think you'd know if she was dead. The Genoveses wouldn't hesitate to flaunt that around and it's more than likely they'll kill her for even helping you." Ned offered that gem right before he refilled Akono's glass.

"What do you know about it?"

Ned shrugged. "A bit. Gossip travels fast among the streets and Old Man Genovese's practically a founding father of Callisto, including Arcas, Calypso and the other cities. He helped corner the club market. Made things respectable, but anyone who's ever worked for him says the same thing, that he doesn't tolerate disloyalty. Heard those words from the mouth of Rina too. If he took her and the old man has any clue what you have planned, then kiss her goodbye."

"Except he loves her." Toni again offered the resounding words.

That was when all hell broke loose, everyone attempting to speak their piece, the echo and volume of each voice rising until Akono heard nothing but squawking. Amid all that, the words about loving Rina...Caterina — those stuck with him. He could recall her laugh, the way she smiled at him with the upturn of her lip, and her catching-her-breath sighs whenever he'd pull back from kissing her. Those things couldn't be replaced and he wanted a life of those sighs, a life of her constant need to feel responsible for things out of her control.

"I do love her."

They could barely hear him above all the debating.

"I love her!" The yell got everyone to shut up. Five pairs of eyes dialed in on him. "But I never told her."

Emilio scoffed. "That was dumb."

"You never told me till the last possible second either, ya arrogant runner." Toni's scolding made everyone laugh.

Stone-cold, Emilio tapped the bar. "Eh, look at me, Sweet. She's right. I waited and, what do they say...oh, yeah acted like a fatching idiot. We could have died not knowing our true feelings, or at least her not knowing mine."

"I get it. So, let's finish up and we'll just have to add breaking Rina out as part of the plan."

Toni slid her empty water glass right off the bar, sending it crashing against the floor. "I like it, but do you even know where they're keeping her?"

"I've got a pretty good idea."

Emilio copied Toni's glass shattering. "You heard the man, back to work. We gotta get the trailer loaded with all the shit Akono's locked up in the basement."

Lee and Zeke sent their glasses flying before joining up with Emilio and Toni. They were on a mission to clear the vault and Akono and Ned would take on the flash-counting room.

"Two more hours. Goddess grant me strength." Ned's whispered words were paired with an extension of interlocked hands to the sky.

"Two more hours?"

"Of having to put up with that Emilio fool. They can be as good-looking as possible, but sometimes the words coming out of their mouths drives me batty."

Akono chuckled and took one last gaze at the front door. The double doors were shut, the wooden arm down, the metal latches at the tops and bottoms secured. No one would get inside until it blew. "If it makes you feel any better, I think Toni gags him from time to time."

"Ooh, a nice mental image to take with me and the canvas bags as we make our way to the vault."

The work occurred with little issue. More like random moans and groans from Lee and Emilio, lamenting his ability to collect junk. Akono kept reminding them that some of the junk would fetch high crinkle in an auction, which was exactly what he planned to do with most of it, once they got off Callisto. Once they were safe.

Finally, all the crinkle and various items were accounted for, trussed up on a wide bed trailer, escorted by four holobikes, with Lee perched on the trailer itself. The helmets and jackets, with proper APUP branding, would discourage greedy types. They'd move quickly to the docks and get everything loaded and up to the cruiser. *No rest for the scheming and devious.*

"Ready to go?" Toni's voice came muffled from the helmet.

Sucks I can't even look at the front of the building. Water gathered in the corners of his eyes. The end of something fabulous, the first thing that was his. But he'd be damned if he left on someone else's terms. *No.*

Sirens could be heard in the streets, coming in their direction. Genovese's pockets went deep and Akono was thankful for Loyda's warning.

"I'm ready."

They hopped on the bikes and began the process of navigating out to the main street. Akono caught flashing lights coming from the downtown direction — they would head in the opposite. Just as they got past the building, headed into an array of tented stores on either side of the street, Akono pressed the button. The explosion had little impact, but the blaze from the front door and windows caught the attention of every Arcan and tourist on the street. Gasps, small screams and panicked voices filled the air.

He hoped they'd remember The Sweet Spot, though it would be forgotten in a matter of months. Instead he offered up prayers of a different nature, silent things to anyone who'd hear him, that he'd rescue the woman he loved before it was too late.

Chapter Nineteen

Rina threw the book across the room, and it gave a dull thud once it hit the carpet. Twenty-four hours. She'd been locked in her room for an entire day. Attempts at picking the lock had been fruitless. A maid had brought a tray, but had been escorted by a guard who'd kept a gun pointed on her and made her stand in a corner the entire time they'd been in the room.

The previous evening, after being brought back by Luca and her father, she'd tried to access a secret entrance to her room, but had discovered it blocked, filled in with wood and concrete. Anything she seemed to think of, they had already considered. Her being captured in her father's house had never been part of the plan she and Akono had discussed. How the hell he'd pull this off...

Then sleep kept eluding her. Every time she did fall asleep, the tiniest creak from the house would have her popping up in bed, ready for a fight, the damn butter knife under her pillow ready to be used. *Fools think I'm completely helpless.*

If it wasn't the fear of Luca making a move, she'd become plagued by images of Akono, Maple, Zeke and Ned dead. The club burning with them trapped inside. The APUPs couldn't do such a thing—at least she hoped not.

Her father had laid out the rest of the plan before she'd been taken back to her room. How the authorities would arrive after finding the evidence to connect her to the murders. Shocking all the guests in attendance. Effectively redeeming him in the eyes of whoever Tuatha was. Rina found him reluctant to talk more about this mysterious person who'd convinced him that killing thousands of people was a great idea.

The number made her shiver, underneath her blankets, curled up in a fetal position. His quota numbers were in the thousands and he'd started this whole operation six months prior, right before he'd killed Dominic. The only redeeming part to his whole confession was that her fiancé had intended to wipe an evil man from the face of the universe. To cast him away so the name could no longer stain the pages of the future. Dominic, at his core, had been a good person. One who would have taken care of her.

Rina could rest her mind on that topic, though she still carried the guilt. Dominic would have had a chance of living a nice life, if he'd stayed far away from her. That was the message she would have sent to Akono, if she had the means. To tell him to follow through with the plan, but abandon the idea of her leaving Callisto and taking down her father. Trouble and death, those were the two things she brought to any situation. The best she could hope for was a shot at killing her father and her brother before the authorities took her away.

The lock on the door started to turn, and Rina bolted upright, shedding her covers. She never changed her clothes, nope. Her bar attire worked just fine as sleepwear in this case. Luca walked in a few moments later, dressed in his finest like some Upper dandy, all solid black suit, white shirt and the bowtie. Bowties were some sort of status symbol of long-forgotten events, and still important on Neptune and Saturn. She found the custom awkward, everyone looking a bit like how a servant would dress, but she'd been told since childhood that some Earth-before-the-nuke practices never went out of style — the extra-long coat tails being another one.

"You're not dressed? You plan on being paraded off to jail in that?" Luca's disgust paired with his arm sweeping up and down, as if he could wave away her appearance. "That closet is filled with half a dozen fine gowns, ones you would have worn at a moment's notice of a party in years past."

"Years past maybe, but I'm now in the present. I think I'll enjoy one more chance to make Father look a fool." He wasn't her father, but she couldn't stop referring to him as such, as he'd participated in the ways of raising her, and shaping her formative years. Vincent Genovese had chosen to be her father, whether he wanted to or not. Therefore, he deserved whatever she could dish out.

Luca sighed and rolled his eyes. "You're predictable. It's a little too late to throw a fit."

Then he stepped closer. A few more steps and he'd be close enough to shove the knife into his throat. *Come on, fool.*

"I'll make you a deal. You throw on a dress, right now, and maybe...maybe I'll tell you how Akono's arrest went down. I can tell you've dying to know."

Bastard. Yes, she wanted to know, but was it worth the dress and bending to another one of her father's whims? "Pick one out for me."

Luca grinned and drew a gun out from his shoulder holster. "Nope. Tricks won't work. I saw you sneak the knife from the dinner table, but figured I'd let you enjoy a little false hope. You're not getting out of this easy. So up you get."

"Always with the mind games. At some point, they get old, Luca." Rina rose from her bed and marched to the standing armoire in the corner. Inside lay beaded and sequined gowns rivaling some of the classic styles of life on Earth. At least that was what the seamstress had told her father and half a dozen other business owners and semi-rich folk on Callisto. Therefore, if the rich had once donned such attire, the ruling class of the sin moon should follow suit.

Rina reached in and picked out the first dress she saw. A beaded purple off-the shoulder thing, it would shimmer in sound and sight as she walked. She pulled it out and moved behind the dressing screen. "I'm putting on the damn dress. I think I've earned the information you promised."

"Information for you wearing a dress, not for you saying you'll wear it and hiding behind a screen. I want to see the clothes fly, literally, or the only thing you'll know is how a bullet in the gut feels."

Anger turned to resounding fury, the dress balling in her fists as she stared at the screen, wishing she could kill with her sight. Luca would be a pile of ash on the floor if that were the case. Except, she needed to know.

Had the pups caught Akono? Had he been gunned down as predicted?

She threw her vest over first, then the shirt. Every single piece of her clothing except her panties went over the screen. Luca whistled in encouragement and her stomach curdled. *Sick fatch.* The dress sat cold and heavy against her skin as she slid into it. The flared bottom fell to the floor. She'd need heels to even make it down the stairs without tripping. Pulling her hair over her shoulder, she stepped out from behind the screen. The sick glaze of lust in Luca's eyes had her lips curling in disgust.

"Now, that's what I call a dress. For being some product of gutter trash, you got a good deal in the genetics department. Too bad you aren't willing to come around to my way of thinking."

The heavily implied message started to sprout some nausea. "I'm in the dress. Speak your piece and let's get this party over with."

"A deal is a deal. The proud owner of The Sweet Spot is no more, but not by the laser shots of our fine law enforcement corp. No, Sweet saved everyone the time and effort, killing himself in an explosion. The club went up and the fire brigade is saying damn thing burned so hot they'll be lucky to find bones. But they did find Sweet's ring and human DNA. I think you can safely count on him not rescuing you."

Relief coursed her body in a swift fashion. The plan was still in play, the club blowing up a huge part of it. Designed to take her father's eye off them... *Looks like it worked. Though a body in the rubble was never discussed.* Now, all she needed to do was get the hell out of this room and find Akono.

She summoned up her best fake sob and bowed her head. *I can play mind games too.*

Luca laughed. "Wow, you really cared about that nobody. I mean, with Dominic, he came from somewhere. Sweet was a whore's son."

"And I might as well have been. Who we come from doesn't matter, it's who we become that does." She lifted her head, staring him down. No way would she feel embarrassed about loving Akono, even if she didn't spend the rest of her life with him. "Let's get this party over with."

"That's the other thing. You won't be going to the party."

Her jaw dropped and she growled. "What the hell are you talking about?"

Luca tapped the side of his head with his free hand then started to tuck his gun back in its holster. "Father never mentioned you or wanted you downstairs. We're holding you until the APUPs arrive. I just wanted to see how far you'd go, and I see you'll do just about anything with the right motivation. Let's say there's plenty of time for a few more games. Enjoy your evening."

She started to follow, to try and catch up to him and overtake him, but the damn dress prevented any fast movement. He'd played her. *Again.* "Hope you have a nice time."

Luca looked up right before he walked out the door. "Don't worry. I will and I'll be back to keep you company."

"Good," she replied with a pursed-lipped grin. *Because next time I see you, you're dead.*

* * * *

The Genovese house looked entirely different packed with people. The main foyer had become a greeting and conversing area, card tables set up in the study, another double-sized room opened up for music and dancing. Dinner would be served shortly, if the word of the cook said anything. And Akono and his crew were already hard at work.

Sleep came due to exhaustion, but not because he wanted to sleep. No, since his proclamation of his love and desire to rescue Rina, his thoughts had kept straying to her, not the task at hand. Still he'd gone through the motions. Eaten food, showered and shaved his facial hair away, slicked his hair back and clambered into the white server's uniform. A hideous thing that contrasted with his dark skin in an alarming way. He'd prefer Ned's purple over this.

"Sweet, we're in." Toni's semi-whisper traveled up the thin set of stairs leading to the vault area.

The one thing Rina had been one hundred percent right about was Vincent's arrogance. A big party like this, Akono would have hired extra security to guard his vault.

Vincent had stuck with the same group of three. One man at the top of the stairs and two at the bottom. All three had met a rather unspectacular death involving snapped necks, thanks to Lee. The woman had deadly hands, and from the rumors, deadlier thighs.

"Good. I'll signal Emilio." Akono secured the last clip of the pulley system Toni's crew had devised. It had been designed to transport whatever was needed up and down the stairs with little work, especially since Sampson had upgraded it to run on motors instead of by hand.

Akono moved away from the little alcove and signaled Zeke, with his tray of champagne glasses. They'd successfully replaced over three quarters of the wait staff hired for the evening.

Zeke approached with a nod. "Are we ready?"

"Alert Emilio, and signal everyone else as you can. They need to drop off. Give me your tray." Akono moved back to the alcove, whistling down to Toni before he moved on, searching for Rina. Never in his life would he have considered they'd make a drop off tonight as well as a pickup, but Luca's actions had made it necessary. As Emilio would say, they had steel nuggets.

Zeke passed over the tray of glasses to Akono and took up position guarding the entrance to the stairs, because Akono had one job. *Find Rina.*

Sure, part of him cared about the ink making it to the vault and the flash from Vincent's stores making it back upstairs, but the future no longer seemed to matter if he wasn't going to share it with Rina. Hell, his bed no longer felt the same without her in it. She'd ruined the simplest pleasures for him and he'd sacrifice what needed to be to get her back.

He used those thoughts as momentum to put on a solemn face and make his way into the first group of people to his right. The study where Vincent had called Akono an idiot for offering protection and assistance to the person who should have mattered the most...Rina.

All around him people laughed. Someone signaled him with a snap of their fingers. *Men and women dressed in finery caught up in their own dramas.* No thought or care given to those who served them. Lord, he was tempted to slip some of the ink into the beverages. *Let all these fools go to reclamation.*

He made it to the other side of the study and passed through a set of opened Venetian doors, leading into a parlor. Couches and chaises sat carelessly flung around, and a thin haze of smoke hung over the room. No Rina, though, and he was starting to run low on glasses.

But everywhere he encountered excess and never once had he found it disgusting, until tonight. He typically held no judgment over people and their vices—more power to them—though this particular group seemed seedier than most, mainly in their dead eyes. Half of them appeared bored, even as they discussed new purchases and races they bet on.

Akono was almost to the edge of the room near the main foyer, and ready to smack the next person who claimed this party was almost boring, when he spotted Emilio.

He tapped the runner on the shoulder and motioned him over to the wall, away from the main group.

"Mother Mary, these rich assholes have no clue. I've been taking special drink requests all night because the idea of going to the bar themselves is too much."

"Have you been back to the kitchen yet?" *Code for 'drop your damn ink'.*

Emilio shook his head. "No, but I've made a decent amount of crinkle in tips."

"Don't let our big plan to walk out of this house richer than we've ever been stop you from your future in catering."

The runner nodded. "Knew you'd understand. My wife already there?"

"Yes. Have you seen Rina?"

"No. I have no clue what she looks like, but her father is on the far side of the entrance, near the secondary bar.

Three men surrounding him and he doesn't leave. He's got some servants moving a chair over for him."

Akono leaned around Emilio, straining to catch a glimpse of the bar and Vincent. "You didn't see a younger woman with him?"

"There are no women over there. Most have been pushed into the couch and smoke room. Seems the women are determined to die from secondhand smoke out of spite. Toni pulls that crap with me, I'll — "

"Why don't you go see what your wife is up to? I'll keep circulating and try to find her."

Emilio moved away and back towards the vault staircase, weaving among the crowd. Damn man didn't even offer Akono a response before leaving.

He glanced at a nearby clock, with no clue when Loyda would get there. They needed to move. Ideally, he would have found Rina by now, the crew would already have half the money up and the servant staff would have started to dwindle. Akono saw a limited number of people.

Then came a commotion, four servants carrying a big, black leather high-back chair. The crowd parted as if Vincent was some sort of god about to be granted a throne, probably part of his intent in the charade. And, from Akono's vantage point, it confirmed Emilio's comments. *No women, and no Rina.*

He almost lost hope completely until he spotted Luca, who appeared less than amused by his father's antics. No, Luca wore the scowl of the angry and signaled to the bartender for something. A bottle of wine and two glasses.

Akono could guess where the bastard was headed, but getting across the room seemed a challenge in impossibilities. He watched Luca head up the stairs as he was stopped, not once or twice, but by nearly every single person setting an empty glass on his tray.

Each one wanted another beverage.

"Bring us whiskey, love. A half leaf in it for you if you hurry."

"A splash of vodka with Fizzy. They have that here, right?"

Oh, the demands came, and Akono suffered them, watching Luca trek a path up those stairs and disappear down a hallway. Rina had said their rooms were hidden in the mini maze of a second floor. Who knew which one they kept her in?

He finally made it past the crowd and to the kitchen, stopping at Zeke, who still stood sentry at the top of the vault stairs. "Do we have it all?"

Before Zeke could answer, Emilio, Toni and Lee stepped out of the stairway.

Lee nodded. "I'm headed to the back, ready for people to come out whenever. We don't want to give our position away, but it's wise to get the important bits out of here sooner than later."

"How about you stick to killing, Lee, and let the rest us do the hard work?" Emilio rattled off.

"You're just pissed because I got to take out the guards and not you, right? I do it better. Less noise."

Toni got between the two of them, staring daggers down at both. "Stuff if or, so help me, neither of you are getting a cut. Put your dicks away and let's get moving. I'll circulate and signal the others. Emilio, go with Lee and make sure she gets no slack. Use that charming tongue of yours to smooth the way."

"Are they always like this?" Zeke was the one who asked, and Akono almost laughed.

Toni chuckled. "Not always. Emilio just likes to be part of the action, and him and Lee have a little competition going. I don't know, don't care. The end of the day, they get the job done. Did you find your girl, Akono?"

"Not yet, but I have a good idea of where they're keeping her. Should be no problem. I'll be back before everyone is out. If I'm not, you know the plan."

Toni had changed her hair for tonight. She'd tucked all of it up tight in a bun at the back of her head. "Don't be ridiculous. We're not leaving you behind."

"You won't be. I'll find a way out. We can steal a hover bike or something."

It seemed there were additional words she wanted to say, but a chef poked his head out of the kitchen doors farther down. "We have trays of drinks that need to be out there. Get in here and hurry up."

Zeke shuffled off and so did Toni.

"I'll be there," Akono said before taking a deep breath and moving towards the back stairs. The ones guarded by two goons on the first landing, and probably more up top.

I'm coming, Rina.

Chapter Twenty

The first sound of footsteps outside her room and Rina assumed the position.

Since Luca had left after teasing her about the party, she'd changed back into her clothes and started crafting her own line of defense. No more waiting for her fate to find her.

The only way to Akono was by getting out of this room. Getting out of this room meant going through her brother, by any means necessary. They shared a mother, but she refused to share anything else.

Any semblance of caring disappeared, like those people who'd died. Oh, guilt proved an even better motivator. She couldn't bring back the dead, but she could certainly avenge them. Which was why she'd worked on developing her own weapons. It was amazing what one could find for defense among regular furniture.

Breaking apart the chair in front of her vanity. Wrapping a scarf around the knuckles on each hand and covering them with necklaces so the sharp edges and shapes protruded. Between that and her chair leg bats, she'd be ready to take him down.

As the doorknob turned, she gripped the bats tighter, the necklace chains biting into her skin even with the fabric. Luca appeared in the doorway, a smarmy smile on his face, similar to the one he'd worn when he left. "I'm back to keep you company, dear sister."

He'd barely crossed the threshold when she charged, swinging the leg bats in a roundhouse motion. Luca caught on quickly and before she could reach him, he'd chucked the glasses in his hand at her, then the bottle. It crashed against the floor somewhere behind her — she didn't give a fatch.

Luca went for his weapon but was too late. Rina slammed one bat into his face and the other on the hand wrapping around the butt of his gun. "Don't you know it's against the law to carry guns?"

Her brother fell to his knees. "You bitch. Forget having you alive. I'll screw your corpse."

She kicked him, and he grabbed her leg. The move threw her off balance and she fell backward, her head slamming against the floor. Luca tried to climb on top of her and panic set in.

As a child, she'd taken defense courses, the best trainers her mother could pay for, because a woman should protect herself. A core belief that had made Rina invaluable to her father over the years. Yet, no matter how many times she'd gotten into a brawl, keeping her mind calm and focused was difficult. Especially against her brother. He could induce panic in anyone.

So as he climbed, she loosened her hold on her bats. Let him get a punch into her gut. She breathed past it and when he finally reached eye level, she smiled. "Surprise, fatcher."

Both bats slamming into his temples got him falling to his side fast and quick. Abandoning her bats, she took the position of power, jumping on him and pummeling at his face with her jewelry-clad hands. "You're a bully, Luca. Bullies get put down."

She relished this moment, one of the few in her life where she finally had the upper hand. He roared beneath her, swatting at her, and finally landing a good punch to give him enough momentum to push her off.

Then it became a roll fest, trading punches as they stayed locked in, arms flying, feet kicking. Some down and dirty stuff she remembered from youthful days. Days when all he'd seemed to want to do was try to force her to submit. Him being younger didn't mean a thing. He liked inflicting pain and she was an object he could try those techniques on.

When they finally broke apart, she jumped to her feet. "Ready to give up? Because I'm going out of that door one way or another."

A door that remained open, and she found it interesting how no guards were running to investigate the problem. No doubt he'd pulled them off so they couldn't hear whatever sick things he'd planned to do.

Luca spat on the floor and rubbed a smear of blood off his lips. "The only way I'll let you out of here is if I'm dead. Do you want to stain yourself with more blood?"

"I think I'll make an exception for you." She formed her fists and saw Luca's gaze land on the gun that sat maybe a foot away from her.

They both dove for it, but Rina got her hands around the damn trigger first. She fired once, then twice, the majority of the sound muffled between their bodies. Her gut hurt from the gun's recoil against her. The smell of singed flesh from the lasers scented the air. He shouldn't have had one of these damn things.

Rina shoved with all her might, pushing Luca onto his back.

His eyes glazed over and stared up at the ceiling. *Dead as a door nail.* She kicked him to be sure, and the bastard didn't move. For good measure she stomped on his balls, because Luca loved his fatching games. Even that got no movement.

"Goodbye, brother." She tossed the necklaces on the floor, tucked the gun into the waistband of her pants and headed out.

Time to find Akono.

She made it out of the room and about twenty paces in the direction of the back stairwell when she saw him. He was wrestling with one of her father's guards. Relief paired with worry, as Akono appeared to be losing the battle.

She drew the gun, but before she could fire, Akono disabled the guard. That was when he saw her. The look in his eyes mirrored her own. For a few hours, she'd almost given in to the idea that she'd never see him again. Had almost believed he wouldn't bother with trying to find her, because it wasn't part of their plan.

He ran towards her. "Rina, thank Goddess."

With his arms outstretched, he looked like some fairytale, unreal and a figment of her imagination. But he reached her nonetheless. "Are you hurt?"

She shook her head.

"Then why are you crying?"

His question was damn silly. She wasn't crying. Her vision was blurry because of poor nutrition. "I'm not."

He chuckled and wiped at the tears on her cheeks before pressing his lips to hers. She closed her eyes and embraced what he gave. The one she wanted every day with. Sweet...sweet, this was Sweet the man. Then at the sound of a laser, Akono slumped against her.

Her eyelids flew open. She lifted her weapon and fired back at the spacehole Akono had disabled. The guard had managed to get off one lucky shot, one that would leave a scar or kill Akono, depending where it had hit. She could barely tell anything with the blood spreading across the white jacket he wore.

Putting one arm around him, she got him against the railing. She glanced down at the four incapacitated guards littering the first landing. "Damn, you took out a fair amount."

Akono tried to laugh, but it came out more like a groan. "You sound surprised."

"I'm not." She lowered him to the floor. "I am upset you got shot."

"I love you." The words hit her like a like a fist to the face. She'd figured he cared about her, but a declaration right off the bat was unexpected. Then the screaming started. Doors burst open on the first floor, followed by the sounds of APUPs charging in. Chaos and distraction, exactly what they needed to escape. A woman's voice, most likely Loyda's, shouted orders.

The din of voices still chattered away. Shocks of outrage, mild gasps — the heads of most of the major businesses in Arcas and surrounding areas were present. Underlings of parliament, and even competing club owners. When Vincent Genovese threw a party, anyone worth wanting to be involved showed up.

Akono gave a sad laugh again.

"Sweet, this situation is not funny." Rina watched as people flooded in, drawn by the commotion, clearing a space for them to make it down the stairs. Though, moving Akono was a horrible idea.

"I'm not laughing at the situation, just the people. They've been complaining about being bored all night. But they aren't right now."

She shook her head. "Sweet. Do you have any way of communicating with Toni or Emilio?"

"No, we kept all communications devices out of this. Didn't want to run the risk of your father's security picking up on our presence." He coughed a little. Hell, she needed to get him out of here.

"Fine. I'm going to leave you here and go get help. Stay out of sight and don't engage." She pressed the gun into his hands.

"You need a weapon."

"I'll get one from that guard I shot on the stairs. Besides, a weapon would make me a target. I need to move fast. You could be in big trouble."

Akono reached for her face, pressing his palm against her cheek. She leaned into it, hating how cold he felt. "I don't care about that. I'm just happy I got to see you one last time."

"Nope. I don't do sad goodbyes or wishy-washy endings. You've got a utopia to build, damn it. So stay awake and stay low." Rina left before he could say anything in rebuttal. Down the stairs. She forgot the gun. People shimmied, ducked and clattered all around her. The APUPs were making a half-hearted attempt to gather them up, but Rina heard Loyda more than saw the woman, taking command near the front door.

She reached the bottom steps of the staircase without issue and turned to head for the kitchens. The plan had been to infiltrate via the servers, so that location made the most sense. *Here's praying they stuck around.*

"Catarina!" Her father's voice rang out behind her, but she refused to turn back. "Look at me. Right. Now."

Just ignore him. A shot fired past her ear and she turned around, the second hardest thing she'd done all day, after fulfilling her promise to end Luca. All the times she'd joked about killing him were now a reality and her mind still wrestled with that. She'd broken some wrists, even a couple of legs, left men twice her size with bruises. Taking lives wasn't on her menu, and now that it was… "What is it?"

"You're not leaving. If I'm going down, you and your brother will need to be here to maintain our family legacy. Accept your fate."

This situation reached peak disaster. Loyda pushed beyond the small group near the front door, two pups flanking her.

"There are two flaws in your plan. One, why would I support a business funded and operated on the suffering and death of people? Two, your son, Luca. He's dead."

Vincent drew a gun and pointed it at her. "I'll kill you where you stand if it's true."

That was when multiple voices spoke.

"Mr. Genovese, put the weapon down."

"Freeze. There's no killing."

"Up here!" The last was accompanied with the sound of something large and heavy falling—a marble bust she'd sworn sat at the top of the stairs. It landed on her father. Glancing up, she saw Akono leaning against the railing. "Rina, tell them I'm sorry."

Those were the last words he called out to her before he slumped back down to the floor. *Damn him and screw everyone else.* She ran up those stairs as if being chased by death itself. Today he couldn't die, wouldn't die...if it was the last thing she did.

Chapter Twenty-One

The club had never looked so good. All the finery, all in purple. Ned had convinced him to remodel away from the classics into something with more flair. Rina stood posted near the bar and Akono strolled to reach her, cultivating a slow stride, even when he wanted to race toward her. She wasn't wearing her hair up. No, those dark tresses were down and flowing around her shoulders. A purple dress, plain coloring, absent the gaudy sequins and glittering jewels women typically adorned them with. His woman liked things simple.

"How long before the next dose?" Rina's question was not remotely what he imagined her asking.

Eights leaned over and looked him straight in the eye. "Soon as he wakes up."

Akono startled, hitting the bed with his arms. Instant pain jolted up his right side and he froze. The stillness brought less pain, but the dull ache remained. "Where am I?"

Emilio stood across the room from him. "You don't recognize it. This is your prized Cruiser, The Sweet

Spot. A good name, since you destroyed your other namesake thing and that's what you plan to do with this fine specimen of a spacecraft soon enough."

He pushed himself up slowly to a sitting position. "Toni ever tell you how dramatic you are?"

"All the time, but she loves me for it."

"How long have I been out?"

"About a week." Emilio pushed off the wall and took a seat on a chair next to his bed. "You scared the ladies for a bit, and should probably pay Doc whatever you can. Anyone else...well, let's just say Doc has more experience working without the fancy tools afforded the Uppers."

"I almost died?"

A chuckle came from the doorway, and Akono's gaze settled on an older man with a full chin of white hair that matched the short-cropped mess on his head, and skin pale like Rina's but far more wrinkled than most Akono had seen. "That's what Emilio would tell you, but no...you weren't going to die. Thanks to that lovely stash of antibiotics you had in your vault."

"Is that what those were?" Akono remembered the transaction, trading for vials of expensive life-saving medicine, although he'd lacked the knowledge about what they cured exactly. "We still have some left?"

"Plenty, and if cultivated properly, you could grow the supply."

"How?"

Doc chuckled. "Toni and Rina were right. You're always working on the next thing, the next angle, but this doctor says you need rest. We can talk more about it once you're healed. I'm happy to teach someone, but the idea of tying down to a planet isn't my style."

"Only because a certain woman would never settle on a planet." Emilio offered this up with a conspiratorial grin.

"Tsk. Emilio, I'm not discussing my personal life. Five more minutes, then let the man rest." Doc left the room, and the doors hissed as they closed behind him.

"Where are we?"

"Yeah, the position of the damn bed doesn't show much. I told Toni that. These cabins are for efficiency, not luxury, not like my *Gina*."

"Emilio, focus, or I am kicking you out until Toni can come back."

For a runner, the man ran his mouth. "We just passed Mars and we're about half a day out from your planet if the streams hold steady. You're nestled between Earth and Mars, and the damn thing worked. I mean, we knew that because we launched it prior, but coming back, this planet has a sustainable core, water. The terraformer in the rocket did its job, and if parliament ever decides to launch to another system, these new machines will get the job done."

But for now, Akono had his own piece of heaven. The government might try to come for it, but the location was undesirable. "Any problems, issues?"

"Nothing major. Whatever deal you had with that APUP inspector worked miracles. No one was pulled in for questioning. Everyone was free to go. We were treated like first-class citizens, members of the union. And it's been smooth sailing ever since."

Too good to be true. "Then where's Rina?"

Emilio shrugged. "Talking with Toni about arranging passage back to Callisto — unfinished business on Arcas."

"Over my dead body." He'd confessed his love for her and had almost died to get her back.

"Exactly, you were almost dead. To quote her words, death follows her everywhere, and everyone she's ever cared about, she's lost. There were also hints about being cursed."

Fatching hell. "But I survived. I'm awake."

And Akono refused to lose her now. Not when they had been through hell and back coming together.

"I get it, but I think you should be telling *her* those words, not me."

Damn the pain and the hurt. "The Doc said to stay in bed, to rest. What if I re-injure —"

"Hey, if my woman was fixing to leave me for some bogus sentiment, I wouldn't settle for waiting till she swung by my room." Emilio made a good point.

Akono had to stop her, had to make a declaration. "How do we do this?"

Emilio grinned like a man with a plan. "I'll tell you this is what I have in mind."

* * * *

"All the evidence your team left in the vault is locked up, but any chance of finding an antidote to the drug's effects is probably solar months or years away. This could have been a moon-wide epidemic if you and Sweet hadn't reached out to me." Loyda's voice filtered through the speakers, the words giving little relief. Sure, the ink had stopped the tattoos from spreading, but the drug in the clubs, and other dealers, still posed an issue.

"We didn't do much. There's still more of the drug out there. The question is, who is Tuatha?" Rina had thought about it a lot over the past week, otherwise she'd have spent all her time worrying about Sweet.

Loyda clucked her tongue. "That I'm not sure about. We did find some ties to money and other body collections off-moon. I'm tracking them and Tuatha, but it's not easy. Especially since no one trusts us pups or gives us information willingly."

"Half of you can be paid off and the other half are either glory hounds or looking to just close a case. You're the first pup I've met who's actually got some sort of do-good bone in her body." Rina rested back in the lounge room chair. Traveling out in space wasn't familiar territory for her. She'd already battled some space sickness, but the Doc, who'd worked magic on Sweet, had told her that was common for someone who'd never been in open space.

"I'll take that as a compliment." Loyda sighed, the frustration and strain present on her face. "It would really help if you remembered anything else. A name, a description, something to give me a direction to head in. Your father may have been a mass-murdering spacehole, but he knew how to hide information and keep conversations from being monitored. I'm surprised we've found anything, to be honest. The books were crisp at the house, but a few of the club managers have been more forthcoming. I guess I can thank you and Sweet for that one too, since Ned is running things now."

"It seemed the perfect fit. Don't thank me until you can take the whole thing down. Let's hope that Ned can continue to pressure them. As for remembering more…" Rina sighed. So much had happened since that fateful night. Any contemplation ultimately led back to Akono, and from there it was a downward spiral. He was lying in a bed, not waking up, and she kept trying to take care of business, making decisions in his stead as the cruiser slowly made its way to this utopia Akono had been willing to sacrifice everything for.

"I can't recall anything more. Akon— I mean, Sweet and I were in a cabinet. Doors were shut and all we heard were voices. The guy who showed up was announced as Jacques. He mentioned Tuatha's name and had a different cadence to his voice. Once he left, Sweet and I moved out of the cabinet through the other door."

"So you might recognize the guy's voice if I can find him, get him to talk?"

Rina shrugged. "Maybe. I think so, but I don't want to make promises to you I can't live up to."

"It's fine. You done a lot, lost a lot. Just know you and Sweet are clear in the system. How is he doing?"

A question Rina hated answering, but she swallowed hard and summoned her words. "He's alive. Still in what Doc called a temporary coma. He's breathing, but he's been in the coma since he passed out at my father's the night of the raid. I'm at my wits' end, and honestly your call is the only reason I'm not sitting there now."

And the fact she'd been forced by Emilio to go shower and clean up. Emilio had chided her for trying to wake Akono with the power of smell. Toni agreed. They were ganging up on her to take care of herself, but she was already doing the best she could under the circumstances.

"I'm sure he'll come around soon. The man is a force to be reckoned with, if having the nuggets to blow up his own property is any indication. He wouldn't have fought so hard for this outcome if he didn't plan on enjoying the result."

Rina nodded, because that was the best she could do. Falling apart came a close second and she'd be damned if she started crying in front of someone she barely knew. "Keep in contact, okay? If you ever need anything or want me to listen to something, I'm sure I'll be available."

"Can I reach you on the cruiser or with Sweet?"

Another big question, one she didn't have the answer for. A solar day prior she'd been unsure of her whether to remain with the ship or go back to Callisto. Staying meant relegating herself to whatever happened with Akono, including the worst. Except, somewhere in the last twelve hours, she'd come to terms with it. "Yes. Wherever he is, I'll be."

"Good luck then. I'll be in touch," Loyda replied with a wave, then the screen went black.

Rina hung her head for a moment, resting it against the palms of her hands.

"Have I told you how beautiful you are?" The familiar sound of Akono's bass voice made her freeze in place. Chill bumps broke out everywhere and she jumped out of her seat, turning to face her man, who sat in a wheelchair. He looked strained, as if the position might be uncomfortable, but still, he was awake. Her entire being rejoiced. She shook her head.

He cocked his head to the side. "How about, have I told you I love you?"

The tears refused to be stopped, and a sob burst from her lips. She came down to her knees, and Akono wheeled forward. At that height, and with her vision blurred by moisture, she could only see the lower half of him rolling towards her.

His legs bumped up against her. "I hate to see you cry, but I can't hold you from down there. Help an injured man out?"

She laughed and pulled herself up, perching on the edge of his legs, and he wrapped his arms around her waist, pulling her closer. *The fool.* "You're going to pull those stitches and re-injure yourself."

"Don't care. It's worth it to be close to you."

She sobbed anew, a ridiculous mess. Why in the hell was she acting like this? She'd always taken care to keep her emotions locked away and not on full visual for everyone to see. Except in the here and now she couldn't help it. "You have no idea how hard this has been. To be told over and over again that you would be fine, but have the hours tick by with no change. Even when you finally broke the fever, your eyes remained shut. I—"

"Shh. I understand, because for me, it was just minutes ago I almost lost you. When your father pointed that gun at you...I didn't hesitate."

"Yes, and you almost robbed me of a chance to tell you I loved you. For once I've been given back something, instead of having it ripped from me."

Akono smiled. "What about you not being worthy of love and that those who love you will have horrible things happen to them? Because I can't change my feelings and I think I might survive."

"It's not my fault you stood in front of me and got shot." She stroked his cheeks and chin, now partially covered with hair.

He pressed his lips against her fingers and heat infused her body. "What are you trying to start?"

She chuckled. "Not the same thing you are. We need to…" She leaned in and pressed a soft kiss to his lips. "Take it slow. For the sake of your injuries."

"Slow as in?"

"Kisses, lots of them." She resumed becoming reacquainted with his mouth, and in between moments where they needed to separate for air, she repeatedly confessed how much she loved him. For once in her damn life, all was right in the world.

Chapter Twenty-Two

One month later

"*Fatch.* Woman, is there supposed to be a continued pinching sensation? My nerve endings are protesting." Akono tried to relax in the chair, but it was damn hard with Rina poking and prodding at his arm repeatedly with a needle.

"You're a tough guy. I think you can handle it." She never glanced up or took her gaze away from her focus.

Has to be a good thing. Since he'd come awake on the cruiser, his life had been a flurry of action. From landing the cruiser on Eden to negotiating with stoners on the moon for a planet-wide defense shield development. He'd barely spent a few days on Eden before business had called him again. Everything was worth it in providing a safe haven for his family, those who'd fled Arcas with him. Emilio and Toni were also constantly asking when Eden would become open for new arrivals. That Akono didn't know.

"All right, I'm done with the outline. Time to fill it in."
Rina sat up straight and twisted away from him, facing
her cabinet of tattoo supplies. He'd built her a small
shop, right here on Eden. Sure, tattoos were frivolous
in the grand scheme of things, but the shop served
multiple purposes, including as an art store where
people might take classes. Something to do after work
and toiling the day away. The goal of Eden was to keep
the criminal element from existing. To be a place of
hard work and fulfilled rest. So far, Akono's plan had
worked.

Akono glanced at the tattoo. A pair of dice, entwined
with his initials and hers etched inside. She already had
one that would match his. "You sure this is what you
wanted instead of rings?"

She turned back and flipped her hair behind her
shoulder. "I'm damn sure. Now hold the fatch on. This
will take me twenty solar minutes."

No objection from him. The tattoos were only the tip
of the slip drive. Within the week, Emilio and Toni,
even Ned would arrive on Eden for their nuptials. Rina
had proposed first, Akono had accepted and they were
going to make it official. A judge was being brought
from Callisto. Akono didn't ask Toni how they'd gotten
one to agree, and he preferred not to know. The
important thing was that it meant they would legally
be bound to one another, not just with promises, vows
and some tattoos. The irony lay in Rina's desire to join.
Akono had planned to let things unfold naturally, not
to pressure her.

He didn't care one way or another, as long as he got
to have her. As long as at the end of things they were
together. Another press of the needle and he growled.

"Tell me there is a reward for sitting still for so long, besides a pretty picture carved into my flesh."

Rina looked up and winked. "Oh, there will be a reward."

Rina sat the needle gun back in its place. She'd need to clean everything up later, but for now…she would show her man exactly what he'd been missing. She moved to the sink to clean her hands. "All done. I've covered the artwork in wrap. You'll need to steer clear of strenuous activity with that arm for at least a day."

"Are you kidding? You are aware of the amount of work I need to get done, and I'll need both arms to do it."

She chuckled as she dried her hands on a towel. "Yes. That would be why I've decided to keep you distracted. For as long as humanly possible."

"How do you plan to do that?"

She walked over to the chair and began wiping the arms down with disinfectant. The air would dry them almost instantly. Then she pulled up the tie loops, the ones meant to help secure anyone who got nervous about needles, because movement was the worst thing a person could do. "I'm going to tie you up and have my wicked way with you."

"Right here?" Akono's eyes had gone wide, the flushed heat of desire present in them.

"Right. Here." She strapped Akono's arms to the chair, stepping back to admire her handiwork before she went and locked the front door.

"I'm not objecting to the idea, but how will…" His words trailed off as Rina came to a halt in front of him and stripped her shirt off.

"You're going to sit there and I'll give you pleasure how I see fit. Your job is to enjoy what's given." She reached for the buckle on his pants and made quick work of them and every article of clothing on his bottom half, leaving him in nothing but a shirt.

She sank between his legs and gripped his dick with a firm hand. It was already rising to the occasion. "You like this?"

He groaned. "I like anything you'll give me."

She guided him to her mouth, licking the tip. He moaned. From there, she gave him the full onslaught, enjoying every last pleasurable moan and whimper that accompanied her efforts. She found a sense of rightness in this, their first sexual act since Akono had been shot. Doc had highly encouraged that they wait until his wounds were fully healed and Akono had departed on various business trips to help benefit Eden. She'd stayed behind to begin the buildings and various other tasks. For the first time in a month, she was finally getting to do something she wanted, something she craved.

Akono tensed underneath her. His legs seized and his dick grew harder, orgasm imminent. She pulled back then.

"Don't stop. Please." His begging was music to her ears, the sound causing her nipples to tighten.

"You can't come yet. I still need you to help me find release." She stood and removed her boots and pants. Her panties stayed in place. She wanted to give Akono a few minutes to cool down before she let him penetrate her.

"Whatever you want. Sweet Goddess, you're a damn wet dream come to life."

"Been dreaming about me?" She climbed up onto the chair and straddled him.

"Every night. About when we first met, the kiss in my office." He pressed his lips to the top of her breast. "When you stood there outside the room of toys in Maple's and I almost begged you to take me there."

Another kiss to her breast was administered, followed by a gentle suck. He was wearing on her patience and muddling her plans with tenderness. The efforts generated a slow, increasing arousal deep with her. Making her so fatching wet.

"Any more fond memories?"

"Our first time is one. But this memory is fast becoming my favorite. You know you're grinding on me? Soaking my dick without even removing your underwear? It's probably the second hottest moment of my life. Next to when you tied me down completely."

She moaned as he pushed upward, rubbing against her in the most delicious way. He was a damn tease, the best kind. "I should have restrained your legs too."

"I think you didn't because you wanted this. You like being tempted, until you don't want to wait anymore."

She leaned forward against him, loving the feel of his lips, the sensation of his tongue on her nipples, the way he bit into her. She returned the favor and nipped his ear. "I'm done waiting."

He chuckled against her chest. "It's been less than a minute."

"I've waited over a month and almost believed I would never feel you move inside me again after the gunshot wound. I've waited long enough." She reached down between them, slipping her hand around his dick. Then, ever so slowly, she guided him to her, pushing her panties to the side. She rubbed him over her entrance, letting her sex lubricate him. His dick jumped in her hand and she smiled.

"So anxious to get in me, are you?"

He shook his head. "No, that thing doesn't listen to me. Mind of its own."

"Well, good thing I like independent thinkers." The last word was punctuated by her inserting the tip of him into her entrance. That independent thinking took over and he impaled her the rest of the way. She sank down, letting him fill her, loving the way he stretched her and completed the longing she had.

They moved together, chasing away all the fears and worries of months past and getting lost in each other. Nothing really replaced this sense of connection. It beat merely holding him at night. No other person could wash away her pain and simultaneously help her reach new moments of joy.

She hit her release first, shocked she could make it all, but the verbal foreplay and restraint had aroused her more than anything. "I'm coming."

He let her ride out her release, moving over him and shaking. "Hold on to me."

Those words were a warning and she grabbed hold right before he became a bucking, rutting man, driving up and into her with a wildness he had only used with her once. The fact that he had to put so much effort into it because of the restraints made it all the more amazing. He finally found his release with a loud shout.

She relished it, reveled in how she'd brought him to such a state, and she'd do it again and again for as long as they both would live. She climbed off him, not caring about herself, and focused on releasing the straps and rubbing feeling back into his arms.

He smiled. "Don't spoil me. I can take care of this. You take care of you."

"All right, but don't say I didn't try." She left and headed to the wash area, cleaning away the evidence of their time well spent before wrapping up in one of the robes she'd purchased for clients. She brought one out for Akono, but he was standing, putting his pants back on.

"Are you in a hurry?"

"Never. Just want to be able to leave here and take this back to our quarters. Somewhere we'll have complete privacy."

"I like your thinking. I can clean up and we can go."

Akono closed ranks, wrapping her up against him. "You're amazing. I'm glad I gambled against you. Also, feel free to light up. I've started missing the scent of cloves."

"I quit."

He pulled back, tears forming in the corners of his eyes. "Now I know it's real."

She leaned up and pressed a kiss to his lips. "You're worth living for."

Want to see more like this?
Here's a taster for you to enjoy!

Clans of Kalquor: Alien Embrace
Tracy St. John

Excerpt

"You're being watched," Ambassador Vrill whispered to Amelia.

Of course I am. I'm the guest of honour and the only Earther here, the redhead thought. Still, Vrill's excited tone raised goosebumps on Amelia's bare arms. She checked the fiery red and gold gown that had been custom sewn for her there on the planet Plasius. It managed to cover her where it should — barely.

She still couldn't believe Vrill had convinced her to wear the almost nonexistent dress. The Plasian must have sneaked something in Amelia's drink before they'd gone shopping. There was no other explanation.

The neck of the sleeveless gown plunged to below her navel. It was bad enough the fabric was whisper-thin — she had to be careful her movements didn't shift the barely there bodice to expose her entire chest to the crowded room. Since she was amply endowed, the meagre bit of fabric was constantly endangering Amelia's modesty.

The halter of the dress would have left her entire back naked but for her hair. Her tresses were caught back from her face in glittering combs. The weight of all that hair flowed in a waved auburn river to her waist.

Amelia found the feeling of her hair on bared flesh wickedly seductive. It was an unfamiliar if titillating sensation—she usually wore her hair in a ponytail. With a shirt on her back.

Beneath the waterfall of hair, the shadowed cleft of her buttocks disappeared into the intricately laced train, which made up ninety-five per cent of the gown's fabric. It was constructed from heavier material that swept the floor. When Amelia walked, the drag of the train pulled at the dress, making the front stretch taut against her torso. She felt sure no one was guessing how she looked naked. Every curve of her body must be blatantly obvious.

The worst part of the dress was its scrap of a skirt. The hem in the front was barely a scandalous inch below her sex. Her long, golden-hued legs were framed by the cascading scarlet and gold fabric.

Dress codes on Plasius were definitely different from morality-driven Earth. The seductive Plasians knew much about allure and cared little for modesty.

"Who is watching me?" Amelia whispered back to Vrill. Her eyes darted over the crowd assembled in Saucin Israla's home. High-ranking Plasians of the government and art guild swarmed the ballroom, flirting with one another. In darkened corners where overstuffed couches lined the walls, movement Amelia dared not watch too long indicated coupling had already begun for some lovers. Their soft moans provided a background hum to the other partygoers' easy conversations. An occasional cry informed anyone who cared that bliss had been realised. To say Plasians were not scandalised by public displays of affection was putting it lightly.

The room was for public functions but still managed to create an aura of seduction. Amber-coloured fabric swathed the walls and golden lighting globes drifted across the ceiling, giving the room a soft, dreamlike quality. The gentle illumination provided shadowed areas for amorous activity.

The globes also highlighted the fantastic but pornographic mural on the ceiling. Amelia sneaked many a glance at the painted figures cavorting overhead, each passionate scene more explicit than the last.

Despite the subject matter, there was no doubting the talent of the unknown artist. If Michelangelo had painted orgy scenes, Israla's ballroom ceiling might have been his work.

Amelia's scan of the room met many eyes and all nodded in respect. The party was for her, Plasius' first Earther artist-in-residence.

Vrill's eyes, streaked like black marble, smouldered. Amelia recognised her friend's arousal with amused embarrassment. The willowy Plasian's bronze skin glistened. The thick olive mane on her head, more like fur than hair, moved as if in a breeze. Her body heat released the perfume globules woven in her scant gown's ice-blue fabric. The air grew heavy with the sharp scent of spice, Vrill's preferred aroma. Her voice rose to its usual husky tone.

"You've caught the attention of a Kalquorian clan. If stares could burn, you'd be on fire now."

Kalquorians! Amelia froze. For a moment she forgot to breathe. "Are you sure there's a Kalquorian clan here? Israla said nothing of them attending."

"I'd know and want a Kalquorian if I was blind." Vrill's dark gaze ran over the Earther's face. "That puts you in a spot, doesn't it? I mean, since Earth refuses to treaty with Kalquor. Your people speak against them at every Galactic Council meeting."

Amelia swallowed. Her voice sounded defensive to her own ears. "Our leaders consider them a threat, especially to Earther women."

Vrill smirked. "That's because your leaders are male and they don't want their women running off to join clans. All of you would, if you had a taste of what the men of Kalquor offer." Her expression changed to one of concern. "Would your government make you leave Plasius if they knew a clan was here?"

"Not if it's just one clan and I stay away from them." Amelia heard the uncertainty in her own voice.

"Good. I don't want you to go. Don't worry, my friend. If you decide not to stay away from the Kalquorians, I'd never tell." She tittered.

"Where are they, Vrill?" Amelia continued to look around but only a forest of tall, bronze Plasians greeted her eyes.

Vrill pulled Amelia a few steps to one side. "Now you should be able to see them. They're in the middle of the room, a little behind you and to your right." She pointed.

Amelia twisted her head to look in that direction. Her tensed neck muscles creaked. She saw the men staring at her immediately. Even from the distance of half the immense ballroom, it was impossible to miss the monumental differences between the Kalquorians and the Plasians.

The three aliens towered over the tall Plasians. Where the Plasians were soft, thin beings, the Kalquorian men looked sculpted from granite. Where the Plasians were slightly curved, the Kalquorians bulged muscle. The Plasians broadcasted their readiness to receive pleasure—the Kalquorians looked capable of taking it by brute force.

Vrill whispered in her ear, "Someone's thinking naughty thoughts. Your skin is as red as your hair."

Amelia's whole body flushed with heat. Her gown's scent wafted over her — the aroma of a summer night's breeze after a thunderstorm. Fresh, new and somehow electric.

The Kalquorians looked like Earthers who'd eaten steroids from birth. There were numerous differences to be sure. Outside of the size disparity, Amelia knew from reports that they had fangs that folded to the roofs of their mouths when not in use. Supposedly, a Kalquorian's bite sent an intoxicating venom into its victim, leaving him or her drunk and incapable of defence.

Otherwise they were very much like Amelia's species. In fact, the resemblance was shocking. It was whispered, though not around those in Earth authority, that Kalquorians and Earthers might have a common ancestry.

According to historians, an alien race had fled a doomed planet millennia ago and settled on Kalquor. Theories abounded that some of the Kalquorian ancestors had also settled Earth. For believers, too many similarities between the two races existed for mere coincidence.

Such ideas were taboo on Earth. Anything that contradicted the Church's edicts was illegal to consider, much less discuss. Earthers were God's chosen people — Kalquorians were viewed as poor copies, perhaps even emissaries of Satan.

Amelia privately prided herself on her more open views. Once off Earth she'd discussed the possibilities of Earther/Kalquorian species ties with her alien friends. Her small circle of Plasian associates had been shocked and delighted to meet an Earther willing to entertain the idea in depth.

For her part, Amelia revelled in the freedom of being away from Earth's religion-based regime. She'd seen too much corruption and too much damage done in the name of God on her home planet. While she still believed in a higher power that would punish evildoers, she felt it was more kind than vengeful, more forgiving than damning. It was this view that allowed her to happily reside on Plasius. Despite the sexual decadence of her Plasian hosts, she tried not to judge them.

If only she could get her emotions to agree with her reason, she often lamented. She was still too conditioned by her restrictive upbringing to be comfortable around the amorous race.

In the brief glance Amelia allowed herself, she noted all three Kalquorians had black hair, wide foreheads and strong jaws. Their skin was dark, like Earthers of Middle Eastern origin. Despite herself, she appreciated the strength of their features, too masculine to be attractive in Earth movie star fashion. Hollywood's current crop of leading men were sometimes prettier than their female co-stars and androgynous enough to pretend sexlessness.

She jerked her eyes away from the clan's penetrating stares. Her clinging scrap of a dress provided no obstacle to their evaluating gazes. She looked down to see the erect buttons of her nipples pressed against the tissue-thin fabric. She blushed anew at the sight of her body's brazen spectacle and crossed her arms over her breasts. How naked she felt. She shivered.

"I didn't realise Kalquorians were so big," she said. "Are clans always made up of three men?"

"Of course. There's the Dramok, the clan's leader. That one is wearing a government insignia, so he's an official of rank. A member of the Royal Council, I believe. He's wearing the black formsuit with blue trim. Those formsuits are nice, aren't they? You can tell exactly what you're getting. That Dramok has a lot to offer a lucky female." Vrill licked her lips.

"He has a commanding presence." Amelia thought about the lean, stern features and piercing gaze of the man Vrill identified as the leader. In that brief glance, his eyes seemed to search her soul. She shivered again and wished she could control her body's reactions. "What about the others? What are they?"

"That monstrously huge Kalquorian wearing the green tunic is an Imdiko, the clan's nurturer. If his face wasn't so sweet, he'd be scary, wouldn't he? I don't know that I've ever seen anyone so big outside the Tragoom race. That's an Interstellar Medical Council badge on his shirt. Only the top doctor from each planet can sit on that council."

"And the third man? The short one?" Amelia almost laughed at calling someone who easily topped six feet tall 'short'. However, he was the smallest of the three aliens.

"He's a Nobek, the member charged with the protection of the clan. He's wearing a Kalquor Global Security formsuit. Impressive credentials on all three," Vrill purred. "The situation must be dire on Kalquor if such an important clan is searching off-world for a Matara."

Matara? Amelia wondered. Her excellent grasp of the liquid Plasian language omitted that term. It sounded too guttural for Vrill's tongue. The ambassador had actually almost barked the word.

Vrill fluttered alabaster eyelashes in the Kalquorians' direction. She flicked her tongue over her lips again. "It's nice to see them here scouting for a female."

Amelia started. "I thought Kalquorians and Plasians aren't compatible."

"Our species can enjoy certain pleasures together, but Kalquorian men are too big to penetrate Plasian females in regular intercourse. Of course, there's always lovely things to do that don't require the typical—I once used my mouth on a Kalquorian to…"

"No, Vrill," Amelia interrupted. Her face flushed.

The Plasian blew an exasperated breath. "You're so repressed. Anyway, I'm betting that clan isn't here for a Plasian fling. I think they're more interested in finding out what the Earther race can do for them."

Amelia's body temperature dropped from hot to cold. "You think they're here because of me?"

Her friend smiled a long, slow smile. "Why don't you ask them, my lovely, prudish friend? Here they come."

"What?" Amelia's head whipped around. Her neck cracked, sending dull pain through her arms and hands. The clan was indeed walking in her direction, their intent eyes riveted on her. She turned back in time to see Vrill disappearing into the crowd.

"Vrill!"

"Excuse me, Amelia Ryan?"

She started and not just because the man spoke to her in her own language. The voice rumbled through her bones. Her whole body seemed to vibrate to the resonance.

She resisted responding to him. She wanted to run away, tried to run away, but the Kalquorian's commanding tone swivelled her body towards the trio of men. She had always obeyed authority, even when it put her life in danger. Now was no different even though the man was not of her species. Any time she sensed someone dominant to herself, Amelia instantly complied with that person's expectations.

As she turned, the clan slid into her line of sight — the bare, muscled arm of the Nobek, his wide formsuited chest and his other arm. Then the sleeved, bulging arms and chests of the other two filled her vision. Her eyes lingered over corded necks, strong jaw lines and three pairs of eyes.

She thought of the concord grapes that grew on the fence surrounding her childhood backyard. She remembered the tart sweetness that slid down her throat like liquid silk. The Kalquorians' sharp eyes were that same cool blue-violet colour, their pupils slitted like those of a cat.

I should walk away without answering him, Amelia thought. Earth would not want me to speak to them. They say the aliens are degenerate, wanting Earth women for unspeakable sexual games. What kind of games, I wonder?

Her body, pinned by their stares, refused to move. Despite her yammering thoughts, her muscles remained locked statue-still.

The Kalquorian standing in the middle, the one treacherous Vrill identified as the leader, spoke again. "Amelia Ryan?"

Her voice floated from her, distant like a dream. "I'm Amelia Ryan."

He bowed, his sleek, shoulder-length hair swinging forward. His eyes never left hers and she was riveted by his stare. He's handsome. They all are, Amelia thought with surprise. With the trimmed moustache and goatee, the Kalquorian speaking to her looked like an old movie version of a musketeer. None of the men looked like the demonic creatures Earth had been warned about.

His voice, despite its strength, was soft. It seemed to envelope her in warmth. "I am Dramok Rajhir. This is my clan. Imdiko Flencik…" He motioned and the largest Kalquorian bowed as well, a hopeful smile softening his strong features.

Flencik's ebony hair fell well below his shoulders in soft spiral curls. His face was clean-shaven and not as narrow as his leader's. Amelia had never seen a man so tall. He was also the bulkiest of the three, but as Vrill had pointed out, his expression was the gentlest. His smile was one of real warmth.

"And Nobek Breft."

The Nobek echoed the others' bows. The smallest of the three, he still stood about half a foot taller than Amelia's five-foot ten-inch frame. His hair swept from his face in waves. Amelia caught herself wondering what it would feel like to stroke it. His moustache and goatee were fuller than Rajhir's, softening the hard planes of his stern but attractive features. The predatory look in his feline eyes suggested he was more dangerous than his larger companions. He looked her up and down, as if wondering how tasty a snack she might be. Amelia could barely restrain a shiver at that evaluating stare. Her heart galloped as if it would jump right out of her chest.

They watched her. She realised they were waiting for her to respond. She struggled for anything to say.

"Um…hello," she said.

Still they waited. Their expressions seemed polite, even patient. Amelia took courage from that.

"I'm sorry if I seem rude." She smiled. "It's just that I've never met Kalquorians before. You're rather imposing."

Rajhir's brow creased. He looked at Breft and spoke in staccato bursts. Breft, looking concerned, answered in the same language, his eyes darting from the clan's leader to Amelia.

Rajhir and Flencik exchanged dark looks and Amelia's stomach turned with sudden fear. What had she said to upset the Kalquorians?

Flencik spoke to her in a halting voice. It was deep like Rajhir's but even gentler. "Your language to us gives confusion. Says Breft our appearance you are threatened?"

Breft interjected, his tenor diplomatic but lined with steel. "Flencik's grasp of your language is not very good yet. He meant to say, does our appearance threaten you?"

"Oh. Well..." Amelia struggled for a tactful tone. "Threaten isn't quite what I meant. When I said you were imposing, I meant I'm not accustomed to your great size. You're much taller than most Earth men. More muscular." Her face heated at the words. She hoped they didn't think she was flirting with them.

The clan relaxed and Amelia mentally sighed with relief. If the Kalquorians found her language confusing, landmines lay waiting within any conversation.

Rajhir smiled at her, the expression warming his stern face. "Our people have misunderstandings, yes? Earth does no like Kalquor, but we have no harmed any Earthers."

Speaking of landmines, Amelia thought, her stomach knotting again. Why am I even speaking to them? Earth would have my tongue cut out if they saw me right now.

She couldn't seem to keep her mouth shut, though. "Your culture is different from ours. Unfortunately,

Earthers have a long history of not accepting what they don't understand."

Her statement prompted another exchange between Rajhir and Breft. After this, Rajhir smiled down at her again as if about to confer a great favour.

"We will discuss Kalquorian culture with you. We will show you Kalquorian ways. When you know the pleasure we offer, you will understand and accept us. Mataras do no—" He paused and looked at Breft. "Grolic?"

"Fear," the Nobek said.

Rajhir nodded. "Mataras do no fear clans."

Matara again. Now Amelia realised why it had sounded strange coming from Vrill—the word was Kalquorian. "What are—?"

Saucin Israla's aide slipped beside her, interrupting the question. The lithe Plasian female inclined her black-maned head towards Amelia before raking greedy eyes over the clan. Once again, Amelia flushed in the presence of overt sexuality. Would she ever relax in this atmosphere of pleasure-seeking decadence?

"Saucin Israla requires Amelia Ryan," the aide purred, still looking at the Kalquorians. She glided away, casting glances over her shoulder. Her fur waved as if to beckon them to her.

The three men ignored the Plasian. Their eyes remained riveted on Amelia. She smiled a nervous apology. "I must go for the presentation. Please excuse me."

Amelia turned from the clan, both relieved and disappointed to be escaping. Relieved, because she feared being close to the aliens. After all, Earth's government violently despised Kalquor. Yet she didn't lie to herself about enjoying the clan's attention. In fact, she knew her trepidation only fed her interest in them.

She was fascinated by how much they resembled her own race.

Plus, they were so unabashedly masculine. Even repressed Amelia had to admit a stab of desire. No wonder Vrill had become aroused at the mere sight of the Kalquorians.

She had taken one step away from the men when a hand slipped around her waist. Before she realised what was happening, Rajhir had pulled her backwards and held her close. She gasped as the hard muscles of his thighs, abdomen and chest pressed against her from behind.

Flencik and Breft moved to surround Amelia, blocking her from the view of the other guests. She stood frozen in shock. Rajhir's hand flattened against her slender belly, his touch hot against the exposed skin. The heat went straight to her sex, making her gasp.

The Dramok pinned her against his body so she couldn't pull away. His other hand stroked her throat with a featherlight touch. It drifted down, sliding over one round breast and cupping it. His forefinger and thumb massaged the tip of her nipple. The sensitive flesh hardened into a hungry nub and strained against the thin material of her gown. The heat of his touch shot from her breast in a lightning bolt to her sex.

The surge of undeniable desire snapped Amelia's paralysis. She gasped and reached to slap his hand away. Breft caught her hands and pressed them to his lips as a smiling Flencik stroked her cheek as if to soothe her. Rajhir switched his attention to her other breast, slipping his fingers inside the dress to pinch the naked nipple. Breft held her hands effortlessly, his lips curling under his moustache in a grin as she tried to pull free. She thought of screaming, but the thought of the Plasians seeing the three men ravish her made her cheeks burn with humiliation. The amorous Plasians wouldn't understand what the fuss was about—sexual play in public was as natural to them as breathing. She'd seen many at the party locked in such embraces already, some indulging in outright public sex. She doubted any would come to her aid. They'd probably cheer the Kalquorians on.

"Do no be afraid," Flencik whispered. "You beautiful be. We show you we like."

"I don't—I don't—" Amelia couldn't think of what she was supposed to say.

"It is all right," Rajhir breathed in her ear. "Be a good girl. We know Earthers do no like others to witness sex pleasuring. You government no discover this. Do no resist and none here will know of our little game."

He'd done his homework on Earthers. More than anything, Amelia didn't want to be seen like this. If Earth found out… Her mind shied away from that thought. The consequences were too horrible to contemplate.

She stopped her struggles, reluctantly surrendering to Rajhir's demanding touch and praying that no one indeed would see her humiliation. Her unlawful behaviour, punishable by torture and death.

"Good, Amelia Ryan. We wish to pleasure you. Show you we make good friends. No fear."

Her heart thundered as the clan's leader rubbed each breast in turn, testing their weight and fullness in his heated palms. Flencik's thumb brushed over her parted lips, his eyes drinking in the sight of his Dramok pulling aside fabric to expose her taut nipples, which flushed rose pink from the attention. An appreciative growl emanated from Breft, who brought her fingers to his lips. He sucked each slender digit into his wet, warm mouth.

Even as she trembled with fear, even as she closed her eyes in shame, wetness crept down her thighs. Desire pulsed through her at the brazen ravishing. As always, her body became a traitor to her better sense, finding pleasure where it had no right to. She tightened her legs together, willing the flow of moisture to stop. Panties had been impossible to wear tonight—the back of the dress dipped too low and the fabric of the gown moulded to her skin so smoothly that underwear would have shown with blatant lines. The Plasians already thought her ridiculously uptight. When she'd dressed for tonight, she'd been willing to go nude under the gown so she wouldn't have to endure the snickers and pitying looks. Now she regretted it. What if the men decided to explore her there, discovering the nakedness, the wetness of her sex? Would her uncontrollable desire encourage them to do more than simply explore with fingers? Would they take her right here in front of the Plasians?

Flencik caressed a breast when Rajhir held it up to him like an offering. The Imdiko licked his finger and whirled his saliva over her areola. Amelia's traitorous body responded against her will. She arched, filling his hand with her breast. Had anyone ever touched her with such gentle knowledge? She moaned. "Please..."

Rajhir's breath warmed her ear. "You are in so great of need. This is wrong you suffer. We know how your society keeps your people from pleasure nature intends."

"I—I have to go," Amelia whimpered, wishing her voice sounded stronger. She tried to pull away again. The Kalquorians held her still as if to show her their physical power. Another bolt of desire shot through